Born in Paris in 1947, Christian Jacq first visited Egypt when he was seventeen, went on to study Egyptology and archaeology at the Sorbonne, and is now one of the world's leading Egyptologists. He is the author of the internationally bestselling RAMSES and THE MYSTERIES OF OSIRIS series, and several other novels on Ancient Egypt. Christian Jacq lives in Switzerland.

Also by Christian Jacq

The Ramses Series
Volume 1: The Son of the Light
Volume 2: The Temple of a Million Years
Volume 3: The Battle of Kadesh
Volume 4: The Lady of Abu Simbel
Volume 5: Under the Western Acacia

The Stone of Light Series
Volume 1: Nefer the Silent
Volume 2: The Wise Woman
Volume 3: Paneb the Ardent
Volume 4: The Place of Truth

The Queen of Freedom Trilogy
Volume 1: The Empire of Darkness
Volume 2: The War of the Crowns
Volume 3: The Flaming Sword

The Judge of Egypt Trilogy
Volume 1: Beneath the Pyramid
Volume 2: Secrets of the Desert
Volume 3: Shadow of the Sphinx

The Mysteries of Osiris Series
Volume 1: The Tree of Life
Volume 2: The Conspiracy of Evil
Volume 3: The Way of Fire
Volume 4: The Great Secret

The Vengeance of the Gods Series
Volume 1: Manhunt
Volume 2: The Divine Worshipper

The Black Pharaoh
The Tutankhamun Affair
For the Love of Philae
Champollion the Egyptian
Master Hiram & King Solomon
The Living Wisdom of Ancient Egypt

About the Translator
Sue Dyson is a prolific author of both fiction and non-fiction,
including over thirty novels both contemporary and historical.
She has also translated a wide variety of French fiction.

The Vengeance of the Gods

Manhunt

Christian Jacq

Translated by Sue Dyson

SIMON & SCHUSTER

LONDON · NEW YORK · TORONTO · SYDNEY

First published in France by XO Editions under the title
Chasse a l'Homme, 2006
First published in Great Britain by Simon & Schuster UK Ltd, 2007
A CBS COMPANY

Copyright © XO Editions, Paris, 2006
English translation copyright © Sue Dyson, 2007

This book is copyright under the Berne Convention.
No reproduction without permission.
All rights reserved.

The right of Christian Jacq to be identified as the author of this work
has been asserted in accordance with sections 77 and 78 of the Copyright,
Designs and Patents Act, 1988.

1 3 5 7 9 10 8 6 4 2

Simon & Schuster UK Ltd
Africa House
64–78 Kingsway
London WC2B 6AH

www.simonsays.co.uk

Simon & Schuster Australia
Sydney

A CIP catalogue record for this book is
available from the British Library

HB ISBN: 978-1-84737-056-3
TPB ISBN: 978-1-84737-057-0

Typeset by Rowland Phototypesetting Ltd, Bury St Edmunds, Suffolk
Printed and bound in Great Britain by CPI Mackays, Chatham

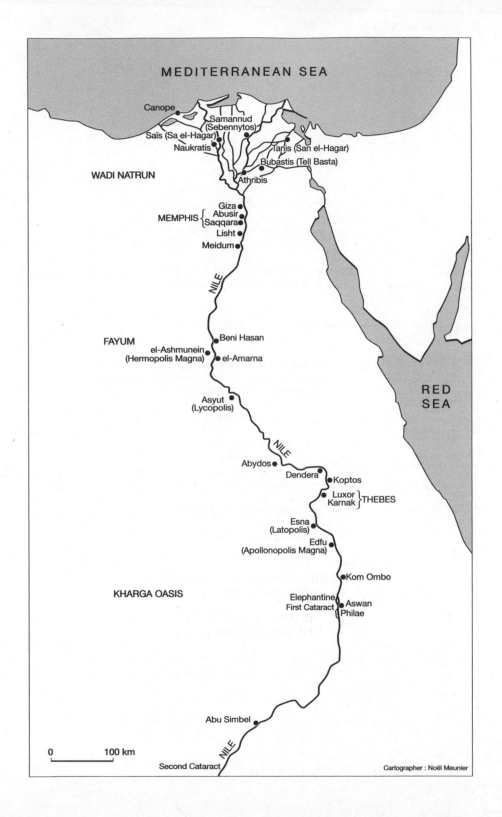

MEDITERRANEAN SEA

Canope

Samannud
(Sebennytos)

Saïs (Sa el-Hagar)

Naukratis

Tanis (San el-Hagar)

Bubastis (Tell Basta)

WADI NATRUN

Athribis

Giza

Abusir

MEMPHIS { Saqqara

Lisht

Meidum

NILE

FAYUM

Beni Hasan

el-Ashmunein
(Hermopolis Magna)

el-Amarna

Asyut
(Lycopolis)

NILE

Abydos

Dendera

Koptos

Luxor } THEBES
Karnak

Esna
(Latopolis)

Edfu
(Apollonopolis Magna)

Kom Ombo

KHARGA OASIS

RED
SEA

Elephantine
First Cataract

Aswan

Philae

Abu Simbel

NILE

0   100 km

Second Cataract

Cartographer : Noël Meunier

Prologue

Normally, sunset was a time of peace and serenity. But on this particular evening the sun was blood-red, and the Divine Worshipper felt a shiver run through her. Once again, human beings had proved treacherous.

The priestess ruled over the sacred city of Karnak, conducting royal rites, undertaking building programmes and governing an enclave which was respected by Pharaoh Ahmose, who was obsessed with Greek culture. Since the foundation of the Saite dynasty,* Lower Egypt had turned towards the outside world, and it seemed as though every day that passed brought further degradation of the country's ideals and customs.

The Divine Worshipper was well aware of the gravity of the situation, and was endeavouring to safeguard the values inherited from the founding ancestors. Only by strict observance of the rituals could her country still be saved from chaos, and even the slightest negligence would have catastrophic consequences. So she demanded absolute dedication from her ritual priests and employees, who were devoted to the earthly wife of the Hidden God, Amun.

The fragile balance that existed in Thebes was threatening to

---

* In 672 BC by Nekau I, who chose the city of Sais in the Delta as his capital.

disintegrate, for the fierce sun indicated that a critical period was beginning. Refusing to tolerate human beings' blindness and mediocrity, the gods would soon take vengeance. The Divine Worshipper stood at the very heart of the tempest, but she would hold fast to the very last moment.

Rather than changing any of her customs or the righteous celebration of the festivals and rites, she would wait. The stormy wind would bring people to her, people who wanted to fight adversity and ward off misfortune. If they proved worthy of that task, she would offer them the treasure preserved at Karnak.

With its help, perhaps they might yet be able to escape the gods' vengeance.

1

Kel woke with a start and leapt to his bedroom window. Judging by the sun's position, the morning was already far advanced. He, a brilliant young man considered very gifted and destined for a fine career, was going to be punished for a heinous crime: being monstrously and inexcusably late for work at the Interpreters' Secretariat.

Recruited six months earlier because of his exceptional talent for foreign languages, Kel had to prove himself every day, and endure the jealousy of some of his colleagues. But he was so happy to have obtained a much-sought-after post that he never complained, and he worked with such zeal and skill that he was highly regarded by his elderly superior, a stern and meticulous scribe.

More than anything in the world, Kel wanted to serve Egypt, the land beloved of the gods. The knowledge of language was that of Thoth, the patron of scribes. By learning more day by day, the young man hoped to attain the wisdom taught by Imhotep, creator of the great stepped pyramid. Writing was a solemn act. It was a case not of transcribing one's personal emotions and preferences, but of drawing hieroglyphs, the 'words of the gods', and embodying them in daily life by practising the Rule established by Maat, goddess of righteousness.

And now, just when he had been entrusted with his first delicate case, Kel had overslept.

A terrible headache gripped his temples like a vice, and the nightmare that had haunted his sleep came back to him: he had failed the examination to become a royal scribe, because he could not translate a Greek text into Egyptian or write an administrative letter correctly. As a result, the authorities had stopped his study allowance and sent him back to his native village, where the peasants jeered at him and made him do the most menial work.

His brow pouring sweat at the thought of such a disaster, Kel washed hastily, shaved clumsily and scrambled into his clothes. Fortunately, in line with the new fashion he wore no wig and kept his hair short. Perfume was still a mark of good taste, but he had no time to primp and preen.

Alas, his nightmare might well become reality. Would the head of the secretariat accept Kel's apologies and merely mete out a suitable punishment? Nothing could be less certain. He was a man who attached great importance to discipline and precision, and had already dismissed several interpreter-scribes whom he considered too light-minded. Kel, after his lateness today, might also be consigned to that category.

How had he come to this? The previous day, he'd been surprised to receive an invitation to a banquet being given that evening by the minister of finance, Pefy. The guests had included notable citizens such as Menk, organizer of the festivals of the goddess Neith, queen of the city of Sais. He wanted a Greek translation of some official documents destined for the senior army officers commanded by a Greek general, Phanes of Halikarnassos.

Located in the western Delta, Sais was a wondrous city, which had become the capital of Egypt nearly a hundred years ago. Its temples were continually embellished by King Ahmose, an ally and protector of the Greeks. With its famous school of medicine, Sais was a beacon of culture and science.

This was where Kel hoped to work, serving the state, until he took a happy retirement. A fine plan, but at the moment it was severely compromised.

The important people at the banquet had overawed him, especially the ravishingly beautiful Nitis, priestess of Neith and pupil of the High Priest; she was destined for high office. For a moment, one short moment, their eyes had met. He would have liked to speak to her, but how could he strike up a conversation when he was sworn to secrecy about everything to do with his work? Even if he'd tried, he'd have sounded ridiculous. Nitis was a beautiful dream, a distant apparition.

All evening he'd been restrained, eating and drinking very little, but when he left the banquet he felt dizzy and he'd had to lie down as soon as he got home. He'd fallen into an uneasy sleep, disturbed several times by the exhausting nightmare that had been responsible for his sleeping so late.

As he was about to hurry out of his house, he realized that he'd forgotten his most precious possession, his scribe's palette. It was made of tamarisk wood, with carved grooves for the brushes, and the round pots were filled with ink which Kel prepared himself, to a standard much envied by his colleagues. He pushed the thin, light palette through the belt of his kilt, tied a stoppered pot to the belt with a piece of string, and rushed off to work.

The Interpreters' Secretariat stood in the heart of the city, at the end of a blind alley near the official government buildings. It carried out extremely important duties: translating documents from foreign lands, notably Greece and Persia; writing summaries for Pharaoh Ahmose; and distributing the Egyptian texts issued by the government, in various different languages. This last task was essential because of the number of Greek and Libyan mercenaries in Egypt – they formed the major part of the army.

From time to time thorny problems arose. Specifically, a week earlier the head scribe had entrusted Kel with a strange coded papyrus which nobody had been able to decipher. Mixing several idioms, it had proved completely resistant to the usual methods of decoding. Although eager to succeed, and thus prove his worth, the young man had come up against a brick wall. But he was dogged and patient, and he wouldn't admit defeat yet. Given enough time, he would solve the mystery.

When Kel reached the entrance to the alleyway, there was no guard there. That was strange. Normally, each interpreter had to identify himself when he arrived, and his presence was recorded. Kel must have arrived when the guard was being changed. Walking faster, he rehearsed the best way to present his apologies.

The door of the secretariat was ajar. Another guard ought to have been there, preventing anyone unauthorized from entering, but he was also missing. That was very strange indeed.

Kel entered and immediately stumbled over a soldier who lay curled up on the floor, clutching his stomach. He had vomited, and the smell of rancid milk filled the antechamber. Kel shook him by the shoulder, but he didn't move.

'I'll go and fetch a doctor,' stammered Kel.

Wondering why the unfortunate man's colleagues hadn't come to his aid, Kel hurried through the antechamber, and entered the large office where he and his three colleagues worked. An appalling sight stopped him in his tracks.

2

There were three corpses, two men and a woman: the three senior interpreters. They had made young Kel's life hard, but never unjustly. He had admired their professionalism and learnt daily lessons from it.

They, too, had vomited, and their faces wore expressions of intense suffering.

Refusing to accept the evidence of his eyes, Kel bent over the bodies. 'Wake up! Please wake up!'

Beside the woman lay the remains of a jar of milk, the milk that Kel, the department's newest recruit, served to his colleagues every day, after receiving the delivery. Everyone appreciated this privilege, which had been granted by the state.

Shocked to the core, wondering if this was some new nightmare, the young man continued his exploration, barely able to set one foot in front of the other.

There were four more corpses in the next room. Then three more, and another five ... The entire department had been wiped out!

There was only the head scribe's office left. Trembling from head to foot, Kel went in. He found the old man seated at his desk, head bowed.

For a moment, Kel thought he was alive, but that soon proved wrong. Although the head scribe had not vomited, he had drunk the deadly milk, as the overturned bowl beside him testified. His faltering hand had scrawled a few words on a piece of papyrus: '*Decipher the coded document and ...*'; there it ended.

The message must be addressed to Kel, whose absence the scribe would certainly have noted. But if he succeeded in breaking the code, what was he to do then?

Stumbling in his shock, he hurried to the room where the archives were stored. The shelving had been destroyed, papyri unrolled and torn to bits, and wooden tablets shattered. Instead of the beautiful, meticulous order that the interpreters had prized, there was nothing but a heap of ruins. Not a single corner was untouched.

Evidently the looters had been searching for a particular document. Had they found it, or had they left empty-handed? And what was it?

Could it be the strange coded text that had been entrusted to Kel? At first, the young man rejected the idea. Then he wondered. In giving it to him, his superior had ignored both the order of seniority and the usual procedures. Had he been suspicious of the authorities? Had he feared outside inter-ference? What absurd questions! And yet ... The Interpreters' Secretariat had been exterminated, with not a single survivor.

Wrong. He, Kel, had escaped being poisoned because he'd overslept. And he hadn't found his friend Demos the Greek among the victims. Hardly daring to believe it, he re-examined the bodies. No, Demos wasn't among them.

What did this lucky absence mean? There were two possible answers. Either Demos had been unable to come to work, or else he'd survived the poison and escaped. The second pos-sibility was hard to believe. Kel thought it much more likely that Demos was ill or was suffering the consequences of too much to drink.

His mind still in turmoil, he headed for the washroom. Under the secretariat's rules the scribes had to wash their hands frequently, and Kel had taken advantage of that fact to make a little hiding-place beneath the store of pleasant-smelling vegetable soap, under one of the tiles; only he and the head scribe knew of its existence.

Nervously, he removed the tile. The coded papyrus was still there, unharmed, rolled up and tied. Should he leave it there or take it away and give it to the security guards?

The sound of a door slamming made Kel jump. Somebody had entered the building. It must be the attackers returning: angry at their failure, they'd come to ransack the offices a second time, in search of the papyrus.

He snatched it from its hiding-place, hid it in a fold of his kilt, and replaced the tile. Then he dashed out of the washroom, down the corridor and out into the secretariat's small garden. As he ran he couldn't help remembering happier times: in this garden, in the shade of the canopy of palm-trees, the interpreters talked and drank cool beer during their rest periods. Here, Demos had encouraged Kel to stand firm, not to listen to jealous people's criticisms and to work without counting the hours. An excellent interpreter could become a royal scribe and, sooner or later, move in government circles.

But right now he must escape. Leaping up, he managed to grab hold of the top of a wall and haul himself up. Once on the other side, he would be safe.

3

Kel was wrong. The men entering the secretariat were neither murderers nor looters. They were soldiers who had seen that the alley-mouth guard was not at his post. After a brief search, they found his body hidden under some palm-fronds.

They hurried down the alley and into the secretariat, where the sight of the carnage left them speechless. The soldiers' leader sent an urgent message to his superior, telling him what they had found.

Less than an hour later, a military detachment was scouring the district and it was the turn of four senior government officials to discover the extent of the tragedy.

'It is unbelievable!' exclaimed Judge Gem,* an elderly man whom the pharaoh had appointed head of all the country's judges. 'What an appalling crime! I shall conduct the investigation myself.'

'I was about to ask you to do so,' cut in the imposing Udja.† He was governor of Sais, royal chancellor, inspector of the court scribes, chief prison scribe and admiral of the war-fleet. Although he was still head doctor at the prestigious school

---

* His full name, Gem-nef-Hor-bak, identified him as a servant of Horus, capable of 'finding, detecting' (*gem*).

† His full name, Udja-Hor-resnet, meant 'Horus of the Southern Temple [in Sais] Flourishes, in Good Health'.

in Sais, he did not give consultations but confined himself to supervising the library, the medical supplies and equipment, and the appointment of new practitioners. A confidant of King Ahmose, he performed the role of first minister. No important matters escaped his notice.

'What do you think, my dear colleague?' he asked Horkheb, head doctor at the palace, who had already quickly examined the victims.

'The cause of death is obvious: a very strong poison. Even a small quantity of milk would be fatal, and nobody could withstand it.'

Horkheb was a handsome, elegant, prosperous man and an excellent doctor. He was very proud of treating the royal family but, despite his position of trust, he took no part in the country's politics and was careful not to overshadow Udja in any way.

'Can you identify the poison?' asked Judge Gem.

'I shall try, though I have little hope of success.'

'Must the corpses be burnt?' Udja asked worriedly.

'There's no risk of an epidemic, but it would be best if these unfortunates were buried soon.'

The judge gave his consent.

The fourth official, Henat, had very dark hair, an inquisitive gaze, and such discreet bearing that he often went unnoticed. He was officially head ritual priest, servant of Thoth and director of the palace. First and foremost he acted as the 'king's ear' – that is, the head of the king's spies.

His presence made Gem uneasy. 'Is there anything you wish to tell me, Henat?'

'Nothing whatsoever.'

'The Interpreters' Secretariat reports directly to you, doesn't it?'

'Indeed it does.'

'Is the cause of this massacre . . . a state secret?'

'I don't know.'

'Can I count on your full and complete cooperation?'

'Within the limits of the duties imposed upon me by His Majesty, of course.'

'I can't help wondering why you're here.'

'You said yourself that the secretariat is under my authority.'

Horkheb had to leave. 'Since you don't need me any more, I shall return to the palace. His Majesty is suffering from a severe headache.'

'Give him your best treatment,' advised Udja.

When he had gone, Udja, Henat and the judge contemplated the body of the head scribe.

'He was a remarkable man, with exceptional skills,' observed Udja. 'He'll be difficult to replace.'

'Henat, it was you who appointed him to his post, wasn't it?' asked Gem.

'That's right.'

'You were in regular contact with him, I assume?'

'He supplied me with a monthly report.'

'Had he recently mentioned anything unusual?'

Henat thought. 'Nothing alarming.'

'Does the secretariat handle sensitive matters?'

'Diplomatic mail is submitted to His Majesty. He orders the necessary alterations, and the interpreters carry them out.'

'Tell us the truth, Henat. Can you – even hypothetically – think of a reason for these murders?'

'Not one.'

A piece of papyrus caught the judge's eye. ' "*Decipher the coded document and . . .*" ' he read. 'What does that mean?'

'It's a routine order from the head scribe. Every month the secretariat examines and decodes dozens of encrypted messages. They come from our embassies or from our agents posted abroad.'

'Unfortunately,' said Gem, 'he didn't have time to make his order clear or give the name of the recipient. These few words don't help us at all. Of course, Henat, you have a list of the scribes belonging to the department?'

'Here it is,' muttered Henat, handing it to the judge.

Gem counted the names: eighteen. 'But we have found only sixteen bodies. I demand a detailed search of the building.'

The search proved fruitless. Two men had apparently been spared.

'Have they run away?' ventured Udja.

'I hardly think so,' retorted Gem. 'As they didn't drink the poisoned milk, they're more likely to be suspects.'

'Let us suppose that they don't like milk or that, for some other reason, they didn't drink it. When they saw the attacker or attackers coming, they probably took fright and ran away.'

'Why this talk of attackers?'

'The archives have been ransacked – no, pillaged! First the staff were poisoned, then documents were stolen. But which ones?'

'Could foreign spies be responsible?'

'Certainly not,' declared Henat. 'First, we know them all; second, none of them would dare do anything like this.'

'Unless they were in a situation where they had no choice.'

'I fail to see what that situation could be, Judge. Egypt is at peace, and all premeditated crime is punishable by death. To my mind, only a madman could have committed such a barbaric act.'

'Could the killer be the man who delivered the milk?' said Udja.

'That is indeed the first lead to be followed,' acknowledged Gem. 'The guards will immediately investigate the whole of this area, in order to find out his name and address.'

'It may be simpler to consult the financial records, if they haven't been destroyed,' suggested Henat.

'I shall do so. Our second lead is the two missing men. How are we to identify them?'

'Henat,' said Udja, 'do you know any of the staff besides the head scribe?'

'Yes, six of them, five men and a woman.'

As Henat gave their names, Gem crossed them off the list.

'Question the guards who were fortunate enough to have their rest-day today,' advised Henat. 'They're sure to be able to identify the victims, and then we'll know which two are missing.'

4

Kel ran and ran, until he was out of breath, then stopped to rest.

Men were queuing up to be shaved by a strolling barber, peasants were leading their donkeys to market, laden with baskets of vegetables, women were gossiping on their doorsteps, and an old man was sheltering from the sun, eating fresh bread ... Life went on, as if the appalling incident had never happened.

Kel could not get the sight of all those bodies out of his mind. To plan and carry out the murders implied efficient organization. It was clearly not the act of a madman, and several people must be involved. He himself could not possibly conduct the sort of investigation needed, so he would go to the authorities with Demos, who might know more.

His friend must be at home, ill or unable to get about. Unless ... Perhaps he'd seen the attackers? If he had, he'd be hiding.

Impatient to dispel this uncertainty, Kel hurried to Demos' home, a small white house in the middle of a working-class district. The Greek had just benefited from a rise in his salary, and was planning to move home shortly. Respected by his superior and by his experienced colleagues, he already occupied a senior post and would soon take charge of a section of the secretariat. A great lover of ancient literature, he also thoroughly enjoyed the charms of Sais, notably the quality of its wines. From time to time, he abandoned his usual moderation and allowed himself to succumb to drunkenness. If the head scribe had found out, he would have dismissed Demos instantly.

Kel crossed the house's small inner courtyard. To the left was the kitchen, partly open to the sky. Demos rarely used it, eating for the most part at the beer-house, so it was spotlessly clean. To the right was the entrance to the living quarters.

He knocked. No answer.

He knocked again. 'It's me, Kel. You can open the door.'

A long time passed.

Kel pushed the door and it opened: the wooden bolt had not been slid across. Suddenly he feared the worst. Suppose the killers had pursued Demos here?

The living-room was empty. Nothing had been disturbed. But a heavy silence reigned.

The young man went into the bedchamber. The bed was made, the linen chest was closed, and there were clothes folded up on a low table, two oil lamps, and a papyrus relating *The Adventures of Sinuhe* – Demos liked reading before he went to sleep.

Kel opened the chest, and looked under the bed. Nothing. All that remained was to explore the cellar where Demos stored jars of fine wine. They were intact, almost as though waiting for him to arrive.

Dejectedly, he inspected the living quarters again, in the hope of finding a clue which would enable him to track his friend down. It was a waste of time.

As he was leaving, a thick-set man appeared on the threshold, blocking his way. Kel tried to close the door on him, but a big hand grabbed him by the wrist.

'What are you doing here, my lad?'

'I . . . I was visiting my friend Demos.'

'You wouldn't by any chance be a thief?'

'I swear I'm not!'

'If Demos is your friend, you must know what he does for a living.'

'He's a scribe, like me.'

'Scribe, scribe, that's too vague: there are thousands of them. Be more specific.'

'I can't.'

'Why not?'

'We're sworn to secrecy.'

The man frowned. 'Go back inside. We're going to check that everything's in order and you haven't stolen anything.'

Kel hesitated. Was this brute going to kill him, once nobody could see?

The man pushed him roughly into the house. 'You certainly don't know how to fight. You're a real scribe, who lives only with his head and forgets about his fists.'

'Violence leads to nothing but injustice.'

'As far as I'm concerned, long discussions . . .'

Suspiciously, the man scrutinized the two rooms. 'Nothing's missing. Now I'm going to search you.'

Kel showed him his scribe's palette and the coded papyrus. It was the moment of truth. If this fellow was one of the attackers, he wouldn't hesitate to kill again in order to get his hands on the document.

'Keep your treasure, scribe. I can only read a few words and I never write.'

'Who are you?'

'The washer-man for this row of houses. Here in Egypt women never do that kind of arduous work. It isn't always pleasant, but I have a good reputation and I earn a good living. Demos gives me his laundry to do. He's a demanding fellow but he pays well. I'm sorry to lose a customer like him.'

'Lose him? Why do you say that?'

'Because he left Sais yesterday evening.'

'Yesterday evening? Do you know where he went?'

'I have an inkling.'

'Then please tell me.'

'Last week, when I delivered his washing, he offered me a cup of wine. It had a funny taste, a bit too sugary for my liking. "It's from the town of Naukratis," he told me, "and I'm very fond of it." Perhaps he's gone to visit his friends there, and empty a few jars. Naukratis is full of Greeks.'

5

While the guards were searching for the financial records among the scattered mass of documents, their commanding officer, who had been absent on the morning of the murder, examined the bodies of his men.

He had difficulty containing his emotion. 'I knew them all . . . Who could have committed such a dreadful crime?'

'Control yourself,' advised the judge. 'Two scribes are missing, and I want their names.'

'Two survivors . . . Yes, Demos and Kel.'

'Tell me about them.'

'Demos is Greek. He's twenty-five, and he's worked here for three years, under the direction of the specialist in diplomacy. He's very well liked, because he's polite, friendly and elegant, and he'll rise quickly through the ranks.'

'Is he married?'

'No, he's a bachelor.'

'Anything on his private life?'

'Not that I know of. The head scribe would have kept records.'

Gem turned to Henat. 'Is that customary?'

'Of course.'

'Did he give you a copy?'

'Regulations demand it.'

'I wish to consult it.'

'The palace must issue authorization.'

'Granted,' said Udja sharply.

Henat summoned his assistant. 'Give the judge all the documents concerning the interpreters.'

Gem was astonished. 'Had you expected my request?'

'When the governor of Sais requested my presence because of several murders at the Interpreters' Secretariat, I immediately thought the investigator would want these documents.'

The judge consulted Demos's file. It painted a picture of a model official.

'And what about the other one, this fellow Kel?' he asked the guards' commander.

'He's brilliant, a highly gifted young man, the latest recruit to the department. His exceptional abilities did lead to jealousies, but he showed such enthusiasm for his work that the envious people confined themselves to muttering. And Demos encouraged him to stand his ground, taking no notice of the unpleasant remarks made by some of his colleagues.'

'Demos and Kel are friends, then?'

'They enjoy chatting together.'

'Accomplices,' murmured the judge. He ran his eye over Kel's file. Nineteen years old, a peasant's son noticed by an important citizen, a study bursary to Sais, the scribes' school, remarkable results, extraordinarily swift progress, a gift for languages, an immediate post in the department, thoroughness, courage and a sense of duty. And, according to his superior's notes, he was soon to be promoted. In short, he might even be a future royal scribe worthy of participating in the government of Egypt.

'Have you heard anything of him?' he asked Henat.

'No.'

'And yet the head scribe was full of praise for him.'

'He was extremely cautious and rarely made a mistake. He was probably waiting for his intuition to be borne out before mentioning the lad to me.'

20

The judge was troubled. The men described in the files did not sound like two criminals capable of committing such a massacre. Nevertheless, they remained suspects.

The files gave their addresses, so he told the guards to go there immediately.

'Perhaps they're ill in bed,' suggested Udja.

'If so, they will be handled with consideration.'

'What if they try to run away?' put in Henat.

'Then they will be arrested without consideration.'

'Judge Gem, we need these men alive. If they're mixed up in some way with the killings, their testimony will be vital.'

'What do you take me for? We are not in a land of barbarians and I respect the Law of Maat.'

'No one doubts that.'

Gem flashed a furious glare at Henat, whose actions were sometimes rather shady.

'Here are the financial documents,' piped up a guard, pleased with himself for finding them.

All expenditure was carefully noted down, from the purchase of papyri of differing qualities to the daily jars of milk.

'We have the name of the milk-seller,' said the judge. 'He's called Stubborn.'

'I know him,' said the commander. 'He certainly deserves his name, but he provides excellent milk at a very good price. His stable's near the Temple of Neith.'

'Bring him to me with all speed,' ordered Gem.

6

Kel did not know where to turn. Even Thoth, the patron of scribes, could not dispel the darkness into which he was sinking. He was even beginning to suspect Demos, his colleague and his best friend.

His best friend? No, that was his companion since childhood, the actor Bebon, who travelled Egypt recounting legends. Villagers and town-dwellers alike applauded his talent as a storyteller, and during the depiction of certain Mysteries which were accessible to the laity, Bebon wore the mask of Horus, Seth or other divine powers. A great seducer, he had made innumerable conquests and had a joyous appetite for life. Always ready to risk his profits in a game, even if it might mean ruin, he never lost his good humour and energy.

Yes, thought Kel, Bebon would be able to advise him – if he was still in Sais.

To avoid all the bother of housekeeping, Bebon had no house of his own, and instead always lodged with his current mistress, though taking care to make it clear to her that, contrary to custom, the fact that they were living under the same roof did not equate to marriage. Since every Egyptian woman eventually demanded marriage, Bebon often had to escape and seek less demanding board and lodging.

His last known address was that of a woman who was a songstress at the Temple of Neith. The heiress to a sizeable fortune, she enjoyed her new companion's humour and his ardour. Her house was large and comfortable, surrounded by a garden where the lovers liked to disport themselves.

Kel approached the door-keeper. 'I wish to see Bebon.'

'What is your name?'

Kel hesitated, then said, 'The Swimmer. Tell him it's urgent.' As children, Bebon and Kel had competed in furious swimming contests and Kel often won, hence his nickname.

'I shall see if he is available.'

He waited for what seemed like an age. At last Bebon appeared, dishevelled and visibly annoyed. 'So it really is you. I was extremely busy and—'

'I need to talk to you. It's a serious matter, really serious.'

'Oh, well, you do look rather solemn. Come in, then.'

'No, I'd rather go for a walk.'

'All right, let's do that. In any event, I was planning to leave this house today. Its owner is becoming rather too demanding.'

'What about your things?'

'I've already had them moved to my new lady-friend's home, on the other side of the city. A month or so of rest, and then I'll tour the South again.'

The two friends set off along a busy main street which led to a market.

'Now,' said Bebon, 'what is this "really serious" matter?'

'All the scribes at the Interpreters' Secretariat have been murdered.'

'*What?*'

'Someone poisoned the milk. If I hadn't arrived late, I'd be dead, too.'

'As a joker, Kel, you have absolutely no talent.'

'It's the truth. What's more, the offices were ransacked from top to bottom. The killers were looking for a particular document, and I don't know if they found it, but I retrieved a coded papyrus the head scribe had entrusted to me.'

'Could that be the treasure and so valuable that it's worth killing several people?'

'I don't know. When the murderers came back, I managed to get away.'

'Why didn't you go to the authorities?'

'Because my friend Demos the Greek wasn't among the victims. I thought he must be ill, and I wanted to talk with him, but he's disappeared.'

'My head's spinning!' complained Bebon.

'So is mine. Was the coded papyrus really the reason for the killings? Is Demos a victim or an accomplice of the murderers? I don't know what to think.'

'One thing puzzles me,' said Bebon, 'the fact that you were late. How on earth did that happen?'

'To my great surprise, yesterday evening I was invited to a banquet attended by senior government officals – I felt very ill at ease, because I didn't understand why I was there. When I left I was feeling dizzy, and when I got home I had to lie down. I had nightmares all night, I didn't wake up till halfway through the morning.'

'Had you drunk a lot?'

'No, only a little.'

'Was there a strange taste in your mouth?'

'Yes, a bit. What are you thinking?'

'That you were given some kind of sleeping-draught.'

'Why would anyone drug me? It's insane.'

'Those senior officials, who were they?'

'I don't know.'

'Could another guest help you identify them?'

Nitis's beautiful face appeared in Kel's mind. 'Perhaps— No, it's impossible.'

'Who is it?'

'Nitis, a priestess of Neith, but—'

'I've got connections everywhere – I'll find her easily. I'm sure you were drugged to make you oversleep, Kel. It remains to be seen why. My new lady-friend's away until the new moon, so you can move in with me at her house. And I'll contact Nedi, one of the few completely honest guard officers in Sais. He'll tell me who's the best person to give your witness-statement to, so you can get free of this horrible affair quickly. Now, go and rest.'

7

Pharaoh Ahmose had reigned for forty-one years.* He was well past sixty, and no longer resembled the proud and fearsome general who, carried along by his men's enthusiasm, had seized the throne of Egypt.

Born in Siuph, in the province of Sais, he had been an immensely popular general. Every day he thought of that incredible time when the army had mutinied against King Apries, an ally of the Libyan prince of Cyrene who was fighting against the Greeks. The men had demanded that Ahmose become pharaoh, and had crowned him with a helmet now piously preserved at the palace. His acceptance had unleashed civil war, which raged until Apries was defeated and killed near Memphis. At least nobody could reproach Ahmose for mistreating his unfortunate rival: Apries had been given a royal burial.

From the agonizing conflict, peace and prosperity had eventually been born. However, as a usurper who had come from the common people, Ahmose had for a long time been regarded with contempt by the ruling classes. The only way of bringing them to submission was by making them appear

* He had taken power in 570 BC. His two principal names were Iahmes-sa-Nt, 'Born of the Moon, Son of Neith', and Khenem-ib-Ra, 'He Who Becomes One in the Heart of Ra'. The king therefore embodied both deities and was endowed with the joint power of day and night.

ridiculous. The king still laughed when he thought of the divine golden statue before which passers-by had bowed. In delight, he had revealed its origin: the remains of a pool used for washing feet. 'I,' he had declared, 'have been transformed in the same way as this metal. A man of humble origins, I have become your king. Therefore you must respect me.'

Now greatly respected, even venerated, Ahmose ruled unchallenged over a powerful country with three million inhabitants.* Priests, scribes, craftsmen, peasants and soldiers did not care about the origins of their sovereign or how he had taken the throne.

A few senior officials did not care much for his way of governing, but at his age he would not change. Early every morning, when the markets were beginning to come to life, he rapidly examined the files his scribes give him, took the necessary decisions, and then joined his guests for a delicious meal served with plenty of wine. Forgetting the cares of power, Ahmose took as much time for himself as he could. To those who called his behaviour unfitting and criticized his lack of seriousness, he answered, 'When one uses a bow, one bends it. After use, it must be relaxed – if it were perpetually bent, it would break. In the same way, if a king worked without pause he would become stupid. That is why I divide my time between the state and pleasure.'

This method had produced excellent results. The Egyptian people lacked for nothing and, thanks to their sovereign's international policies, enjoyed a lasting peace. To prevent another invasion,† Ahmose relied upon firm alliances with the Greeks and never missed an opportunity to show them consideration. For example, when the Temple of Apollo at Delphi burnt down in the twenty-second year of his reign, he had been the first to offer substantial aid for its reconstruction. Rhodes,

* Some scholars put the figure as high as seven million.
† In 661 BC, Assyrian invaders had reached Thebes, destroying monuments and massacring the people.

Samos, Sparta and other cities appreciated the generosity of Egypt's ruler, whose army was made up mainly of Greek mercenary soldiers, who were well housed and well paid. And the pharaoh had married a princess of the royal family of Cyrene, herself the inspiration for a remarkable project: the development of the coastal town of Naukratis, where trade with Greece would be concentrated.

While the king was preparing to enjoy a peaceful boat-ride on the canal near the palace, Henat requested an urgent audience.

Ahmose detested this kind of inconvenience. 'What is it now?'

'I have two important pieces of news, Majesty.'

'Good or bad?'

'Let us say . . . worrying.'

The boating trip was ruined. Weary at the thought of difficult problems which he must resolve quickly, Ahmose sat down heavily in an armchair.

'Emperor Cyrus of Persia is dead,' Henat said solemnly. 'His son Cambyses is to succeed him.'

The pharaoh was shocked. After crushing King Kroisos of Lydia, an ally of the Egyptians, Cyrus had founded an immense empire whose limits were the River Indus, the Caspian Sea, the Black Sea, the Mediterranean, the Red Sea and the Persian Gulf. He constantly improved his war-fleet and his armies, but dared not attack Egypt, which was powerfully armed. As Ahmose had foreseen, Cyrus had been content with his vast territory and had put an end to the time of conquests.

'What is known of Cambyses?'

'He has governed Babylonia with an iron fist and promises to follow in his father's footsteps.'

'Then we have nothing to worry about.'

'He may not mean what he says, Majesty.'

'Has Cambyses retained our friend Kroisos as the head of Persian diplomacy?'

'Yes, he has.'

'So the new emperor wants peace.'

The career of Kroisos of Lydia, was most unusual. Introducing a monetary reform which had made him wealthy, he had proved to be a generous protector of temples, philosophers and artists, and had believed that he would always live the peaceful life of a wealthy despot.

When the Persians attacked, Babylon, although it had signed an alliance with him, made no move to help, and the Egyptian troops arrived too late. To general surprise, Cyrus spared Kroisos' life and even granted him a small territory. Better still, he appointed him head of Persia's diplomacy. Now the faithful servant of the man who had vanquished him, Kroisos constantly sang the praises of Persia's greatness, and guaranteed Egypt eternal peaceful coexistence.

'Have you forgotten, Majesty, that Kroisos married Nitetis, daughter of Apries?'

'That happened a long time ago, and everyone has forgotten it.'

'Cambyses is young, and may be ambitious and eager to extend his empire.'

'Kroisos will calm him down. He is aware of my network of alliances and knows that the Greeks will always defend Egypt against Persia. Attacking us would be suicidal.'

'Majesty, I must nevertheless emphasize the danger and—'

'The matter has been noted, Henat. And what is the second piece of news?'

'There have been some horrifying killings.'

The king tensed. 'Is there an insurrection?'

'No, Majesty. But all the scribes in the Interpreters' Secretariat have been murdered – at least almost all. Two of them were spared, and we are actively searching for them.'

'Was the head scribe one of the victims?'

'Unfortunately, yes.'

Ahmose was devastated. 'I liked him a great deal. He was

29

incorruptible, and always selected the best scribes and did impeccable work. We have lost a precious, irreplaceable man. Who committed this vile crime and why?'

'Judge Gem has taken charge of the investigation himself.'

Ahmose appeared displeased. 'I appointed him senior judge because of his integrity, but he is old and slow-witted. An affair of this magnitude is surely beyond his capabilities, is it not?'

'That is for you to decide, Majesty.'

'Do not play games of flattery, Henat! What is your opinion?'

'We have never before been confronted by a such a great tragedy. Is this the act of a madman, vengeance or an attack on the security of the state? As yet I have no idea. Judge Gem and I will both continue our investigations, he in his way and I in mine. We must try to set everything in motion in order to discover the truth.'

8

Ahmose was angry, and drank two cups of strong wine before going to see the queen, a fine woman some years younger than himself. Formerly Ladike of Cyrene, she had taken the name Tanith, or Ta-net-Kheti ('Woman of the Hittites', though that race had long since vanished), recalling her foreign origin. She had a friendly nature, and was elegant and noble. She forgave her husband's fleeting infidelities and organized the court's celebrations with peerless talent.

'Cyrus is dead,' announced the king.

'One tyrant the less. Who is his successor?'

'His son Cambyses.'

Tanith frowned. 'That is bad news.'

'Why do you think so?'

'He is young, ambitious, a warlike spirit . . . He may try to invade and conquer us.'

'He is aware of our military power and wouldn't dare attack.'

'Are you sure of our systems of defence?'

'Phanes is an excellent general, and I know about these things. Moreover, our war-fleet is far superior to the Persians' and well able to prevent them reaching our shores.'

'What about an attack by land?'

'Our finest troops, comprising experienced Greek mercenaries, will block the way. Have no fear, Tanith: not a single

Persian will enter the Delta. And our alliances with the Greek kingdoms and principalities are stronger than ever. Egypt is in no danger, and Cambyses will be content to administer his own vast empire. Internal conflicts will take up all his time. Besides, we have our dear Kroisos. He constantly pleads our cause and advises the emperor to adopt a policy of moderation, similar to my own. War is ruinous; peace benefits everyone – I have made this country prosperous and happy, have I not?'

'Everyone is grateful to you, Ahmose, and nobody wishes to endanger this happiness. But why, if you are not concerned about the Persians, do you look so troubled?'

'All the scribes at the Interpreters' Secretariat have been murdered.'

Tanith thought she had mis-heard. 'There have been murders? Here, in Sais?'

'Yes, a veritable slaughter. Old Gem is conducting the investigation.'

'Is he capable?'

'Henat would probably be more effective. I fear we may be dealing with espionage. Eliminating our best interpreters partially disrupts our diplomatic activities. Many sensitive documents passed through the hands of the head scribe, who was a skilled and dedicated servant of the state. I must find a replacement, and the prospect exhausts me.'

'Leave it until tomorrow, and let us enjoy the charms of the countryside today. We shall eat lunch beneath shady trees, far from the hurly-burly of the palace.'

Ahmose kissed his wife. 'You are the only one who understands me.'

Light of heart, the king went to the cellar, where he himself chose several fine wines. This opportunity to escape would enable him to forget his cares.

*

'What is your name?' asked Judge Gem.

'Stubborn.'

'And your profession?'

'Milk-seller.'

'Your family circumstances?'

'Divorced, two sons and one daughter.'

'And you deliver milk to the Interpreters' Secretariat every morning?'

'At dawn on every working day. Since they're my most prestigious customers, I go there myself. With Stubborn, you can be sure you are getting the finest produce at the best prices.'

'This morning, did you deliver your milk as usual?'

'Yes, of course. With Stubborn, there are no delays or incidents. My competitors can't say the same.'

'So you noticed nothing unusual?'

'No, nothing. But why are you asking me all these questions? Has somebody complained about my services? If so, I want to see him right away and sort it out.'

'Calm down,' ordered the judge. 'To whom did you hand the jars of milk?'

'Always to the same scribe, ever since he arrived at the office. A young man, very polite, whose job it is to serve it to his colleagues – and he says they really enjoy my milk. It's the best in Sais. With all respect to your honour, you should try some and you'll see that I'm not lying.'

'Do you know the name of this young scribe?'

Stubborn looked embarrassed. 'Well ... I shouldn't. But a guard told me: he's called Kel. A really gifted scribe, apparently.'

'And you handed your jars to him this morning?'

'Of course, same as I always do.'

Gem summoned an artist and ordered Stubborn to describe Kel. Half an hour later, the judge had a remarkably accurate likeness.

9

There was such frenzied activity at the guard-post that Bebon had to wait a long time before seeing his friend Nedi.

The officer was stocky, rugged and rather sad-looking, but punctilious and honest. A blunt man, he could lack tact and his superiors did not care for him much, although they were obliged to acknowledge his skills.

Bebon amused him. And when the occasion arose, since the actor travelled often, Nedi entrusted him with small fact-finding missions. No other officer was so well-informed.

At last, as the sun was setting, Nedi emerged from his office. 'Let's go and get some beer,' he said to Bebon.

There was a suitable beer-house nearby, and they found seats outside.

'Have you got a problem?' asked Nedi.

'I haven't, but a friend of mine has.'

'Has he committed a crime?'

'Absolutely not!'

'Then what's he worried about?'

'Nothing,' Bebon assured him, 'but he needs to give a witness statement.'

'Tell him to go to the guard-post closest to his home, and his deposition will be registered.'

'My friend isn't just anyone, and the affair he has un-wittingly got mixed up in is liable to cause a stir – a big stir. So he needs to meet a senior officer who's completely honest.'

'That sounds interesting,' said Nedi. 'What affair are you talking about?'

'The murder of the interpreters.'

Nedi almost choked on his beer. 'How do you know about that?'

'My friend escaped with his life.'

'What's his name?'

'Kel. He's an exceptional lad.'

'Exceptional – and accused of the murders.'

Bebon paled. 'There must be some mistake. I tell you, he only just escaped with his life.'

'According to Judge Gem, the highest legal authority in the land, your friend is a monstrous assassin.'

'That's ridiculous!'

'Where is Kel?'

'That's the problem,' said Bebon. 'I don't know. He's vanished and I'm very worried. The real murderer must be on his trail.'

'Don't take the wrong road. All guards have orders to arrest him. He's a savage beast, and anyone who helps him will be accused of being an accomplice to the murder.'

The actor hung his head. 'So Kel lied to me. How naive I've been.'

'Your lucky star has enabled you to avoid the worst. Where are you living at the moment?'

'In a good area of the city, with a singer called Neith.'

'Don't leave Sais. Your testimony may be necessary.'

Neith's apartment was most agreeable. It occupied the upper storey of a recently built house, and benefited from a terrace equipped with sun-shades and mats. His nerves on edge, Kel watched the sunset, a magical spectacle whose beauty enabled him to forget the tragedy for a few moments.

But it soon resurfaced. Why had his peaceful world, which

had promised such a fine future, suddenly gone awry? Fortunately, Bebon's friendship would extricate him from this nightmare. First thing tomorrow, he would appear before a judge and be cleared of all suspicion.

Reassured, he dozed off.

The bang of a door awoke him with a start.

'It's me, Bebon.'

Kel ran down the staircase that led from the terrace to the apartment.

'Did you contact your friend?' he asked urgently.

'You're accused of the murders,' said Bebon.

Kel froze. 'Is this some kind of joke?'

'I'm afraid not. Judge Gem has solid proof.'

The scribe seized his friend by the shoulders. 'It isn't true! I'm innocent, I swear it!'

'I don't doubt it, but that's not what the authorities think.'

Kel swayed. 'What is happening to me?'

'Above all, we mustn't lose our grip.'

'I'm going to let myself be taken prisoner, so that I can explain. My innocence will be recognized.'

'Don't deceive yourself,' advised Bebon.

'Aren't you confident in the legal system?'

'This is such a dreadful crime that they need to find a culprit very quickly. You might be chosen.'

'I'm innocent!' Kel declared again.

'On its own, your word won't be enough.'

'Then what can I do?'

'Find the real murderer.'

Overcoming his emotion, Kel tried to think clearly. 'The milk-seller! Either he poisoned the jars, or he was involved in it.'

'Do you know his address?'

'His stable's near the Temple of Neith.'

'That fellow is going to talk,' decided Bebon.

10

Thanks to the artist's clever work, Judge Gem now had about thirty portraits of Kel, which would soon be distributed to all the guard-posts in Sais.

Overburdened as usual by the thousand and one duties his multiple offices demanded of him, Governor Udja interrupted his long list of meetings to receive Gem.

Every time they met, the judge was impressed by Udja's broad shoulders and imposing stature. The governor had a rare energy, and his authority was undeniable. Age had no hold on him and, although he had known King Apries, Ahmose's predecessor, he seemed to enjoy eternal youth.

'Good news, Judge Gem?'

'Excellent! We know the identity of the murderer. He is a young scribe called Kel. Unfortunately, he was not at his home. The guards are searching for him.'

'Have you any proof of his guilt?'

'The testimony of Stubborn, the milk-seller, duly registered before two witnesses, is the determining factor. Yesterday morning he delivered his jars to Kel. According to custom, Kel himself served the milk to his superior and to his colleagues in the secretariat, And before he did so, he poisoned it.'

Udja seemed only half convinced. 'That's a plausible reconstruction. But why did he commit such a horrible crime?'

'It was probably an attack of homicidal madness. But if he

had another motive he'll confess it during his interrogation.'

'Act as discreetly as possible,' advised the governor. 'We cannot yet exclude the possibility of a conspiracy aimed at destroying the Interpreters' Secretariat. In that event, Kel would be a cat's-paw.'

'Will the murders strike a severe blow against the state?' asked Gem worriedly.

'That is overstating it, but we must rebuild the secretariat with all speed, and staff it with reliable, skilled professionals, and that won't be an easy task.'

'Even if espionage is involved, I have discovered the guilty party, and I shall have him arrested and judged according to legal procedure. In other words, you, the head of the spy service, must not place obstacles in my way.'

'What about the second suspect? Udja asked.

'Demos is also missing. Questioning the inhabitants of the district has given us nothing. Here, too, the situation seems clear: Kel and Demos are friends, and therefore accomplices, and the Greek helped the Egyptian in one way or another. Perhaps they have fled together. With the aid of Kel's portrait, we shall soon find him.'

'Should you not also have a likeness of Demos made?'

'Good idea. Conspiracy to murder is severely punished, and the Greek is bound to confess the truth in order to avoid the supreme penalty.'

Kel knew Stubborn well. Each morning, just after dawn, he brought him the jars of milk which the interpreters so appreciated. Their number was noted down, and every ten days the secretariat's accounting scribe paid the bill.

The tradesman and the scribe liked to exchange a few words. A former soldier, Stubborn had used his savings to buy a fine stable near the main government offices and had proceeded to conquer a very profitable market. True, he complained about everyday difficulties and poor profits, but his good reputation and the quality of his produce ensured that he always had plenty of buyers. Heavy taxation sometimes made him think of changing his profession. Nevertheless, he was planning to develop his business.

Kel, the secretariat's newest recruit, served the milk to his colleagues. He did not object at all to this custom. Some merely murmured 'Thank you'; others were more effusive. One day a newcomer would take Kel's place and he or she would then provide the interpreters with their first small pleasure of the day.

This custom had made Kel the prime suspect. It would indeed be easy to pour poison into the jars, but who had committed the crime? It must have been the milk-seller. An expert had provided him with the poison; but who was behind the expert? The extent of the conspiracy made Kel's head spin.

If the murderers really were looking for the coded document, they had failed, and he was in mortal danger. The guards didn't want to arrest him, they wanted to kill him. The contents of the papyrus must be terrifying if they could cause such carnage. Stubborn must be made to talk.

'Together, the two of us will manage it,' said Bebon.

'The fellow will know how to defend himself.'

'I'll use my club.'

'No violence,' Kel objected.

'Get your head out of the clouds, my friend! You've been accused of murder, and only Stubborn can clear you. So forget your outmoded moral principles and defend yourself. That fellow belongs to the band of murderers; we needn't treat him gently.'

The young scribe swayed, caught up in a dark world where the rules of harmony no longer existed.

At the dairy, all seemed calm. A red-haired fellow was milking a fine brown and white cow with gentle eyes.

'Stay back,' Bebon advised Kel.

The actor stepped forward. 'What magnificent animals!' he

exclaimed. 'And what a beautiful stable. Are you the owner?'

'I wish I was. What do you want with him?'

'I'm looking for work.'

'I'm not even sure I'll be keeping my own job.'

'Is Stubborn having problems?'

'He's just sold the stable and all the cows.'

'Why? Isn't the business flourishing?'

'He complained he wasn't earning enough and decided to go back to being a soldier. He's taking up an officer's post at Naukratis.'

11

'Naukratis?' Kel was astonished. 'That's where Demos has taken refuge, according to his washer-man.'

'The milk-seller accuses you and then disappears,' exclaimed Bebon.

'It's only a hypothesis.'

'Don't be foolish. Here you are at the centre of a cunning plot. The real culprits have scattered and you make an ideal target.'

Bebon's observation was accurate. Demos and Stubborn were mixed up in the conspiracy and had disappeared, and the forces of law would be unable to trace the affair back to the mastermind who was behind it. To them, Kel was the perfect candidate for murderer.

'We're being watched,' whispered Bebon. 'Take that little alleyway on the left, and put a considerable distance between us, as if we don't know each other.'

'That's the murderer!' shouted a guard, pointing at Kel.

He and his colleagues rushed at the scribe, but Bebon threw himself in front of them.

'Run away!' he yelled.

His hands immobilized by wooden manacles and his face dripping blood, Bebon was dragged before Judge Gem.

'This bandit is the murderer's accomplice,' said the guard. 'He helped him escape.'

'Before he is interrogated, have him treated by a doctor. And give me a written report.'

When Bebon reappeared, he looked more like a human being again.

'What is your name?' asked the judge.

'Bebon.'

'Your profession?'

'I travel Egypt, telling the old myths, and I play the parts of the gods during public performances of the Mysteries.'

'Do you have a family?'

'There's nobody left. And I'm not married.'

'According to this report, you prevented the guards from arresting a criminal.'

'No, I didn't. First of all, I didn't know they were guards; second, they charged at me and knocked me over, and then they beat me.'

'You shouted "Run away!" to your accomplice.'

'No. I was so afraid of those brutes rushing at me that I shouted "Keep away!" And I haven't got any accomplices.'

'Do you know a scribe called Kel?'

Bebon appeared to think. 'I don't see many scribes. The name doesn't mean anything to me.'

The judge was disconcerted. The suspect's story was plausible, and he did not have the profile of a dangerous conspirator.

'One of my assistants will question you again, and note down what you say.'

'Am I going to be beaten again?' asked Bebon, trembling.

'Certainly not!' Gem replied indignantly. 'What is more, I shall conduct an enquiry, and if unjustified violence has been used the guards will be punished.'

The actor hung his head. 'I don't understand what's happening. I've never done anything wrong.'

'If you are innocent, you have nothing to fear. Tell the truth, and all will be well.'

This poor fellow, thought Gem, had found himself in the wrong place at the wrong time. Once the routine checks had been carried out, he would be set free. And if he complained about the guards' brutality, his complaint would be investigated.

'I have called you all together in order to review the situation,' said Udja. 'I shall then inform His Majesty. Has the poison been identified, Horkheb?'

'Unfortunately not. But it was particularly virulent one, often used by Asians.'

'Persians, for example?'

'For example.'

'Which might incline us to think in terms of espionage,' observed Udja.

'We mustn't jump to conclusions,' advised Judge Gem. 'It will take more than this to justify charging Kel with spying on behalf of the Persians.'

'What do you think, Henat?'

Henat frowned. 'I agree with the judge.'

'We have identified the guilty party,' Gem continued with satisfaction, 'and his arrest is merely a matter of time. However, we still have to establish his real motive. I shall interrogate him myself, and he will tell the truth.'

'I am not sure that a public trial would be a good idea,' said Henat.

'That is for me to decide,' snapped the judge, 'and even the pharaoh himself may not intervene. Everyone in this country must know that justice is handed down in accordance with the Rule of Maat, and not for personal interests. Both rich and poor trust it, and they must not be disappointed.'

'Indeed,' agreed Henat. 'But if the murders are linked to state secrets . . .'

'In that event, I shall take the sensible course.'

'Up to now,' went on Udja, 'this terrible affair has been kept quiet. I dare to hope that the guards will be both efficient and discreet.'

'I've given orders to that effect,' said Gem. 'An investigation is not a public spectacle, and all that matters is its success and the respect for law.'

12

At last Kel stopped running. He was exhausted and famished.

Instinctively, he had left Sais and made for the village of his birth, near the great city. Now that Bebon had been arrested and imprisoned, and perhaps even killed by guards in league with the killers, he was once again alone and friendless.

Where could he take refuge? The only option was an old uncle, the last living member of his family. He had a small farm; perhaps he would grant his nephew hospitality, at least for a few days. Kel would have to explain himself, and prayed that he'd be convincing.

It calmed him to see the verdant countryside again, filled with palm-groves and small, well-tended gardens. He encountered peasants and their donkeys, laden with baskets filled with vegetables, and greeted the farm-hands as they worked. Beneath a merciful sun life went by, changeless and peaceful.

Surely he must be having a nightmare, which would soon fade away? Alas, closing his eyes, going to sleep and waking up again were not enough. Dreadful reality continued to make his heart pound.

There was a crowd of people at the entrance to the village, engaged in animated discussion. A tall beanpole of a man, his arms raised to the skies, was having a loud argument with an old woman. Eventually they stopped shouting and the crowd dispersed.

In the shade of a palm-tree, Kel waited for lasting calm to return, then made for the little white houses which were shaded by sycamore trees. Here, his parents had lived happily before leaving for the Beautiful West, where their souls lived in company with the Just. The scribe remembered his childhood games, swimming, laughter, running crazy races. Taking part in the harvest was not a punishment but a pleasure. And he had loved taking care of the pigs and the geese. Their intelligence fascinated him, and he spent hours talking to them. His future as a peasant had seemed mapped out.

But one evening, during a celebration, the scribe appointed to oversee the harvest had shown him some lines of writing. Suddenly, another world had opened up. Nothing was more important than those signs, the brush used to draw them, the pots of ink and the eraser.

Braving his parents' hostility, little Kel had presented himself – without any letter of recommendation – at the scribes' school attached to the nearby temple. Ignoring his colleagues' criticisms, the director had admitted him, while stating clearly what was expected of the boy.

Studious, eager to learn and tireless, Kel had soon become the best of his pupils. Not wishing to stifle such talent, the director had spoken about him to a teacher in Sais. After checks had been carried out, it was clear that the little boy did indeed have uncommon gifts.

Although caught in a kind of whirlpool, Kel had not forgotten his village.

Seeing it again today, should he lament his destiny? No, he was trying to realize an ideal, and no amount of regret would enable him to overcome adversity.

The beanpole barred his way. 'You aren't from here.'

'Yes, I am.'

'Did the guards send you?'

Kel smiled. 'Don't worry, I've only come to see my uncle.'

The beanpole scowled. 'What's his name?'

'Changeless.'

'Ah . . . Haven't you heard?'

'Heard what?'

'Are you hungry?'

'I'm starving.'

'Come and eat at my house. My wife makes the best stew in the province.'

The beanpole wasn't boasting. Chunks of mutton, stuffed aubergines and a cumin sauce made a delicious meal, and the local red wine added to the feast.

After exchanging a few pleasantries, Kel broached the subject of his uncle. 'Is he in trouble?'

A heavy silence fell.

'Tell him the truth,' said the beanpole's wife.

'His house burnt down, and he died in the fire. Most of the villagers want to believe it was an accident, but I don't: I saw a stranger set fire to it. And our head-woman has forbidden me to talk to the authorities.'

'She's right,' cut in his wife. 'It would simply bring us trouble. These matters don't concern us. Look to your family and hold your tongue.'

'When did this happen?' asked Kel.

'Two days ago.'

Suddenly, everything became clear. Nothing was due to chance. The murderers had chosen Kel as their victim and – by killing his uncle – had removed his one source of help. Bebon thought Kel had been drugged during the banquet so that he awoke halfway through the morning and arrived late at the office. Kel was the designated murderer, and had no chance of escaping from justice. And the real culprits would never be identified.

'Thank you for your hospitality,' he said. 'Now I must go.'

'Won't you have some more stew?'

'It's wonderful, but I'm pressed for time.'

If Bebon was right, the invitation to the banquet was the

final stage in the machinations devised by one or more influential men close enough to power to know the importance of the Interpreters' Secretariat.

Who could help Kel identify the important people who had been present that evening? The face of Nitis, the beautiful priestess, appeared to him.

13

Nitis was eighteen years old, with eyes of a deep, almost unreal blue; she had devoted herself to the service of Neith since her adolescence. A singer and weaver, she had discovered that the goddess was the prime embodiment of the living being, at once 'Mother of mothers' and 'Father of fathers'. Neith was a creative tide, a primordial energy, constantly weaving the universe. Death and life lay in her hands and, by creating the ritual fabrics, the initiates carried on her work.

The young priestess lived in her family's modest home, near the goddess's great temple. Her mother had recently died, after many years as a widow; she had never recovered from the death of her husband, a carpenter, in an accident.

If Nitis proved worthy of the great Mysteries, she would live inside the sacred domain. But she had still to prove her worth, working with thoroughness and patience, and proving herself worthy of her ideal.

After passing through a gate in the outer wall of the temple, she headed for her home. As she was thinking about a symbolic text describing two crossed arrows, one of the Neith's symbols, a young man stepped in front of her.

'Forgive me for troubling you. My name is Kel, and I wish to speak to you about a serious matter.'

Nitis remembered those intense eyes. 'You were one of the guests at the finance minister's banquet, weren't you?'

'Yes, and I believe that that was the origin of all my misfortunes. Without your help, my life is in danger.' Kel surprised himself with his own boldness. How dared he speak like that to a priestess of Neith, whose beauty and charm overwhelmed him?

'You seem very shaken,' she observed.

'In the name of Pharaoh, I swear to you that I'm innocent of the crimes I'm accused of.'

Kel was taking a huge risk. Either Nitis would agree to listen to him, or she would send him away. And he couldn't blame her if she didn't trust a stranger who behaved suspiciously and made disturbing declarations.

'Come to my house.'

He felt like taking her in his arms and kissing her, but managed to contain the impulse, the like of which he'd never felt before.

The residential district was very peaceful. Here and there, oil lamps were being lit and dinner was being prepared.

Nobody saw Kel cross the threshold of Nitis's house, with its bare interior.

'Let us pray to the ancestors,' she proposed, 'and beg for their wisdom.'

The two young people knelt down, side by side, facing limestone busts of a man and a woman. They raised their hands in a sign of veneration, and Nitis spoke the ritual words celebrating the Light that emanated from the world beyond, lighting up the paths of the living.

Nitis's perfume intoxicated Kel. A subtle mixture of a thousand scents, in which jasmine was the key fragrance, it was both sweetness and fire.

'Are you hungry?' she asked.

'I can't stay in your house, I must—'

'You can explain everything to me over a good meal. To judge from your state of exhaustion, you need one.'

'I don't want to endanger your reputation, and—'

'I live alone, and nobody knows you're here.'

'Then you . . . you believe me?'

Nitis smiled. 'I don't yet know the details of your story.'

They walked through into the reception room, which was equipped with armchairs and an elegant low table. Nitis liked the simple style of furniture from the Old Kingdom, which was being recreated by some contemporary craftsmen.

She laid out several small dishes: sweet onions, cucumbers, baked aubergines, dried fish, figs, fresh bread and red wine from the oases. Despite his great hunger, Kel tried not to eat the lot.

Nitis ate, spoke and moved with the same distinction, an alliance of femininity and magic. He would have liked to gaze at her for hours, to become her shadow and never leave her for a moment.

'What happened to you, Kel?'

He drank a cup of wine to give himself courage. 'I was the latest recruit to the Interpreters' Secretariat in Sais.'

'You're very young for such an important job.'

He scribe blushed. 'Work is my only passion, and I've been lucky.'

'Or is it a question of precocious and exceptional skills?'

'I tried to show myself worthy of the responsibilities entrusted to me by the head scribe, and he gave me a strange coded papyrus which no one could decipher. Here it is.'

Kel took it out of a pocket in his tunic. Nitis looked at it but, despite her learning, could not read a single word.

'It is possible that all my colleagues were murdered because of this document.'

'Murdered?'

'Yes, with poisoned milk. They were all killed except my Greek friend, Demos, who has disappeared, as has the milk-seller, I'm accused of being the murderer. Two days before the killings, the last member of my family died when his house was deliberately burnt to the ground. Yesterday evening, at the

51

banquet, I was drugged, so I arrived late at the office. And there you have it: I'm the ideal culprit.'

Nitis gazed at him for a long time. His fate hung on her decision.

'I believe you are innocent, Kel.'

14

For a moment, Kel closed his eyes. She had not rejected him, so he still had a future.

'Once a person's word is given it is sacred,' she reminded him. 'Since you have taken an oath, you have committed yourself before both gods and men. Only a twisted person could lie to that point.'

'I have told you the truth. If I'm arrested I'll be killed – probably in a regrettable accident, in order to avoid a trial.'

'All this suggests the most incredible conspiracy.'

'I know, Nitis, but there's no other explanation.'

Kel summed up his experiences, point by point. And he didn't hide the involvement of his friend Bebon, who was now under arrest.

'The Interpreters' Secretariat dealt with many sensitive matters,' he said, 'and my superior was in permanent contact with the palace. The pharaoh used our work to direct his diplomatic policy, our guarantee of peace. Such a massacre can't have been the act of a madman. It was carefully organized, and its instigators chose me as the ideal culprit. My running away will have confirmed my guilt – an innocent man should have presented himself to the authorities and proclaimed his good faith. The manhunt will be intense, evidence will be accumulated, and the investigation will be closed quickly.'

'Can the legal system not distinguish truth from falsehood?'

'Circumstances are against me. And if the judge is in league with the murderers, he won't even listen to me.'

Nitis's peaceful world was crumbling. Suddenly crime, violence, falsehood and injustice were being unleashed, aspects of *isefet*, the force of destruction that was opposed to the serene harmony of Maat, goddess of righteousness. Why did she believe this young man? Why was she listening to these horrors, which overturned her tranquil, carefully mapped-out existence?

Kel saw that she was troubled. 'Forgive me for upsetting you like this. My position is untenable, I know, and I have no intention of dragging you into the depths of the abyss. May I simply ask you for the names of the people present at the banquet?'

Overcoming her emotion, the priestess spoke in a steady voice. 'First, the owner of the house, or Pefy, the minister of finance and agriculture. He knew my parents well and helped me to enter the Temple of Neith – his full name, Pef-tjaou-aouy-Nt, means 'His breath depends upon Neith'. He is an upright, hardworking man, who manages the Double House of Gold and Silver very well indeed, and watches over the country's prosperity. As the director of fields and overseer of the river-banks which flood, he created the post of planner in order to prevent future damage. Moreover, he is an initiate of the Great Mysteries of Osiris and conducts the rituals of Abydos, whose cause he often pleads to the pharaoh. On account of the development of Sais and the other cities in the Delta, he feels that the sacred city of the master of resurrection is being neglected.'

'He's one of the most important men in the country,' said Kel. 'Why did he invite me, an insignificant scribe?'

'In view of the brilliant start to your career, he probably wanted to get to know you.'

'If that were so, he'd have spoken to me at least once.'

'Pefy can't be the organizer of a murderous conspiracy.'

'Isn't he senior enough?'

'You're on the wrong track, I am certain of it.'

'Well, what about the other guests?'

'There's Menk, the organizer of festivals in Sais. He's in charge of the upkeep of the goddess's boats, checks the stocks of incense, face-paint and oils and ensures that the processions take place without a hitch. He is an affable, pleasant man, with nothing of the assassin about him.'

'Is he at all involved in politics?'

'Not at all.'

'Nevertheless, he knows the king and spends time with his ministers.'

'Yes, but his only preoccupation is ensuring that the rites are correctly celebrated.'

'But what if that's only a façade?'

Nitis's gaze faltered.

'I may be quite wrong,' conceded Kel. 'But listen to me, I beg you. Our world seemed well-ordered, governed by the Rule of Maat, yet now I've been accused of several murders.'

'I understand,' she murmured. 'Only the truth can re-establish harmony.' Suddenly, the future seemed disturbing. 'There was a third senior official at the banquet,' she said, 'Horkheb, head doctor at the palace.'

'A doctor? He'd have all kinds of drugs at his disposal.'

'Horkheb treats the royal family,' explained Nitis. 'He's said to be an excellent doctor, proud of his skill, and cautious. He never misses a big reception, cares what people think of him, but doesn't get mixed up in affairs of state, and his main concern is to accumulate a huge fortune. Why would he have become involved with such a conspiracy?'

'He'd have been handsomely paid.'

'That's only a suspicion.'

'Nevertheless, it's a first lead, thanks to you. You've helped me a great deal, Nitis, and I thank you with all my heart. Now I must go.'

'In the middle of the night? That would be madness! You must sleep here.'

'I refuse to put you in danger. And your reputation—'

'Nobody knows you're here, and I cannot simply abandon you in such circumstances. My master, the High Priest of the Temple of Neith, is an influential and respected man – the pharaoh himself takes account of his opinions. I've decided to talk to him about you and ask his advice.'

15

Every morning, High Priest Wahibra, whose name meant 'The Heart of the Divine Light is Lasting', celebrated the cult of Neith with ever-increasing veneration.

Shortly before dawn, he purified himself in the sacred lake, put on a white robe and, entering the heart of the shrine, gently awakened the Great Mother, from whom radiated the secret Light, source of all the many forms of life.

This daily duty did not weigh heavily upon him; quite the contrary. Aware that he was contributing to the maintenance of harmony on earth and fighting against the forces of destruction, the High Priest thanked destiny for granting him so much happiness. Consequently he oversaw every detail, so that the ritual might be the most perfect work of art possible.

In his eyes, nothing equalled the spiritual power of the pyramids of the Old Kingdom. Nevertheless, he appreciated the splendour of the main temple in Sais, an ancient city raised to the rank of capital. Situated at the centre of the western half of the Delta, it occupied a strategic position, the cause of its impressive development over the last few decades. Protected by a wall built by Milcsians, Greeks who originated from the city of Milet, the port harboured impressive warships, clear evidence of Egypt's defensive capacity.

The High Priest trusted Pharaoh Ahmose to safeguard the Two Lands. An experienced and skilful ruler, a former soldier who now hated war, the king had consolidated a peace which had often been threatened. Despite their warlike nature and their thirst for conquests, the Persians would not dare attack such a well-protected adversary.

Detaching himself from external realities, Wahibra congratulated himself on the attention the king paid to the Temple of Neith. Resembling the sky in all its moods, which housed all the gods and goddesses, the temple had benefited from many embellishments: a pro-pylon, a path lined with sphinxes, royal colossi, a sacred lake sixty-eight cubits long and sixty-five wide,* two stables dedicated to Horus and to Neith, a place of rest for the goddess's sacred cow, and many examples of restoration, carried out using enormous blocks of granite from Elephantine.

Inside the temple stood several statues of Neith, wearing the Red Crown of Lower Egypt, symbolizing the birth and development of the creative principle. She was depicted holding two sceptres, the *ankh*, Life, and the *was*, Power. Aided by the statues of her sons, Osiris, Horus, Thoth and Sobek, and her daughters – the vulture-goddess Nekhbet, guarantor of the royal office, the snake-goddess Wadjyt, who ensured the prosperity of creation, the terrifying lion-goddess Sekhmet, possessor of the power of the cosmos, and the cat-goddess Bastet – the queen of the great Mysteries opened the gates of the heavens to initiates.

Their function was neither to propagate a doctrine nor to convert people, but to carry on the work of Maat by correctly conducting the rites of the First Time, that perpetually renewed moment when the light of the Word was revealed. Its energy was concentrated in the temple and must be handled only by experts, with extreme caution.

At the end of the morning office, Wahibra went to the weaving workshop. There, priestesses were preparing the

* The estimated length of the cubit is 52cm.

fabrics used during the celebrations of the rites of Osiris, and the youngest, Nitis, was by far the least able of them. Always listening to her Sisters, filled with an inner joy and light which calmed angry people and energized the mournful, Nitis had accomplished a sort of miracle: attracting favourable opinions from the entire temple priesthood.

At the sight of the High Priest, the weavers stood up and bowed.

'Come, Nitis,' he said. 'I must speak with you.'

The young woman followed Wahibra to a building called Per-Ankh, 'the House of Life'. It was enclosed by high walls, and only those who had been initiated into the Mysteries of Isis and Osiris were allowed to enter.

'The time has come for you to pass through this door,' he said.

Nitis almost recoiled. 'I am too young, I—'

'I appoint you Superior of the songstresses and weavers of Neith. Inside the House of Life, you will find the sacred archives, which have been preserved since the birth of the Light, and the ritual texts we must constantly reformulate. I am old and sick, and the knowledge must be passed on. That is why I am finishing your training: so that you may succeed me.'

The weight of the entire temple suddenly weighed upon the young woman's frail shoulders. 'My lord, I—'

'Protest is pointless. By developing your magic and your sense of the abstract, you yourself have brought about this irrevocable decision. I did not wish to occupy high office, any more than you do. One must forget all ambition, and serve the gods, not human beings. Only this rigorous approach will enable you to bear your burden.'

The door of the House of Life opened.

A shaven-headed priest greeted Nitis and led her to the centre of the building, a square courtyard where she gazed upon the symbol of Osiris reborn. Then Wahibra showed her the texts, written by the ancient seers, from which Egyptian spirituality had been formulated. She allowed these words of power to imprint themselves upon her soul, knowing that she would never exhaust their significance.

16

Although still dazzled, Nitis could not hide from Wahibra the grave concerns disturbing her. While they were eating lunch together, she decided to confide in him.

'I am very sorry to remind you of the torments of the outside world,' she apologized, 'but because of the gravity of the situation, I need your advice.'

Her serious expression worried the High Priest.

'I have met an interpreter-scribe, Kel,' she went on. 'He is accused of having murdered his colleagues at the secretariat, but he swears he is innocent. And I believe him.'

Wahibra was stunned. 'The Interpreters' Secretariat is vital to state security,' he said. 'Without it, our diplomacy would be deaf and blind. Since I have not been informed of this tragedy, it seems it has been kept strictly secret.'

'Kel believes he is the victim of an incredible plot,' said Nitis. 'If there really is a conspiracy, senior officials are necessarily implicated in it.'

'A criminal matter of such importance ... Are you sure the scribe isn't merely a fantasist?'

'His sincerity convinced me. He's the newest recruit to the secretariat, and he was drugged during a banquet so that he'd oversleep and not be poisoned by the milk he usually served to his colleagues. Unfortunately, he made the mistake of panicking and running away, taking with him a coded document which the real murderers were probably looking for.'

'Has he deciphered it?'

'Not yet.'

'Did he show it to you?'

'Yes, and I didn't understand a single word of it.'

'Why doesn't he go to the authorities?'

'He's afraid he'll be killed before he can explain.'

'The authorities conspiring with criminals? Ridiculous!'

'If Kel's telling the truth, we can't rule out that possibility.'

'How long have you known him?'

'Since . . . yesterday evening.'

'And you don't doubt his word?'

'He swore on oath that he was telling the truth, he speaks in a direct and candid manner, and has a steady, open look in his eyes. At first I found it all hard to believe, but I am now completely convinced of his innocence.'

The High Priest was silent for a long time; then he asked, 'Does he accuse anyone of the murders?'

'Horkheb, head doctor at the palace, may have drugged him. If so, was Horkheb obeying orders from somebody else?'

'Kel must have made up this absurd story.'

Nitis felt a cruel pang of doubt. Had the young man been making a fool of her?

'Study the papyrus devoted to the seven words of Neith,' ordered the High Priest. 'I shall go to the palace, in the hope of dispelling this nightmare.'

'The lord Henat will see you immediately,' his private secretary told Wahibra.

Henat had a remarkably sober office. There was no decoration, and the furniture was austere. As soon as he stepped across the threshold, Wahibra felt uneasy.

'Is there a problem, dear friend?' asked Henat.

'Have the scribes at the Interpreters' Secretariat been murdered?'

Henat avoided the old man's gaze. 'That is a very direct question.'

'Is this rumour well-founded, or not?'

'You embarrass me.'

'Have you been forbidden to tell the High Priest of Neith?'

'No, indeed not. But the gravity of the situation—'

'So the killings did indeed happen.'

'I'm afraid so. Fortunately, the investigation soon brought results, and we know the identity of the murdered.'

'What is his name?'

'My duty of secrecy—'

'Must I remind you who I am?'

'He is a scribe called Kel, the newest member of the secretariat.'

'Is that a certainty, or merely an assumption?'

'Judge Gem, whose integrity and competence no one can doubt, has solid proof. Kel had an accomplice, a Greek scribe called Demos, who is also a fugitive. They will soon both be caught.'

'Why did they kill their colleagues?'

'We don't know – we're impatient to hear their reasons.'

'Do you suspect espionage?'

'At the present time, it is impossible to rule it out definitively, but there are no definite indications to that effect.'

'Without any senior-level interpreters, won't our diplomatic service suffer grave difficulties?'

'His Majesty is working to resolve them.'

Of course, Henat was conducting a parallel investigation and would not say a word about it. Judge Gem observed the usual legal procedures, whereas the head of Egypt's spy service operated in the shadows. And he was evidently convinced, despite his reserve, that the elimination of the Interpreters'

Secretariat could not be classified as an act of madness or simple villainy.

'May I ask you to observe the utmost discretion?' said Henat.

Wahibra nodded. 'Don't worry. I am not known as a talkative man.'

'I didn't think for a moment that you were. Merely, it's best not to frighten the general populace and to maintain secrecy about this abominable incident. Judge Gem agrees and is working discreetly. After all, the most important thing is to punish the murderer and rebuild the Interpreters' Secretariat, isn't it?'

17

Two days and two nights had passed, and Nitis had not come back. Refusing to consider the idea of treason by the sweet and attentive young woman, Kel could not escape the reality: she had been arrested on the orders of the High Priest. Brave Nitis must have refused to denounce him, otherwise the soldiers would have come for him.

Lost in admiration, Kel reproached himself for having dragged the priestess into this disastrous adventure and ruined her career. Because of him, his friend Bebon had suffered the same fate. Had he survived being beaten and tortured? And what tortures would be inflicted on Nitis? He must leave this house and rush to her aid.

But how could he free her, except by going to the authorities and stating that she was not his accomplice? Alas, she had sheltered him in her home. If both of them denied this detail fiercely, perhaps the judge would show mercy. The judge . . . Was he seeking the truth or was he being manipulated by the killers?

Kel heard the front door open. Was it the guards . . . or the murderers? There was no chance of escape. Kel grabbed a stool. He would fight.

Nitis appeared, looking resplendent.

'Don't worry,' she said. 'I'm alone. High Priest Wahibra wishes to see you. The meeting will be a crucial one.'

'You were gone so long . . .'

'I had to fulfil the first duties of my new appointment as Superior of the songstresses and weavers. And I was counting on you to stay calm while the High Priest went to the palace to verify what you told me.'

'Helping me any further would be mad, Nitis. Don't endanger yourself any more.'

'Hurry, Wahibra is waiting for us. The guards won't look for you at the temple.'

Kel was filled with wonder when he saw Neith's immense domain for the first time. Nitis guided him to a shrine on the northern side. An acacia tree grew in front of it, and the High Priest was seated in its shade.

His stern demeanour made a strong impression on the young man. Could he convince this dour old man?

'What do hieroglyphs mean to you?' asked Wahibra, his voice hard.

'I don't confuse them with the writing of the outside world, used in daily tasks. Hieroglyphs are the words of the gods, and are reserved for the temples. They contain the secrets and the forms of creation that embody true thought, beyond human capacity. Forming a secret language, they are the basis of our civilization and, before the incident in which I've become involved, I was hoping to discover a part of their mysteries.'

'Judge Gem is in charge of the investigation, and has proof of your guilt. Do you still deny that you are a murderer?'

'In the name of Pharaoh, I declare my total innocence.'

'A false oath destroys the soul.'

'I am aware of that, High Priest. And I maintain what I have said. It's the only freedom I have left.'

'You persist in claiming that you're innocent, in the teeth of the evidence?'

'The evidence is fabricated! I haven't killed anyone, and the murderers chose me as their perfect scapegoat because I can't defend myself.'

'Are you accusing your friend Demos?'

'His disappearance is disturbing, and I want to find him so he can explain.'

'Since you swear in the name of Pharaoh, how do you visualize the hierarchy of powers?'

'At the summit stands the creative principle, One in Two, at once male and female. Then come the gods, organizers of life and of the Rule of Maat, which Pharaoh must ensure is applied in this world by building temples, celebrating the rites and practising justice. If these tasks are not performed correctly, the country will return to chaos. The pharaoh possesses the testament of the gods and is the servant of the creative power; he drives back the forces of darkness and guarantees prosperity.'

'Have kings never failed?'

'Our history proves that they have.'

'When the king is a bad ruler,' declared the High Priest, 'the people become guilty and barbarism triumphs. A pharaoh's first preoccupation must be the gods, not men. If he chooses the wrong priority, he leads us to disaster.'

Kel thought he must have misunderstood: was Wahibra actually accusing Ahmose of being a bad ruler?

The High Priest stood up and looked deep into the young man's eyes. 'I believe you are innocent, my boy, for I have sounded out your heart. We are therefore in the presence of an exceptionally serious affair of state. The state powers are allowing a false accusation to be made, senior officials are mixed up in a conspiracy, and abominable murders have been committed without hesitation.'

'This may perhaps be the reason,' ventured Kel, showing the High Priest the coded papyrus.

Despite all his scholarship, Wahibra could not decipher it. 'The Interpreters' Secretariat is linked to the spy services,' he recalled. 'Henat directs them and reports to the king, who is favourable to the Greeks. To him, corruption and the abandonment of certain values matter little, as long as his allies can settle in great numbers in Naukratis, Memphis and other towns and cities in the Delta.'

'Is Ahmose himself responsible for the tragedy?' wondered Nitis.

'We cannot rule that out.'

'If that is the case, the authorities are carrying out his orders without taking account of the truth.'

'Kel shall hide here,' decided Wahibra. 'His knowledge will enable him to carry out the duties of a junior priest. You and I shall conduct our own investigation and assemble pieces of evidence enabling us to prove his innocence. If the guilty parties are government officials, I shall find the necessary support to destroy their sinister plans.'

18

'I have just heard of your appointment,' Menk told Nitis, 'and I'm delighted about it. Together, we shall do excellent work organizing the festivals. May I say that you look absolutely radiant?'

'In view of my inexperience, your help will be very valuable.'

'Whatever you do, don't quarrel with anyone. You'll have to give orders to priestesses who are older than you, sensitive and rather self-important. If you hurt their feelings, they'll become enemies and will cause you a thousand and one problems. Learn how to charm them, use your magic, and you will go on enjoying everyone's support. As for ritual problems, I'll always try to make your task easier. If you have the slightest difficulty, call on me and I'll come running.'

'Allow me to thank you in advance,' said Nitis.

'The High Priest was right to choose you as his pupil. Thanks to you, the future looks bright.'

'I shall do my utmost to serve Neith to the best of my ability.'

'Never compromise on the quality of the products used in ceremonies. The High Priest demands the best incense, the best oils and the best perfumes, and the items made in our workshops must be flawless. There remains one aspect which is always delicate: the songstresses' voices. Some, alas, sometimes forget to practise, while others wrongly believe that they are gifted. Correcting these faults will demand a great deal of you.'

'Since it is a question of honouring the gods and not humans, I shan't run out of energy.'

'The next festival takes place next week. All is ready, with the exception of the processional boat, which the temple carpenters have just finished restoring. We shall examine it tomorrow morning.'

The young woman seemed vexed. 'In view of the enormous amount of work facing me, I shall no longer have time to attend banquets like the one organized by the finance minister.'

'On the contrary, it's vital that you learn how to relax. If you work too hard, you won't be able to think clearly. Besides, your rank obliges you to take part in these revels, at which the prominent guests will appreciate your attendance. It's vital that you meet them and benefit from their good graces.'

'There was one guest there, that evening, whose presence surprised me.'

'Really? Which one?'

'A young interpreter-scribe. Didn't you notice him?'

'He didn't make an impression on me.'

'Why did the minister invite him?'

'I have no idea,' said Menk.

'People are whispering that this fellow Kel, if it really was him, has committed terrible crimes.'

Menk seemed ill at ease. 'Do you know any more about it?'

'Apparently, he murdered several colleagues.'

'What? Here, in Sais? That's impossible.'

'You haven't heard anything about it, then?'

'No, nothing.'

'And you don't know Kel?'

'This is the first time I've heard of him.'

'I have summoned the songstresses to a meeting and rehearsal late in the afternoon. Would you like to come?'

70

'I'm so sorry, but I have another commitment. Next time, certainly. I wish you luck, Nitis.'

Menk left the sacred enclosure and hurried off to consult his superior, Udja, governor of Sais and the king's first minister.

The offices of Udja's secretariat occupied one wing of the vast royal palace. A hard worker, Udja met the king every day and presented him with a summary of all the matters to be dealt with. Ahmose made swift decisions, and Udja carried them out.

Menk had to wait for a whole hour before being received. When he was shown in, Udja was standing by a broad window, admiring Sais.

'A splendid city, isn't it?' said the governor. 'At sunrise and sunset, I give myself the infinite pleasure of gazing at it. And we are constantly making it even more beautiful.'

'Indeed, my lord, indeed.'

Udja turned and looked at Menk. 'You seem agitated. Are there problems?'

'No, but there is a rumour – a most alarming rumour.'

'Go on.'

'Someone has committed murders, here, in Sais.'

'Who were the victims?'

'The scribes at the Interpreters' Secretariat. And the murderer is apparently one of their colleagues, a scribe named Kel, whom I met at a recent banquet. I still shiver at the thought of it. But this can't be true, surely?'

'Who is spreading the rumour?' asked Udja.

'A lady friend ... a great friend, who's respectable and trustworthy. That's why I'm so troubled by it. I want to show her that she's wrong, and only you can help me.'

'What is her name?'

'Discretion ...'

'I demand her name.'

'But it's only a wild rumour.'

'The scribe Kel did indeed murder his colleagues,' said Udja.

'He will be arrested, tried and sentenced. Since this is an affair of state, His Majesty demands the utmost discretion, and all the officials concerned are sworn to silence. Now, what is the name of your friend?'

'Nitis, the new Superior of the songstresses and weavers of Neith.'

'Confidentially, I must inform you that my spies and informers are taking charge of this affair, whose eventual ramifications are not yet known. One good piece of advice: keep well away from this horrible incident.'

'I shall be completely dumb,' promised Menk, 'and I don't want to hear another word about these crimes.'

'Warn Nitis to be extremely careful. The sages state that too much talk is harmful.'

'I shall pass on your wise advice, my lord.'

'Prepare us a fine festival, Menk. Our city must remain joyful.'

19

Pefy, minister of finance and agriculture, was angry. Once again, Ahmose had refused him the credits necessary for restoring the temple at Abydos. All that mattered to the king was the beautification of the capital, Sais.

'The High Priest of Neith wishes to speak with you,' announced his secretary.

'Show him in immediately. You didn't make him wait, I hope?'

The secretary stammered that he had not, and showed Wahibra in.

Pefy and Wahibra embraced.

'I'm delighted to see you again at last,' exclaimed Pefy. 'At our age, we shouldn't let such a long time pass without talking about the good old days.'

'Your burden of office does not leave much leisure time.'

'Neither does yours. I'll cancel my lunch with the director of taxation, and we'll enjoy a few quails roasted in red wine.'

The minister's cook was as good as the king's. As for the wine, it was just about perfect.

'The king is neglecting Abydos,' said Pefy angrily. 'To him it's merely a small town of no economic importance, but in fact it's vitally important because of its link with Osiris, whose magic ensures the equilibrium of the Two Lands. Developing the North to the detriment of the South runs the risk of destroying that balance.'

'But the Divine Worshipper, of Thebes, is both the king and the queen of Upper Egypt, isn't she?'

'Her spiritual and temporal power is limited to the sacred city of Amun, though her administrative skills please Ahmose. For my part, I'm having to use my own resources to do all the restoration work needed at the temple in Abydos – planting trees and vines, building a brick curtain-wall, dredging the sacred lake, making offertory tables of gold, silver and hard stone, and ensuring the proper functioning of the House of Life, where priceless written records are preserved. You, my old friend, do not have such cares.'

'The king enables me to maintain the Temple of Neith in excellent condition, I agree, but the recent tragedy has disturbed my peace.'

Pefy frowned. 'What tragedy?'

'The murder of the interpreter-scribes.'

'You aren't the kind of man to make sinister jokes. What do you mean?'

'Hasn't the king told you?'

'I never know what's going on.'

'A scribe called Kel is accused of poisoning his colleagues.'

'What, all of them?'

'Including the head of the secretariat. Apparently Kel had an accomplice, a Greek named Demos. Judge Gem is leading the investigation, and Henat is conducting his own enquiries.'

Pefy was thunderstruck.

'And that isn't all,' added Wahibra.

'What could be worse?'

'You invited Kel to your last banquet.'

'I didn't! Never!'

'But he was among the guests. He's an accomplished scribe, I grant you, but not to the extent of receiving such an honour.'

'I shall clear this up immediately.'

Pefy summoned his steward, an experienced man with an unblemished record of service, and demanded, 'Did you invite an interpreter-scribe called Kel to last week's banquet?'

The steward avoided his master's gaze. 'Forgive me, my lord. I was ill, and I gave the list of guests to my replacement and hoped he would do a good job. The name Kel isn't familiar.'

'Might your replacement have invited him?'

'Unfortunately, yes. I had a fever and aching joints, so I couldn't conduct my usual checks. All manner of ne'er-do-wells try to take advantage of official receptions.'

'Who treated you?' asked the High Priest.

'The palace doctor, Horkheb. He had me back on my feet in two days.'

Pefy dismissed the steward, and nervously chewed a piece of bread. 'Why has the king distanced me from such a serious matter? His love of the Greeks is going to his head. Surely the death of Cyrus and the succession of young Cambyses, who's probably greedy for conquests, ought to worry him?'

'Our army is more than capable of repelling the Persians, isn't it?'

'Any attempt at invasion seems doomed to failure,' conceded Pefy. 'Udja has built up a formidable war-fleet, and Phanes of Halikarnassos is an experienced soldier. All the same, we still need intelligent and active diplomacy, and the destruction of the Interpreters' Secretariat has deprived us of it.'

'Won't it be reconstructed very quickly?'

'That's easier to say than to do. The head scribe was exceptionally skilled, able to deal unerringly with delicate situations. Replacing him may take a long time.'

'Who will benefit from the situation? Who had an interest in committing the murders?'

'At first sight,' replied the minister, 'a secret agent in the service of the Persians. By depriving us of eyes and ears, the enemy can develop a strategy without our knowledge.'

'Kel, a young scribe who'd only recently joined the secretariat . . . Is he a plausible culprit, in your opinion?'

'Youth is no guarantee of innocence.'

'If I'm seeing things clearly, Judge Gem's investigation will serve as a decoy. Only Henat will discover the truth.'

'I've had enough of this mockery,' decided Pefy. 'This time Henat cannot hide behind his files.'

20

Wearing an expression of fury, Pefy burst into Henat's office, where he found his quarry dictating an urgent letter to his secretary.

'I want to talk to you – alone,' snapped Pefy.

Without waiting for his superior's orders, the secretary beat a hasty retreat.

'What is this about?' asked Henat in surprise.

'Don't play games with me. Why was I not informed about the murder of the interpreters?'

Henat gestured to indicate his powerlessness. 'Everything moved very fast. The murderer, a scribe named Kel, will soon be arrested, and Judge Gem will hand down a just sentence.'

'And what about the results of your own investigation?'

Henat's face hardened. 'Only Judge Gem is authorized to—'

'Stop treating me like an imbecile!' thundered Pefy. 'I demand the truth, and I demand it now!'

'These were appalling crimes, and we must find out what lies behind them.'

'Destroying the whole secretariat implies a conspiracy on an extraordinary scale.' Incarcerating the actual perpetrator will not be sufficient. What precisely do you know, Henat?

'Investigations are continuing.'

'And you continue to keep me in the dark!'

'His Majesty demands the utmost secrecy. Frightening the

population would be pointless. The king himself has undertaken to rebuild the secretariat and is ensuring that our diplomacy proceeds satisfactorily. For your part, ensure that the economy does likewise.'

'Is that a veiled threat, by any chance?'

'Come, come, Pefy. Everyone knows the weight of your responsibilities and appreciates your efficiency. Next week Sais will celebrate a wonderful festival, and we shall continue to enjoy prosperity and peace.'

In his capacity as organizer of festivals in Sais, Menk was authorized to attend the rehearsal of the songstresses of Neith, under the flexible yet firm direction of the beautiful Nitis.

Ye gods, she was ravishing! Clearly she must one day be his. Already they were working together; soon they would taste the joys of love. He must be very careful not frighten her, but win her over little by little – and, of course, prevent her from making regrettable mistakes. Forgetting all about the singers, Menk had eyes only for the Superior and her exquisite elegance.

The rehearsal ended, and the priestesses dispersed.

'So you found time to come,' observed Nitis. 'Did the singers seem more unified?'

'Oh yes. Thanks to you they're much, much better.'

'You seem moved. Is the music for the festival too emotional?'

'It isn't that. I saw Udja, and he confirmed that the interpreters have been murdered. It's a terrible thing, and the news must not get out. Judge Gem and Henat are dealing with the affair, and the murderer is indeed that young scribe, Kel, whom we met at the banquet. I still shiver at the thought of it – what if that madman had decided to murder all the guests? I only hope he doesn't kill again before he's arrested.'

'Will the investigations decide that it was an act of madness?'

'I don't know and I do not want to. We must keep well clear of the whole dreadful business, my dear Nitis, and concern ourselves only with our duties. However, there's one thing I must ask you; how did you learn of the tragedy?'

'It was just a rumour,' she replied with a smile.

'Well, don't listen to it again, and don't pass it on. Udja requires our silence, and we must obey him. A serious error could destroy your career, couldn't it?'

'That's wise advice,' agreed Nitis.

Menk relaxed. 'You are as intelligent as you are beautiful. When one knows how to keep in one's proper place and not annoy those in positions of power, fate is kind. And we have a great deal of work ahead of us.'

'Serving the goddess to the best of our abilities will be our sole priority,' said Nitis. 'I shall see you tomorrow, for the next rehearsal.'

'Henat treats me like a fool,' Pefy complained to Wahibra, 'and he refuses to tell me what he really knows. If he's handling matters, this is certainly nothing to do with the crimes of a madman. We're talking of an affair of state with unforeseeable consequences.'

'Would you use the word "conspiracy"?' asked the High Priest.

'Whatever it is, I am excluded from it. I still think it was a sinister crime by Persian spies with orders to disrupt our diplomacy by depriving us of information.'

'In other words, Cambyses is preparing to invade Egypt?'

'I think that's unlikely,' said Pefy. 'On the other hand, he may well be thinking of getting his hands on Palestine by infiltrating spies there, along with traders and propagandists. Our lack of interpreters will prevent us, for a certain time, from knowing any more. But above all, my friend, keep your distance from this affair. Henat is no joker.'

'Would he dare attack the High Priest of Sais?'

'I have lost count of the underhand blows landed by his men! Don't forget that Ahmose won power by force, and he won't tolerate anything which calls his authority into question again. We owe him our peace and prosperity, it is true, but will they be lasting?'

'You seem very gloomy,' said Wahibra.

'If Ahmose reconstructs the Interpreters' Secretariat quickly, and if the murderers are punished in accordance with their crimes, the future will be brighter.'

21

Kel took enthusiastically to his new duties as a *wab*, a 'pure priest'. Every morning, before dawn, he went to the sacred lake and filled two alabaster vases, which he handed to a ritualist. Next, he examined the list of fresh produce destined for the temple and checked the suppliers' descriptions. He was quiet and reserved, and indistinguishable from the other scribes in the service of the Superior of songstresses and weavers.

He willingly carried out the elementary tasks given to a new *wab*: cleaning palettes, washing ink-pots, and rolling papyri. Cleanliness was an absolute rule, so he swept the premises occupied by the pure priests and carried the kilts to the washer-man.

This new life would have satisfied him fully, but pangs of anguish kept bringing him back to reality: he was nothing but a fugitive, a supposed criminal, taking advantage of temporary shelter. His brilliant future, his planned career and the security expected by a good worker were all lost to him, and the present beautiful mirage would soon melt away.

'The Superior is asking for you,' a colleague told him.

Kel went to the House of the Weavers, where he was greeted by Nitis and High Priest Wahibra.

The young woman closed and bolted the door. 'Is all well?' she asked.

'Nobody has asked me any awkward questions.'

'The pure priests stay in the temple for only a short period,' Wahibra reminded Nitis, 'and faces change frequently. As long as he does his work well, Kel will go unnoticed.'

'Have you learnt any more about the affair?' asked the scribe anxiously.

'At first I thought Menk knew nothing about it,' said Nitis, 'but his behaviour makes me wonder. He assured me that he did indeed know nothing and wanted to keep his distance from the drama. Nevertheless, he rushed straight to Udja, to tell him I'd spoken about the murders, and then in veiled words he ordered me to keep to my new duties and allow the authorities to act.'

'Menk is in love with you,' said the High Priest. 'He wants to prevent you from doing anything wrong.'

'Couldn't that be evidence of his complicity? He knows the identity of one or more of the criminals, and is trying keep me from finding out the truth.'

Kel felt profoundly depressed. So Menk was in love with Nitis – and he probably wasn't the only one to want her. She would marry a dignitary of her own rank, with a spotless reputation.

'Menk seems frightened,' she added, 'he may merely be pretending to be a coward. He's very skilful and very persuasive – but is he mixing sincerity with lies? One can't trust him.'

'And yet,' objected Wahibra, 'he told you he'd been to see Udja.'

'That might be part of his plan,' suggested Kel. 'If Menk's in Udja's pay, and is carrying out his dirty work, he could be pretending to be obedient in order to protect Nitis.'

'How can one imagine such duplicity?'

'So many murders have been committed!'

'And you are still the only one accused of committing them' Wahibra reminded him. 'Your friend Demos's case seems hardly to interest the authorities. He might be your accomplice, perhaps, but not the culprit. Judge Gem has shown that he's convinced you will soon be arrested and will reveal the reasons behind the affair.'

Kel felt like a broken man. In those few words, the High Priest had summed up the whole situation. It was impossible that he could escape his fate.

Wahibra laid his powerful hand on the young man's shoulder. 'Don't despair. I believe that you are innocent.'

Nitis smiled comfortingly at Kel. 'The High Priest and I know that the real criminals chose you as the ideal scapegoat, and we are determined to identify them.'

'My friend Pefy didn't enlighten me very much,' said Wahibra. 'To listen to him, he knows nothing about what's going on, and Henat refuses to tell him anything.'

Nitis was astonished. 'The minister for finance and agriculture treated like that? Is that plausible?'

'Up to now, Pefy has never lied to me.'

'Are you sure that he isn't playing his own game?' Kel asked.

'He is deeply attached to the Law of Maat, and has never done anything contemptible.'

'Nevertheless, he carries out the king's orders.'

'That's true, but he is clear-headed about it, and he's thinking in terms of Persian spies trying to weaken Egypt by disrupting diplomacy. According to him, Cambyses is hoping to extend his influence without actually invading us. His goal is probably Palestine. Since Ahmose wishes to avoid another war, he would be unlikely to take military action.'

'Why did he invite me to his banquet?'

'That point seems to have been cleared up,' said the High Priest. 'Normally, his steward submits a list of guests to Pefy for approval, and then issues the invitations. But he was ill, and passed that task on to a replacement. Pefy was unaware of your existence, and was himself made use of. He told me one important detail: it was Horkheb who treated the steward, and

83

he isn't usually interested in any but high-ranking patients.'

'At last something solid!' exclaimed Kel. 'Horkheb drugged the steward and chose his replacement, so as to be sure I'd fall into his trap.'

'He has always scrupulously avoided getting mixing up in politics,' the High Priest recalled.

'Yes, but he spends a lot of time with senior officials – and he treats Pharaoh,' the young man insisted.

'Horkheb's main interest is increasing his wealth and his possessions, which are already considerable. A large fee might have persuaded him to take part in the ruse without knowing its real significance.'

'This is an important lead,' said Nitis. 'Horkheb must be made to talk. His testimony could clear Kel and enable the investigation to begin again on a new basis.'

'Unfortunately,' said Wahibra, 'Judge Gem is stubborn and his only thought is to arrest Kel. Approaching him directly seems risky to me.'

'I have an idea,' said Kel.

22

Summoned as a matter of urgency, Horkheb hurried up the ramp and into the royal palace. The whole place was a veritable hive of activity, where butchers, bakers, brewers and many other craftsmen worked, all extremely well-paid and eager to keep their jobs. Given the size of the building and the considerable number of rooms, stone-cutters, sculptors, carpenters and painters were often at work. The king's dwelling, which was compared to the horizon, must not suffer from a single imperfection.

Each morning, Pharaoh rose like the sun, in order to spread forth life and light. The part of the palace that was constructed from brick was a reminder of the human and fleeting nature of the individual who embodied the royal office, while the stone-built section served as a reminder of his divine origin. At the heart of the palace were an immense pillared reception hall and shrines with granite doorways, enabling the king to remain in contact with the gods.

Horkheb greatly admired the luxury and beauty of Ahmose's palace. Rich colours, varied floral motifs, superb paintings of birds frolicking above lotus flowers . . . He never ceased to marvel at it all.

At each entrance, members of the king's personal body-guard were posted. Heavily armed, they applied the king's security directives to the letter. Ahmose never forgot that he had seized the throne by means of an insurrection, and had had to wage a civil war before gaining control of the whole of Egypt.

Although he was the royal family's doctor, Horkheb yielded with good grace to the rule that required everyone entering the monarch's private apartments to be searched. He even opened his leather pouch containing precious remedies.

Queen Tanith came to meet him. 'My husband has been taken ill,' she whispered. 'I am very worried.'

Stretched out on a bed with feet shaped like a bull's hooves lay Ahmose, his eyes half closed.

'Here I am, Majesty,' said Horkheb. 'What is the trouble?'

'I have a terrible headache and dizziness,' said the king. 'I think I lost consciousness, and now I cannot stand up.'

The doctor laid his hand on the nape, chest, wrists and legs of his illustrious patient. 'It's nothing serious,' he concluded. 'The channels are expressing the way of the heart, and energy is circulating freely. I shall prescribe you a potion made from figs, aniseed, crushed ochre and a little honey. You shall take it for four days, and your system will be refreshed.'

Reassured, the queen smiled and left the chamber.

'Majesty,' murmured Horkheb, 'there is one part of the treatment which only you may apply.'

Ahmose sat up. 'What is it?'

'An excess of wine and beer seems to me to be prejudicial to your health. It's true that you have a robust constitution, but these excesses—'

'Let me be the judge of that.'

'Permit me to insist.'

'I do not permit you anything of the sort. Do your work and dispense with your comments.'

Horkheb returned to the sumptuous house in the centre of the city where he received his wealthy patients – he no longer treated poor or low-class folk. Now the owner of two substantial properties, one in the capital and the other in Upper

Egypt, he worked only three days a week and took full advantage of his reputation as the royal family's physician. An expert in general medicine, and therefore at the summit of the medical hierarchy, he referred any difficult cases to specialists.

'There's an emergency,' his assistant informed him.

'Involving whom?'

'The Superior of the songstresses and weavers of Neith.'

'A repulsive old woman, I take it?'

'On the contrary, she is young and very pretty.'

'Then present my apologies to my first patient, and bring her into my examination room.'

The assistant had not lied: Nitis was delectable.

'We met at the minister of finance's last banquet, did we not?' said Horkheb.

'Indeed.'

'I did not know you had been promoted.'

'It happened only very recently.'

'Permit me to congratulate you and to wish you a brilliant career. Now, what is troubling you?'

'I am very well, but a priest at the temple in Sais has had a serious accident.'

Horkheb coughed. 'I don't deal with that sort of emergency.'

'High Priest Wahibra would be infinitely grateful to you for your help. On one hand, you may fix your own fee. On the other, he will speak to the king of your generosity.'

'My duty as a doctor obliges me to act,' decided Horkheb.

He told his assistant to tell his patients to come back the next day, and followed Nitis, whose jasmine-tinged perfume enchanted him.

'What kind of accident was it?' he asked.

'A heavy fall.'

'Is he unconscious?'

'No, he's remained alert.'

'That's a good sign. Have you moved him at all?'

'We merely applied balm to his wounds.'

Nitis took Horkheb to an external annexe of the temple, where the serving pure priests lodged. Thinking of the enormous fee he'd charge, Horkheb cheerfully crossed the threshold.

Suddenly, he stopped in his tracks. There, in front of him, was the scribe Kel.

'Why did you drug me and who ordered you to do it?' demanded Kel.

The doctor's reaction astonished the young people. He dropped his pouch, pushed Nitis out of the way and fled at top speed.

Kel immediately chased after him. This was as good as a confession. Recognizing his victim and the designated scapegoat, Horkheb had proved he was involved in the conspiracy. Of course, he had been promised that he'd never see Kel again, and would hear no more about the affair.

Despite his fear, too many over-copious meals meant that Horkheb could not keep up the pace for long. As he turned along a busy side-street, he ran full tilt into the leading stallion in a troop of donkeys laden with sacks of wheat, and found himself on the ground.

Several animals reared up, some charged, others brayed in protest. A sack of wheat came loose from the leading donkey's load and fell on top of Horkheb. The furious donkey-driver wielded his staff several times, hitting the thief who was trying to run off with his property. And two loose donkeys trampled all over the attacker.

'Stop!' roared Kel.

His face bloody and his limbs broken, Horkheb moaned piteously.

'That thief deserved his punishment,' declared the donkey-driver.

'I must question him.'

'Are you a guard officer?'

'Isn't that obvious?'

The peasant drove his donkeys back, eventually managed to calm them, and retrieved the heavy sack of wheat.

Kel addressed the wounded man. 'Talk to me, Horkheb. Who employed you? Why were the interpreters murdered?'

But real guards, armed with clubs and short swords, were running towards them.

'Tell me!' begged Kel.

Horkheb fainted. Kel took to his heels.

23

Horkheb's condition was critical, and he would not live much longer. His skull had caved in, he could no longer speak, and he was hardly breathing. Three eminent doctors from the Sais medical school had all given the same diagnosis: 'It is an illness which we cannot treat.' All they could do was give the dying man a powerful drug to relieve his suffering.

Although barely conscious, Horkheb made out a silhouette entering his bedchamber; it was that of the originator and supreme leader of the conspiracy.

The visit owed nothing to compassion. The leader wished to extract a little information from this gullible imbecile. Basically, the accident was rather convenient. The conspirators had decided to get rid of Horkheb, who had become a liability, but the donkeys had done the job for them.

'Are you really unable to speak?'

The dying man painfully raised his right hand.

'According to the official report, a donkey-driver mistook you for a thief, and his beasts trampled you. Was it really an accident?'

With a great effort, Horkheb managed to shake his head.

'Who killed you?'

The hand rose again. The conspirator helped him hold a brush and placed a piece of papyrus under his fingers. Horkheb traced three barely readable signs: *K . . . e . . . l.*

'Kel! So he's still hiding in Sais. Do you know any more?'

The stiff, clumsy fingers gripped the brush again and traced a few, almost indecipherable signs.

The conspirator could just make out the word 'temple', which might possibly be followed by a name.

'Make an effort! Who is protecting the scribe?'

The brush fell on to the papyrus. Horkheb was dead.

The leader of the conspiracy did not hide the truth from his followers. 'Not only is that damned Kel still alive, not only has he evaded the authorities, but he even managed to follow the trail as far as Horkheb. Fortunately, the trail stops there – he cannot go any further.'

'He certainly has the coded papyrus.'

'It ought never to have reached the head of the secretariat! That stupid administrative error has forced us to take radical action, and that is deeply regrettable. Nevertheless, with regard to the overall situation, we must continue to develop our plan.'

The conspirators gave their assent.

'Have no fear,' said the leader, 'our code cannot be broken. One awkward fact is that Kel certainly has protectors.'

'Do we know who they are?'

'Before he died Horkheb gave me a clue, and we're going to exploit it. Once Kel has been arrested and the papyrus retrieved, we can go forward in complete safety.'

Pharaoh Ahmose glared at Udja and Henat. 'I cannot do without Horkheb!'

'Alas, Majesty,' said Udja, 'my eminent colleague has just passed away. He will receive the finest mummification and will be buried in a magnificent tomb.'

'What was the cause of his death?'

'A stupid accident. Destiny can sometimes be cruel.'

'I have decided that you are to replace him.'

'Majesty, I have long since ceased to practise medicine, and my duties—'

'Everyone agrees that you were the finest ever medical director of the Sais school. I shall be your only patient and you will run to my aid whenever necessary.'

Udja bowed. He knew the king's penchant for full-bodied wines and strong beer, and would have to try to maintain his body in good condition despite his excesses.

'Majesty,' said Henat, who was visibly troubled, 'my office has received an anonymous letter accusing the Temple of Neith of hiding the fugitive scribe Kel.'

'That's impossible!' scoffed Udja.

'It's not impossible that the monster has abused the good faith of a priest,' said Henat. 'Such a dangerous man is capable of absolutely anything. Knowing that he is lost, he won't hesitate to use more violence.'

Ahmose thought for a moment, then said, 'I am going to give Judge Gem the order to cordon off the temple and search it. If the murderer is there, he will be arrested.'

'Won't such forceful action upset the High Priest?'

'He rules neither the country nor this investigation! Must I remind you that I have abolished the temple courts and that they are now subject to royal jurisdiction? No religious precinct may give refuge to a criminal. Moreover, my government has restored the temples' finances by granting them fiscal privileges and profitable lands – let them remember that. Despite his authority and his reputation, the High Priest must obey me and allow the judge and his men to enter.'

'Majesty, I would advise a degree of subtlety,' ventured Udja. 'If the operation is too visible, it may worry the population.'

'Permit me to agree with Udja,' said Henat. 'And we should consider the possibility that he might take hostages. By killing them he would spread panic, and the peace of our capital city would be gravely disturbed.'

'We should be wary of the anonymous letter, too,' empha-sized Udja, eyeing Henat as though he were its author. 'It may be a complete lie.'

'To what purpose?' Henat asked in surprise.

'The High Priest's spiritual stature has made him enemies, and there are ambitious men who covet his place.'

'Let us forget that,' snapped Ahmose, 'and concern our-selves with finding out if the murderer is hiding in the temple. Udja, fetch Judge Gem immediately. I myself shall give him the necessary instructions.'

24

'Horkheb lost consciousness before answering my questions,' Kel told Nitis and Wahibra. In view of the seriousness of his injuries, he has little chance of survival. But his behaviour proves his guilt. As soon as he saw me, he realized that I'd uncovered the truth.'

'Evidently,' said Wahibra, 'he was merely carrying out orders. His death may well suit whoever was employing him – by dying he will keep silent for ever, and our only lead ends in a blind alley.'

'No, it doesn't,' Nitis protested. 'Menk was at the banquet, too. And let us not cross Henat and Udja off the list of suspects.'

'I would add to it the king himself,' declared Kel solemnly.

'Let us not become unrealistic,' advised Wahibra. 'Why should Ahmose destroy one of the major strengths of his diplomacy, his Interpreters' Secretariat?'

'It infuriates me not to be able to decipher the coded papyrus. It would undoubtedly give us all the answers.'

Nitis looked significantly at the High Priest, who instantly understood what she meant.

'The House of Life may contain crucial information. Give the papyrus to Nitis; she will try to find the key to reading it.'

Kel hesitated. What if this was a clever ruse? Nitis had also been at the banquet. Was it her plan to inveigle him into doing this very thing? Without the papyrus, Kel would have no means of defending himself, and his pursuers would have no further need to keep him alive. Nitis was the pupil of the High Priest, and the High Priest obeyed the pharaoh. Instead of being protected by true allies, had Kel fallen into the hands of the conspirators?

He gazed intently at the young priestess and saw such a light of truth in her eyes that he instantly regretted his suspicions. 'I wish you success, Nitis.'

Someone knocked at the door.

Kel quickly hid behind a screen, and then Wahibra opened the door. He spoke briefly to the visitor, then closed the door and turned back to Kel and Nitis.

'Juge Gem demands to search the temple and all its annexes,' he told them. 'Kel cannot go back to his quarters.'

'We must leave at once,' said Nitis. 'Try to delay the judge while we get out of the enclosure.'

'Where will you go?' Wahibra asked anxiously.

'They won't catch Kel – you need have no fear of that.'

'The door of the archive chamber is open. When you go out, follow the wall along as far as the first guard-post. The guard is unlikely to question the Superior of songstresses and weavers, accompanied by a pure priest.'

Once again, Kel was gripped by agonizing suspicion. He didn't doubt Nitis's sincerity, but was this the High Priest's way of delivering him up to the authorities?

'Come quickly,' said Nitis.

Wahibra went out to meet Judge Gem, who was flanked by two burly soldiers.

'What is happening?' asked the High Priest.

'Just so that you are aware of the situation: it seems that Kel, the murderer of the interpreters, may be hiding here.'

'Upon what evidence is this unbelievable supposition based?'

'An anonymous denunciation.'

'And you, an experienced judge, give credence to such a thing?'

'I must check everything.'

'I will not permit a complete search of the temple.'

'Pharaoh has ordered it. Don't oblige me to use force and to deploy the hundred men who accompany me. From this moment on, all ways in and out of the domain of Neith are being watched.'

'You are violating a sacred place!'

'Temples no longer have independent jurisdiction,' Gem reminded him, 'and we are pursuing a savage creature capable of killing again. Do not refuse to help me, High Priest. On the contrary, guide me and let us disturb the peace of this place as little as possible.'

'Very well, but on condition that you enter neither the innermost shrine, which is reserved for Pharaoh and his representative, the High Priest, nor the House of Life, where the sacred archives used by initiates in the Mysteries of Isis and Osiris are kept.'

'Will you swear in the name of the king that the murderer is not hiding there?'

'How can you even consider such a monstrous thing? I am the guarantor of the secrecy of these pure places and willingly give the oath you demand. May the gods strike me down if my tongue lies!'

The High Priest's cold fury impressed the judge. 'My task is highly sensitive – you must understand that.'

'Come with me,' ordered Wahibra. 'Let us examine each part of the goddess's domain together. And you may question whoever you wish.'

Deep down, the judge had little faith in the anonymous denunciation. Ordinarily he tore up that kind of rubbish and took no account of it during trials. But this time the king had been most insistent that he should check. Gem could have refused, but the affair was so serious that he preferred not to leave any lead unexplored.

And so, together with the High Priest and a detachment of experienced men, he explored the sacred and profane places, from the chamber where very ancient ritual objects were stored to the bedchambers of the pure priests. He did not leave out the four shrines arranged at the four points of the compass, nor the storehouse for linen fabrics and the numerous workshops; and he even visited the shrines overlooking the tombs of the kings who had been buried close to the temple.

When Gem wished to enter the Temple of the Bee, Wahibra blocked the entrance and said, 'Only you, a servant of Maat, may enter. Outsiders may not.'

Having nothing to fear from the High Priest, the judge agreed.

The Temple of the Bee housed the cult of Osiris, which was linked to that of the ancestors. This was where the rites were celebrated, linking Neith to the god of resurrection and those 'of just voice'. This was the dwelling-place of the mysterious chest containing Osiris's body of light.

Gem was so impressed by the majesty of the temple, whose façade resembled those of the House of the North and the House of the South at Saqqara, built in the reign of Djoser, that for a moment he forgot about his quest.

As he emerged from the temple, the sight of his men jolted him back to reality.

25

'Are you satisfied, Judge?' asked the High Priest.

'My guards prevented anyone from leaving the sacred enclosure before the end of the search. However, there is one small thing. A priestess, accompanied by a man, got through the first guard-post by arguing that she was the Superior of the songstresses and weavers. Who is that?'

'Nitis.'

'A mature woman of great experience, I assume?'

'No, a young priestess whose excellent qualities are recognized by all. Her appointment was unanimously approved.'

'Did you choose her?'

'Indeed.'

'Why has she run away?'

'Run away? Whatever do you mean?'

'Where does she live?'

'The improvements to her official residence will be finished by tomorrow.'

The judge's tone hardened. 'Where does she live ... at present?'

'In her family home, near the temple.'

'Will you take me there?'

'What if I refuse?'

'I shall inform the king of your uncooperative attitude and will ask that you be closely questioned in order to learn the truth. Your position as High Priest of Neith does not place you above the law. If you have sheltered this criminal, and if Nitis has indeed fled with him to hide him at her house, you will both be punished in accordance with the law, and the court will show you no lenience.'

'Your accusations are insulting and grotesque. And I shall speak to the king about the manner in which you have conducted your investigation, casting suspicion upon innocent people.'

'I repeat, will you take me to Nitis's house?'

'I bow one last time to your demands.'

The High Priest led the way with ponderous slowness. Though he gave no sign of it, he was anxious. How would Nitis explain herself? Had she really been unwise enough to take Kel into her home? In the event of an arrest, she and Wahibra would both convicted of being accomplices to murder, stripped of their status and belongings and imprisoned. Nobody would believe that the young scribe was innocent.

The door of Nitis's modest house was closed.

A soldier knocked. 'Open up! Judge Gem wants to speak to you.'

The young woman appeared. 'Judge Gem? And you, too, High Priest?'

The magistrate went instantly on to the attack: 'Why did you run away?'

'I? Run away?'

'You left the temple with a man and passed through a guard-post despite my orders.'

'Yes, I did, because there was an emergency.'

'What emergency?'

'A serious leak on my terrace. The next time there's a storm, my bedchamber would have been flooded, so I asked a stone-cutter from the temple to repair it straight away.'

Judge Gem smiled ferociously. 'And I suppose this stone-cutter is at work right now?'

'Of course.'

'I shall check.'

Wahibra was filled with consternation. Nitis was naive and thought that she was safe at home, underestimating Gem's pugnacity. Even if Kel succeeded in getting away by jumping from roof to roof, the soldiers would capture him.

'Do not move from here,' ordered the judge.

Two sturdy soldiers went first. They climbed the stairs four at a time, leapt on to the workman and flattened him to the ground.

'Well, well, Kel the scribe!' exclaimed the judge in delight. 'You thought you were safe, but the chase ends here.'

The man, a short, brown-haired fellow with a scarred forehead, did not look much like the portrait of the murderer.

'I'm not a scribe,' he protested in a frightened voice. 'I'm a stone-cutter at the Temple of Neith, and I came here to mend a leak, at the Superior's request.'

'Let him go,' said Gem, bitterly disappointed. 'We shall search the rest of the house.'

The High Priest could tell from Gem's expression that things were not going as the latter had hoped.

When the judge came back up from the cellar, he approached Nitis.

'Scribe-interpreter Kel is a dangerous criminal on the run. Has he contacted you in any way?'

The young woman was most indignant. 'Why would a murderer approach me?'

He showed her the portrait. 'Take a good look at his face. If you see this monster, inform me immediately.'

'There is no chance that I shall encounter him at the temple, which is where I shall be living from tomorrow.'

'Judge Gem knows that perfectly well,' confirmed the High Priest. 'And now, if he has no more need of us, we are going to celebrate the evening ritual. I dare to hope that these guards and soldiers will return to their barracks.'

'For your own safety,' said Gem, 'I shall leave a few men here to keep watch. Since you've done nothing wrong, it shouldn't trouble you.'

'I deplore this pointless show of force,' said Wahibra, 'and I shall inform the king of it.'

With that, he and Nitis walked away.

'Where is Kel hiding?' he asked as soon as they were out of earshot.

'He didn't leave the temple. When I saw that the guards were there, I told him to keep moving, following you step by step. I was sure that, by taking the stone-cutter with me, I'd attract the judge's attention and thus prove our innocence. Kel has returned to your archive chamber and is waiting for us there. After such a public failure, the judge won't dare search Neith's domain again.'

26

Wahibra was in no doubt: Judge Gem was obeying the killers, who wanted everyone to believe that Kel was guilty. The way he was conducting his investigation proved his bias, and the libellous denunciation was nothing but his own invention. Acting on orders, he was placing the Temple of Neith under guard to deter any thoughts of helping the suspect.

Hoping profoundly that the king was innocent, the High Priest decided that he must inform him of Gem's actions and ask him to remove Gem from the case in favour of a more honest judge, who would be able to listen to Kel without preconceptions.

Wahibra had never seen so many soldiers near the palace. They were dispersing all passers-by, and preventing access to the ramp leading to the main entrance. He found his way barred by an officer, who told him, 'No one may enter.'

'The king will receive the High Priest of Neith.'

'Wait here.'

The officer went off to find his superior.

When he returned he said, 'Please come with me.'

'Has something serious happened?'

'I don't know, High Priest. I've been ordered to take all important guests to Lord Udja.'

Udja had just dismissed a senior official, and his forbidding appearance did not bode well.

'I wish to speak with His Majesty,' said Wahibra.

'I'm sorry, but that isn't possible.'

'Why not?'

'That is a state secret.'

'Are you trying to make mock of me, Minister? Drive me out, if you dare!'

'Please try to understand. The circumstances—'

'I wish to see Pharaoh immediately.'

'As I told you, that isn't possible.'

'It concerns an affair of state, Minister, and it will suffer no delay.'

Udja appeared to lose patience. 'The queen may agree to receive you.'

'I shall wait as long as is necessary.'

The High Priest did not have to wait long. A steward took him to the queen's reception hall, where the paintings, in the Greek style, mingled with a floral Egyptian design of the most traditional type.

Dressed in a long green gown, with a necklace made up of five rows of multicoloured beads at her throat, Tanith looked marvellous.

'Is the king unwell, Majesty?' asked Wahibra.

'Let us say . . . somewhat troubled.'

'I am sorry to inconvenience you, but I must speak with His Majesty.'

'Is it really urgent?'

'Extremely.'

'I shall try to persuade him . . .'

This time, the wait went on and on.

The queen herself took the High Priest to Ahmose's office.

'Leave us now,' the king her. 'Well, High Priest, what is this emergency?'

'Judge Gem is persecuting the Temple of Neith, Majesty. He is conducting his investigation in a wholly unacceptable way. Searching for a murderer does not imply dragging innocent people through the mud.'

'The nature of this affair has recently changed,' said the king, 'and only an experienced, honest judge like Gem can discover the truth without showing partiality to anyone.'

'Permit me to protest vigorously.'

'You have no idea what is going on! Someone has stolen my helmet of power.'

'Your helmet of . . . ? You mean—'

'Yes, the one a soldier placed upon my head to crown me pharaoh, in front of my army. At first, I refused the heavy responsibility and that way of acquiring power, but then I accepted my destiny and the decision of the gods. That helmet was the symbol of it, and magically guaranteed my legitimacy. Without it, my power will disappear.'

'The practice of the rites will maintain it, Majesty. When you wear the crown of Osiris, you are no longer a victorious general but Pharaoh, spreading the light of the world across the Two Lands.'

'Someone is trying to destroy me,' confided Ahmose. 'The murder of the interpreters and the theft of the helmet are linked.'

'In what way?'

'I do not yet know. Henat and his spies will find out.'

'Their methods, Majesty—'

'I have given them complete freedom of action.'

'But violating the Rule of Maat will bring misfortune.'

'Kel the scribe is the criminal who killed his colleagues. Despite his young age, I suspect him of also being the mastermind behind the plotters seeking to overthrow me. There is no point worrying about the Persian threat. It is here inside Egypt that people are conspiring against me. But my enemies are very much mistaken if they think they have brought me low. I am a warrior and I shall emerge victorious from this new battle. As for you, High Priest, celebrate the rites and preserve the gods' favour towards me. Above all, do not try to interfere. This affair goes beyond you, and you do not have the weapons necessary to resolve it. Any impetuous action which might compromise the success of the investigation will be severely punished.'

His thoughts whirling, Wahibra withdrew. Was Ahmose sincere or was it all an act? And why was he distancing the High Priest of Neith from power? Depriving himself of the priest's support and counsel in this way could easily lead to the pharaoh becoming isolated, or even coming to harm if he listened to his enemies.

Only one thing was certain: the fate of the innocent young scribe was sealed, and nobody and nothing could enable him to escape from injustice.

27

When the door of Wahibra's archive room opened, Kel tensed.
Had soldiers come to arrest him? Pleading his innocence
would be futile, so he would defend himself tooth and nail –
he'd sooner fall beneath their blows than rot away in prison.

'It is Nitis,' said the priestess's musical voice.

Hugely relieved, Kel emerged from his hiding-place.

'The affair has taken a new turn,' she told him. 'Someone
has stolen the palace treasure, the helmet with which a soldier
crowned Ahmose to proclaim him Pharaoh. The whole city
has been placed on alert, guards and soldiers are everywhere,
and the High Priest has temporarily restricted the activities of
the temples.'

'Ahmose must fear that a usurper may imitate him,' said
Kel, 'by putting on the helmet, taking command of the rebels,
and declaring himself to be the new king.'

Nitis disagreed. 'The generals, from Phanes of Halikarnassos downwards, are loyal to Ahmose, to whom they owe
everything. How could the rebels possibly overcome the
army?'

'You may be right, but the helmet has been stolen, thus
depriving Ahmose of the symbol of his power. Magically, the
king is much weakened. And the thief must intend to take
his place, a plan which only a very senior official could have
devised.'

'The king has complete trust in Gem,' said Nitis. 'He refuses to remove him from the case, and believes that the theft of the helmet and the murder of the interpreters are linked.'

'How?' asked Kel in great surprise.

'The link is you: for you are supposed to be not only the murderer but also the mastermind behind the plot against the king.'

Thunderstruck, the young man sat down on a folding stool. 'I shall have to run away. But why am I being persecuted in this insane way?'

'There is nothing insane about it, and it corresponds to a carefully constructed plan in which you play the role of the ideal scapegoat.'

'And the king himself is demanding my death. What if it was he himself who decided that my colleagues should be killed?'

'At the moment, he seems more like a victim,' Nitis pointed out.

Kel clutched his head in his hands. 'It's like being caught in a sandstorm and unable to see even two paces ahead. Everything's becoming dark and incomprehensible. I'm lost, Nitis.'

She moved nearer, and he caught the scent of her perfume.

'Someone is trying to make you lose your reason and your courage, and the High Priest has been forbidden to take action. However, we shall not stand idle. And nobody knows that I am by your side.'

He had the feeling that her smile was not merely that of a friend or a confidante, but he refused to let his thoughts wander. 'You're taking too many risks.'

'In Egypt a woman is free to act as she sees fit. That is one of the finest aspects of our civilization. And in future you—'

'I have no future, Nitis. Quite the contrary, in fact.'

'What if you were to recover the stolen helmet?'

Kel's jaw dropped.

'If we are to believe Ahmose,' she reminded him, 'the theft

and the murders are linked. Does he have secret information which enables him to say that? We must not let our imaginations roam freely. We must emerge from this storm and come back to the facts.'

'My best friend, the actor Bebon, is in prison because of me. He may even already be dead, unless he has been sentenced to forced labour in an oasis.'

'I shall try to find out,' promised Nitis. 'But the most important thing is still the coded papyrus. In my opinion, that is indeed what the murders were looking for – and still are. I've begun studying it, using the archives in the House of Life, but I'm afraid it will be a long and difficult process.'

'And we have no guarantee of success,' sighed Kel. 'We have no guiding thread.'

'Yet it must exist. You can count on my patience and determination.'

How he would have loved to hold her tightly to him! But she was the Superior of the songstresses and weavers of Neith, a woman of extraordinary beauty and uncommon intelligence, and destined to succeed the High Priest. She was bound to marry a high-ranking official.

'Let us each make a copy of the papyrus,' she suggested, 'and then we'll hide the original.'

'Where?'

'Where nobody will look: in the funerary shrine prepared for Pharaoh Ahmose, behind the cult statue. You shall keep the copy I make, and I will keep yours. In that way, our destinies will intersect and we can work at all times.'

Kel agreed, and the two young people set to work. The future depended upon these few incomprehensible signs.

'We mustn't forget Stubborn or Demos,' said Kel. 'Stubborn delivered the poisoned milk, and may even have administered the poison. As for Demos, his role is still unclear. Is he an accomplice or a victim?'

'He wasn't among the corpses,' Nitis reminded him.

'Like me, he must have run away, fearing that he'd be wrongly accused.'

'Why didn't he drink the milk?'

'A conjunction of circumstances . . .'

'I find it hard to believe in his innocence.'

'His testimony will be vital, as will Stubborn's. Both men are now in Naukratis, the Greek city in the Delta which is constantly expanding, thanks to the generosity of Pharaoh Ahmose. I must go there and meet them.'

'If they're guilty, they'll kill you.'

'I shall take precautions.'

'You don't know anybody there,' she said anxiously.

'Yes, I do: my Greek teacher, Glaukos, who now lives there in retirement. His help will be vital.'

'Won't he denounce you to the authorities?'

'I don't think so.'

'It's too great a risk.'

'It's my only chance.'

'Do be careful, I beg you. And, above all, come back.'

28

All the members of the Great Council were present: Udja, first minister of Egypt and governor of Sais; Henat, palace director and head of the king's spies; Pefy, minister of finance and agriculture; Judge Gem, head judge; and Phanes of Halikarnassos, commander-in-chief of the armies.

As usual, Pefy reported on the economic figures and congratulated himself on excellent results.

'Nevertheless,' he concluded, 'I deplore the constant increase in the number of state officials. Their sheer numbers are beginning to strain the state budget.'

'As a body, they support me loyally,' countered Ahmose, 'and as it happens I have decided to take on more tax-collectors in order to draw up a proper inventory of the country's wealth. In the past we had competition from the temples and their administration. They have now been reduced to silence, and we have again taken control of affairs. I also demand more customs duties and an obligatory declaration of each inhabitant's income, so that taxes can be imposed at the appropriate level.'

Pefy was indignant. 'There are already sufficient taxes, Majesty, and—'

'The discussion is closed. This idea, which was devised by my Greek friends, pleases me greatly and its application will enable me to pay my soldiers the best wages. The courts are to punish all attempts at fraud severely. Now, Henat, what have you to report?'

'Good news from the island of Cyprus, Majesty. Our new trading-vessels will soon be launched from its boatyards, enabling us to reach Phoenicia and the Greek ports more quickly. Our military protectorate in Cyprus is functioning extremely well. In addition, the tyrant Polycrates of Samos assures you of his friendship; and all the Greek cities confirm our treaties of alliance. Nevertheless, once again I permit myself to urge Your Majesty to guard against the ambitions of Cambyses, Emperor of Persia.'

'Have you had new information?'

'No, but—'

'Then let us trust my friend Kroisos, head of Persian diplomacy and unfailing supporter of Egypt. If Cambyses had warlike intentions, we would be immediately alerted to them.'

'I have a duty to be suspicious,' insisted Henat.

'Do you still doubt Kroisos' word?'

'Indeed, Majesty. After all, he is the husband of Nitetis, daughter of Pharaoh Apries, whom you overthrew, and so might harbour a desire for vengeance.'

'Nonsense! Those old events are forgotten, and the world has changed. There will be no clash between the Persian and Egyptian civilizations, for we all wish to live in peace.'

'Unlike Egypt,' Udja reminded him, 'Persia has a warlike, conquering spirit. Might Cambyses not intend to gain a foothold in Palestine and use it as his base to launch an attack on Egypt?'

'That would be madness. You yourself, commander of my war-fleet, control a powerfully persuasive force, do you not?'

'I strengthen it more every day,' declared Udja, 'and the Persians will have no chance of defeating it.'

'And by land,' thundered Phanes, 'they will have no greater success. I propose a show of strength, led by His Majesty. The

111

warning will extinguish any flickers of aggression Cambyses may have.'

'Organize it with Udja,' ordered Ahmose. 'Solid alliances, and an army of well-equipped, battle-hardened professionals: those are my answers to a young emperor's desire for conquest – he will find other fish to fry. And Kroisos will persuade him to consolidate peace instead of launching himself into a disastrous venture.'

'Nevertheless,' murmured Henat, 'recent incidents . . .'

The pharaoh ignored him and turned to Pefy. 'I did not think it useful to inform you of the murder of the inter-preters, but that was intended to distance you from the centre of power. Today, the whole of the Great Council must be informed of an equally serious incident. Here, in this very palace, my general's helmet, symbol of the power granted by the people, has been stolen. In other words, a usurper intends to wear it and proclaim himself pharaoh.'

'You were the commander-in-chief,' Phanes reminded him, 'and the entire army chose you as king. It remains absolutely loyal to you. No senior officer would dare defy you – and I'll cut off the head of the first man who does, for high treason!'

'I would prefer a properly constituted trial and sentencing,' cut in Gem.

'The danger may come from a civilian,' added Ahmose, 'the young scribe who murdered his colleagues. I have the feeling that the killings are linked to the theft of my helmet, which must be retrieved with all speed but without news of the theft leaking out.'

'My agents are already at work,' said Henat.

'Apart from the members of this council,' said the king, 'only the High Priest of Neith has been told of the theft. He knows how to hold his tongue, will confine himself to his vital ritual activities, and will not interfere in the investigation.'

'Am I also to involve myself in this matter?' Judge Gem asked.

'All the members of the Great Council must work together effectively,' decreed the king. 'When are you finally going to arrest that murderer Kel?'

'The search of the temple uncovered nothing, Majesty, and no one would dare imagine the High Priest as an accomplice to a criminal. The anonymous document was merely an attempt to compromise him. Once the truth has been established, all that remains is for us to catch the guilty man and make him talk. As far as I can tell, neither Kel nor his friend Demos appears to be in any position to harm you, for they are nothing but hunted fugitives. However, assistance from the army and the spy network will be welcome.'

'To work,' ordered Ahmose.

Udja let the other members of the Great Council leave the room, and said, 'May I speak with you in confidence, Majesty?'

'I am listening.'

'Henat is a true professional, but is he not interested in too many matters?'

'Are you advising me to be wary of him?'

'I would not go that far. However . . .'

'Do you know anything specific?'

'No, it is merely an impression, and probably an erroneous one. Given the situation, I prefer to confide my doubts to you before it is too late. You are the one who directs and decides.'

'I have not forgotten that, Udja.'

29

A canal linked Sais to the Greek city of Naukratis,* situated west of the capital on the Canopic branch of the Nile. It was there that Ahmose had decided to concentrate trade with Greece, which was increasingly flourishing. Seething with life, home to Greeks of all origins – Ionians, Aeolians, Dorians, Eginites, Samians, Milesians and Lesbians, as well as Phoenicians and Cypriots – Naukratis was an open city without fortifications. It contained several temples, notably that of Aphrodite, the Greek equivalent of Isis-Hathor, patroness of sailors and protector of travel by water.

In the port Greek was spoken, and Kel was grateful that he had been taught several different dialects by his teacher, Glaukos, who had stayed at the palace for a long time in order to teach this language to the king and his counsellors. The young man took a narrow side-street leading to the artisans' district, where potters, goldsmiths, amulet- and scarab-makers and blacksmiths worked. They were authorized to produce iron blades and arrowheads for the Greek soldiers who were Ahmose's elite troops.

Kel approached an old man, who was sitting in front of his house. 'I'm looking for Glaukos the teacher.'

* Naukratis (today, Kom Gi'eif) was about 20km from Sais. It was perhaps founded in about 664 BC by Psamtek I, but it was Ahmose who developed it.

'Go and ask at the customs post. They know everyone who lives here.'

Ahmose levied taxes and duties on goods, and no trader could evade the customs scribes.

But of course Kel wanted to avoid any contact with the authorities. He asked a dozen or so craftsmen, but without luck. Perhaps he would have better luck if he consulted a public letter-writer or a priest. So he went towards the Temple of Apollo, which was clearly visible at the centre of its esplanade. It was surrounded by a curtain-wall, which made it look like a citadel.

A delivery man was staggering along, bent double beneath the weight of silver vases destined for the temple.

'May I help you?' offered Kel.

'If you would. Up to the top of the staircase. These steps are an ordeal! Do you live around here?'

'I'm looking for Glaukos the teacher.'

'That name rings a bell ... I had to deliver some writing-tablets to him last month. We'll make the delivery to the temple, and then I'll take you to his house.'

The house occupied the far end of a quiet side-street lined with comfortable dwellings where citizens of note lived.

A door-keeper watched them approach. 'What do you want, my boy?'

'To see Glaukos the teacher.'

'And who might you be?'

'A former pupil.'

The visitor was clean, neatly dressed, and had the manners of an educated young man; he didn't seem like a lowly beggar. So the door-keeper agreed to go and inform his employer.

'Glaukos will see you,' he said on his return.

According to the Egyptian custom, Kel took off his sandals and washed his feet and hands before entering the house, which was full of Greek vases of different sizes and shapes, whose decorations depicted passages from the *Odyssey*.

Glaukos was sitting in an elegant ebony armchair, his hands gripping a walking-stick.

'I am almost blind,' he said, 'and I cannot make out your face. What is your name?'

'Do you remember Kel the scribe?'

A smile lit up the old man's face. 'My best pupil! You were the only one who could manage several Greek dialects, and you learnt remarkably quickly. Are you happy with your career?'

'I cannot complain.'

'One day you will enter the government. The king is bound to notice an exceptionally gifted fellow like yourself, and you'll eventually become a minister.'

'And you? Are you enjoying a happy retirement?'

'Old age offers nothing but disadvantages, but my staff are dedicated. My cook feeds me well, and a friend reads Greek poetry to me every day. Life disappears slowly, and I try to remember the good times. But tell me, why are you in Naukratis?'

'Dinner is served,' announced the cook.

'Help me up,' said Glaukos.

Kel did so, and the two men went to the dining-room, where they had an excellent meal of beef boiled with garlic, cumin and coriander, together with a local wine flavoured with aromatic herbs.

'I must hand over a document to a Greek colleague, Demos. He has been living in Naukratis for a short while. Have you heard of him?'

'I no longer take any interest in the scribes appointed here by the king. Naukratis is constantly growing, and new faces appear every day. To be honest, the lion's share goes to the traders and the army.'

'As a matter of fact,' said Kel, 'I also wish to contact a milk-seller from Sais, who apparently came to Naukratis recently and re-enlisted as an officer.'

'Are you interested in the army?'

'It's a simple combination of circumstances.'

'Have a taste of this cake. It's made with ground carob,*
and it's absolutely delicious – I adore it.' The old man ate his
own cake with relish, and drank a cup of wine. 'If I understand
correctly, you are carrying out some kind of secret mission.'

'It's a simple administrative matter.'

'My friend Ares could help you. He lives a stone's throw
from where the scarabs are made, and knows everyone in the
barracks at Naukratis.'

* Regarded as the Egyptian version of chocolate, because it tastes similar
to cocoa, carob is the fruit of a small tree greatly appreciated by the ancient
Egyptians. It was called *nedjem*, 'the sweet one'.

30

'I am looking for Ares' house,' Kel said to a bearded fellow who was a good head taller than he was and whose right arm was covered in scars.

The man looked him up and down. 'That's odd . . . Ah well, each to his own. I'd have had you down more as a scribe with a brush in your hand. Ares' office is down the side-street to the right. Join the queue and wait your turn.'

About ten men were waiting, standing one behind the other.

The last one turned round and watched Kel approach.

'You look a mite frail to me, my boy. Ares prefers strong men. If you want to be a soldier you need muscles.'

So Glaukos was getting rid of Kel by sending him to a recruiting-office. Not believing a word of his story, Glaukos had not denounced him to the authorities but was offering him the only possible way out. He probably thought Kel had committed some serious crime, no longer belonged to the central government, and was trying to hide in Naukratis. And the army would be the ideal hiding-place.

'All the same, I'll try my luck.'

'Ah well, you may be right. They're taking on men at the moment. There's a need for men on the boats, and the fortified encampment near Bubastis has just been enlarged, as well as the barracks at Memphis and Marea, on the Libyan border. Me, I'd like to be posted to Daphnai, near Pelusia, over towards Asia. Apparently the food's decent there, there are girls on hand and the pay is good. And the Greek traders give us little presents, in return for us protecting them. Egypt – what a wonderful life! I don't miss my native Ionia one bit. Here, people have everything they need, and a man can live to a peaceful old age.'

'What if you have to fight?'

'With the army we've got, nobody will dare attack us. It was a real work of genius on the part of Pharaoh Ahmose to develop a such powerful army. Even a crazy warmonger would think twice. And everybody knows that Greek mercenaries are the best of all warriors. That's why Egypt has entrusted her safety to them – an excellent course of action, believe me.'

When he emerged from the recruiting-office, the man looked pleased. 'I'm leaving for Daphnai tomorrow. It's your turn now, my boy, and good luck.'

Ares was stocky, stiff and in a hurry. Maps on the walls of his office showed the location of camps and barracks throughout the country.

He seemed surprised by Kel's appearance. 'I warn you,' he said, 'my role is only to direct people according to the needs of the moment. On-site and after tests, an officer decides whether or not to enlist you. Where would you prefer to be based?'

'Here, in Naukratis.'

'War-fleet, cavalry or footsoldiers?'

'I'd like to join a former milk-seller who enlisted recently.'

'What's his name?'

'Stubborn.'

'Where's he from?'

'From Sais. Given his military past, he should be an officer.'

Ares frowned. 'And what do you want with this officer?'

'To serve under him.'

'Are you from Sais, too?'

'From a nearby village.'

'Have you ever handled weapons?'

'I'd prefer to deal with stewardship and administration.'

'That's not my domain. I select future soldiers, and you aren't the right type. No camp commander will take you on. Go and find another profession.'

'I must talk to Stubborn.'

'I don't know him. And even if I did, I wouldn't talk to a stranger who doesn't belong to the army.'

'I must insist: it's very important.'

'This is a recruiting-office. I don't hand out information.

'I assure you, I—'

'Outside, lad, and don't come back or you'll regret it.'

Dejectedly Kel left the office. He'd failed yet again. By hiding in Naukratis, even though it was close to the capital, Demos and Stubborn knew they were beyond reach.

Deep in thought, he bumped into a passer-by. She was a tall, beautiful woman aged around thirty, her hair piled up in a perfumed chignon and covered in jewels.

The queue of waiting men had fallen silent. Each one was staring at this superb – and completely inaccessible – woman.

'I – I beg your pardon,' stammered Kel.

'Did you want to enlist?'

'Yes and no, I—'

'We have enough soldiers in Naukratis. On the other hand, there is a shortage of qualified scribes. Can you read and write?'

'Indeed.'

'My name is Zekeh, but I'm known as "the courtesan" because I'm the wealthiest businesswoman in the city and I'm free and unmarried. To the Greeks, that makes me virtually a prostitute. They aren't accustomed to the rights Egyptian women enjoy, and they certainly don't want to import them into their own country. Many of them would like to veil us and confine us to the home – they think a woman's sole function is to be a sexual slave to her husband, cook his food and bring up his sons properly. I was born in Sparta, but I take full advantage of Naukratis and I'm showing the way. I've just bought some more land and vineyards, so I need a steward. Could you do a job like that?'

'I don't think so.'

'How curious, I am convinced of the opposite. Will you at least discuss it?'

'As you wish.'

'Then let us go to my house.'

Kel thought he must be the only man present not to fall under the spell of the fascinating Zekeh. He would go with her, in the hope of obtaining information which would enable him to pick up the trails of Demos and Stubborn.

The would-be soldiers watched the pair walk away.

'By Aphrodite,' one of them exclaimed in astonishment, 'that young lad amazes me! How did he manage to seduce that superb filly?'

'She'll soon trample all over him,' predicted his comrade.

31

The lady Zekeh's house stood in the centre of the city and comprised four floors. A door-keeper guarded the entrance day and night. He bowed very low before his employer, and noted with interest that she was accompanied by a new suitor, much younger than the previous ones. This fabulously wealthy businesswoman's appetite seemed insatiable.

'I have a horror of the countryside,' she admitted to Kel. 'Too many little beasts of every kind.'

On the ground floor, a weaving workshop provided the beauty with clothing made to measure, household linens, bed-sheets and pillows. Bakers and brewers produced fresh bread and beer every day, and there was a dining-room in which the servants could eat.

On the first and second floors were the private apartments and washrooms, on the third the offices, and the fourth served as store where records and foodstuffs were kept.

The furniture was unbelievably luxurious: high-backed arm-chairs, low chairs in precious woods, folding stools decorated with painted flowers and plants, rectangular tables, side tables, storage chests and a multitude of many-coloured cushions. On the walls were heavy hangings made from linen dyed green, red and blue.

'We shall have lunch,' decided Zekeh.

Two servants hurriedly laid out the food on alabaster trays and poured red wine into glass cups.

'This dish is goose, cooked for a long time in a large cooking pot with the finest fat,' explained the cook. 'It will be followed by quails' eggs hard-boiled in salted water, to which chopped onion and butter have been added. Permit me to hope that you enjoy your meal.'

'I like light meals,' said Zekeh. 'If I was forever digesting food it would slow down the pace of my work, and I have so many matters to deal with. This wine won't make your head spin: it contains neither honey nor aromatic herbs. It's twenty years old, as light as air, and it clarifies the mind.'

Kel tasted it: Zekeh had not exaggerated.

'This is the best country in the world,' she declared. 'You should see the faces of the Greeks disembarking at Naukratis. They cannot bear a woman to be free to marry according to her own taste, to get divorced, to enjoy her own possessions, to bequeath them to heirs of her choice, to go alone to the market, to trade and to run a business. Their male vanity is shaken to its stupid core, and I am delighted to see those pretentious idiots become soldiers in Pharaoh's service and ensure the independence of Egypt and the Egyptians.'

'So you aren't married?' ventured Kel.

'Divorced, I am very happy to say. As soon as I arrived, I married a ship-owner from Milet, but I soon caught him sleeping with a servant-girl. The separation was pronounced in my favour, and I received substantial compensation, which I immediately invested. In short, I had gained freedom and wealth. A few ideas, a lot of work, and ... success. The Egyptian traders like me, I import quality goods and buy land, and pay my employees the correct wages. Now I own several large buildings in Naukratis, and the leading citizens are delighted to be my guests. You, on the other hand, seem embarrassed.'

'I don't deserve such honour.'

'That is for me to judge. You interest me, young man, for you aren't an ordinary person. Who are you, and what do you want in Naukratis?'

Kel's mind raced. Should he find a means of escape or reveal some of the truth and take the attendant risks? This woman was a veritable cobra; she did not practise free generosity. In the end, a stranger in this closed, if not hostile society, he had no choice.

He took the plunge. 'I am an interpreter-scribe from Sais, and I'm looking for two men who have taken refuge here. One is my former colleague Demos, the other is called Stubborn – he's a milk-seller who wants to re-enlist as a soldier.'

Zekeh seemed surprised. 'Why do you say "taken refuge"?'

'Both are mixed up in a criminal matter, and I assume that they're hiding in Naukratis.'

'A criminal matter? Are they criminals or innocent people who are under threat?'

'Frankly, I don't know, so I must talk to them and hear their explanations.'

'Are you involved, too?' asked Zekeh slyly.

'I have been accused unjustly.'

'What is your name?'

'Kel.' She did not react. So the murder of the interpreters must have been kept secret, and Naukratis knew nothing of it. But how long would that last?

'Demos and Stubborn,' she repeated, accentuating each syllable. 'Do you really wish them well?'

'Demos is my friend,' protested Kel. 'As for Stubborn, I enjoyed chatting with him and regarded him as a good fellow. If they ran away, perhaps they have information which will enable me to prove my innocence.'

'A criminal matter, you said. Who was killed?'

'Some interpreter-scribes. And I would prefer to call it an affair of state. It's in nobody's interests to get mixed up with it.'

'A salutary warning. I probably ought to inform the authorities.'

'That's right.'

Zekeh smiled strangely. 'Wrong, young man. First, I am not an informer; second, your training as an interpreter-scribe will be extremely useful to me. Since you read both Greek and Egyptian, you'll have no difficulty in studying administrative documents and will extract the important material much more quickly than my own clerks. For you need my help and you're in a hurry.'

'Can you find Demos and Stubborn?'

'If they've gone to ground in Naukratis, they won't escape me. Here is my proposition, and you can take it or leave it: you will be housed and fed, you will work for me in accordance with my demands, and I shall provide you with the necessary information. If you refuse, you must leave Naukratis immediately.'

'I'll stay,' decided Kel.

32

Two of the shrines in the sacred domain of Neith were devoted to the weaving of the many fabrics used during the celebration of festivals and rituals. Having climbed through all the ranks of the priestesses and all the stages of her profession, the young Superior would not let herself be exploited by any lazy workers.

None of the other priestesses had contested her appointment, and all were happy to have avoided such heavy responsibilities, so they were all working eagerly. The senior weaver presented Nitis with linen garments finished the previous day and mummification bandages designed for a sacred crocodile. They would make its soul happy and enable it to pass through the gates of the celestial paradise.

'The hour is come to weave the Eye of Horus,' said Nitis.

Both sun and moon, the light of the day and the night, the Eye was embodied in a brilliant white cloth of the very finest quality. With the surest hand, Nitis fashioned the first bundle of linen fibres while her assistants prepared the looms. And the song of the spindles began to ring out.

The woven Eye would also be the shroud of Osiris, the garment of resurrection for the body of Light that shone forth beyond death. Few weavers were initiated into the great Mysteries, but all the women were aware that they were accomplishing a vital act. By creating this offering, by seeking perfection in their work, they were participating in divine immortality.

Looking at her Sisters, Nitis was reassured: the work was proceeding exceedingly well. There was no spirit of competition, just a quest for excellence and the gift of skills. The power of Neith was guiding their hearts.

As night fell, the workshops closed. The guard checked the bolts, and the priestesses went their separate ways.

Nitis was heading for her official residence when Menk approached her.

'Are you pleased with this first day of hard toil?' he asked.

'The weavers have proved worthy of their duties.'

'You can charm even the most recalcitrant of them.'

'I attribute this miracle to the magic of the Eye of Horus. Within it, that which was scattered is reunified.'

'Do not underestimate your personal magic,' advised Menk. 'The High Priest chose well when he appointed you to this post.'

'I shall do my best not to disappoint him.'

'Making sure that such a vast temple functions properly presents many difficulties,' observed Menk. 'Every morning all those who work here must be purified according to the Rule, not according to his or her own fancy. We must have enough linen robes and enough sandals, clean the basins and fill them frequently with fresh water, ensure that no items are forgotten, and care for the well-being of the divinities who are present in their shrines. Not to mention all the festivals . . .'

'Are you feeling discouraged?'

'Indeed not, but I would like to talk to you about the many problems that need to be solved. Together we would be more effective.'

Nitis was very surprised. 'Doesn't the Rule fix the framework of our cooperation?'

'It does not forbid less . . . formal encounters. Above all, be wary of certain scribes and administrators, whose only concerns are furthering their own careers and becoming wealthy. They will try to obtain your favour and will set traps for you.'

'Thank you for your valuable advice, Menk. I shan't forget it.'

'Don't hesitate to consult me. I know all the leading citizens, and nothing happens in Sais that I don't know about.'

'Except that horrible murder of the interpreters, it seems.'

'Don't talk about that monstrous crime,' said Menk angrily.

'It's difficult not to think about it.'

'It doesn't concern either of us. The authorities are dealing with it, and the murderer will be caught and punished. It's because the authorities have hushed it up that the city isn't buzzing with a thousand frightening ill-founded rumours.'

'What if someone's trying to hide the truth?'

'This affair is too great for us, Nitis. It is up to the state to resolve it. Listen to the voice of reason, I beg of you, and don't overstep the limits of your position.'

'I have no intention of doing so.'

'I find that most reassuring. When may we dine together?'

'Not in the immediate future, because of my burden of work. I must consult the many archives in order to rewrite certain rituals and restore to them the vigour of the Old Kingdom.'

'An admirable task,' agreed Menk, 'but don't forget to live. Those old documents cannot pay fitting homage to your beauty.'

'Sleep well, Menk.'

'You also, Nitis,' and he bowed and walked away.

The young woman was puzzled, unable to make up her mind. Was Menk merely an ordinary seducer, or were his words covert threats? And was he somehow involved in the conspiracy? Mingling with Sais's high society, he had access to the palace and maintained close links with the men in power. He enjoyed an excellent reputation, and had only friends.

The next day Nitis explored the mathematical papyri in the House of Life, hoping to find information about codes. In certain periods, the interplay of signs had made it possible to conceal the meaning of texts touching upon the nature of the gods. Her task seemed likely to be long and difficult, and she might well not succeed. Meanwhile, Kel was risking his life in Naukratis. His knowledge of Greek was a precious advantage, but were Demos and Stubborn setting a deadly ambush for him?

As she imagined the young scribe's death, Nitis felt overwhelmed: never to see him or hear him again, never again to share hopes and fears . . . Unable to work, she slowly rolled up the papyrus and replaced it on the shelf.

'You look troubled,' said High Priest Wahibra.

Nitis gave a start. 'Oh! I did not know you were there.'

'I came to fetch you to introduce a strange individual to you. He is a Greek, on a quest for knowledge which he has not found in his own country. He wishes to consult us and I would like your opinion about his sincerity.'

'What is his name?'

'Pythagoras.'*

---

* Two writers of antiquity who were initiated into the Mysteries, Porphurio (AD 233–304) and Iamblichas (AD 250–330), wrote lives of Pythagoras which tell of his long sojourn in Egypt and his contacts with sages and scholars.

33

Pythagoras had a high forehead and wore a solemn expression. He bowed before the High Priest and Nitis.

'Thank you for agreeing to meet me. I have come from the palace of Pharaoh Ahmose, who granted me a long audience to determine whether I had obeyed him unfailingly. In fact, I did indeed go to Heliopolis, the sacred city of Ra, god of the Divine Light, and then to Memphis, city of Ptah, master of the Word and of craftsmen.'

'Were you put to the test?' asked Wahibra.

'Yes, and harshly; but I don't regret it.'

'You Greeks are still children. There are no old men in your temples and you have no knowledge of the true Tradition. That is why your philosophy can be reduced to a mere babble of words.'

'I acknowledge that, High Priest. Like a certain number of my countrymen, I realized that Egypt is the homeland of Wisdom. For a long time, I was rejected and advised to return home. Only perseverance enabled me to convince the priests that my quest is an authentic one. Here, and nowhere else, the science of the soul is taught, and understanding is distinguished from knowledge, the second being suborned to the first.'

'What did you learn in Heliopolis and Memphis?'

'Geometry, astronomy and the symbolic methods leading to

the perception of the Mysteries. My mind was awakened to the power of the gods during several initiation rituals.'

'Did you see the acacia?' Nitis asked.

Pythagoras gave the correct answer: 'I am a son of the Widow and a follower of Osiris, the perpetually regenerated one.'

'You have already travelled a long way,' said the High Priest.

'I also went to Thebes, where the Divine Worshipper tested me for a long time, then initiated me into the Mysteries of Isis and Osiris.

'A man obeying a woman,' observed Nitis. 'Is that not shocking from a Greek point of view?'

'In that area, too, we have a great deal to learn. When I return to Greece to found a community of initiates, I shall open its doors to women, and they will gain access to knowledge of the Mysteries, as they do in Egypt. By excluding them from high spiritual office, the world is condemned to violence and chaos. Moreover it is a woman, the lady Zekeh of Naukratis, who has facilitated many of the steps I have taken. She prizes the freedom she enjoys in Egypt and would like to see it spread everywhere.'

'So you have decided to found an order of initiates in Greece and to pass on Egyptian esotericism as you perceive it,' said Wahibra.

'I believe that to be a vitally important task. I could remain here and progress along the path of knowledge until my last hour, but that would be the act of an egotist. My vocation is to reveal to the Greeks the treasures I have glimpsed in your temples, and thus raise up their souls. They must have greater respect for the gods and the Law of Maat, must keep a promise once it is given, and practise moderation and harmony, while following rituals that will enable them to attain the isles of the blessed – that is to say, the sun and the moon, the two components parts of the Eye of Horus.'

'What is the most important thing, in your opinion?' Wahibra asked.

'The Number,' replied Pythagoras. 'Each human being possesses his or her own, and knowing it leads to Wisdom. Both one and multiple, the Number contains the vital forces. It is up to us to discover them in order to perceive the universe of which we are a limited expression. Our origin and our goal are the sky of fixed stars, the resting-place of the gods where the liberated souls of the Just dwell.'

'What do you expect from me, Pythagoras?'

'Founding my order implies the unanimous agreement of the High Priests who granted me their teaching and judged me worthy to pass it on. If you refuse me yours, my path will be blocked.'

'Will you give up?'

'I shall try to persuade you, for I believe in the importance of this mission.'

'I shall use the same method as my colleagues,' decided Wahibra, 'and put you to the test. Tomorrow morning Nitis will take you to one of our principal ritual priests. He will give you several tasks to fulfil. After that, we shall meet again.'

Pythagoras bowed again and returned to the royal palace, where he was staying.

'A learned and determined man,' commented Nitis.

'But a Greek,' the High Priest reminded her, 'and he has the favour of King Ahmose.'

'Do you suspect Pythagoras of being a spy, sent to watch us?'

'I cannot discount it. He seems to have unlimited curiosity, and certainly does not lack intelligence.'

'The Divine Worshipper initiated him into the Mysteries of Osiris,' Nitis pointed out. 'She had a reputation for being exceedingly stern and severe. No hypocrite could deceive her.'

'That is a valid argument,' conceded Wahibra. 'Nevertheless, we must remain vigilant.'

'If Pythagoras has mathematical and geometrical talents, perhaps he could help us to decipher the code?'

'We must not rush things, Nitis. Before showing him such a dangerous document, we must be absolutely sure that he is sincere.'

'But time is pressing.'

'I am aware of that, but one false move would be fatal, and Kel would be doomed to the abyss.'

'I shall return to the House of Life,' said Nitis. 'There are many mathematical papyri there, and I have noticed some interesting details.'

'Don't go without sleep,' the High Priest advised her. 'Your duties are far from simple, and you will need all your strength.'

34

Judge Gem was presiding over the court that was held in front of the monumental doorway to the Temple of Neith. He wore an old-style wig, and a pendant depicting Maat, the goddess of justice, seated and wearing on her head a feather, the rectrix, which enables birds to direct their flight. Making no distinction between lord and servant, serving-girl and mistress, he heard many plaintiffs, whose affairs went beyond the competence of the local courts. Village councils settled most disputes, and judges from the nearest town dealt with the difficult cases. If no satisfactory solution was found, plaintiffs and defendants resorted to the highest level of the legal system.

Gem opened the audience by touching the figurine of Maat. Thirty judges heard scribes read out the detailed complaints, concluding with the amount of damages demanded, and the defendants' responses. Given the complexity of one quarrel between heirs, the opposition to these arguments was heard, followed by a final counter-attack by their opponents.*

Gem could have summoned both parties, but the documents

* According to Diodorus Siculus (first century BC), 'It is thus that all cases were conducted in Egypt. Egyptians were of the opinion that lawyers only obscure causes with their speeches and that the art of the orator, the magic of action, the tears of the accused often lead the judge to close his eyes to the law and to the truth.'

clearly established the facts. So he placed the figurine of Maat upon the plaintiff's file. A mother had legally disinherited her children, who were ungrateful and dishonest, and instead had left everything to a loyal servant-girl, whom the cohort of embittered offspring had tried to discredit. They had gone to the extent of producing a forgery, and would be sentenced to pay heavy damages and compensation.

Justice having been done in the name of Maat and the pharaoh, Gem returned to his office, where the latest reports on the Kel affair awaited him. There was no trace of the fugitive, even though all informants were on the alert, and the forces of order were making every possible effort.

Kel must have left Sais. Unless he was hiding inside the sacred enclosure of Neith ... No, the search had been very thorough, the judge could not doubt the word of the High Priest.

All towns in the Delta must be alerted. Was Kel benefiting from the help of accomplices? Was he wandering the country-side? And if he headed a network of criminals, had they helped him to leave Egypt? Henat might well know the answers to these questions but, despite the king's intervention, he remained tight-lipped.

Gem's secretary interrupted his thoughts by asking, 'What is to be done with that fellow Bebon?'

'Bring him to me.'

The judge consulted Bebon's file: it was empty. And the authorities were constantly arresting innocent people whose sole crime was that they looked like Kel. Groaning beneath the weight of pointless cases, Gem decided to rid himself of this one.

When the actor appeared he was grubby and dishevelled, and seemed not at all cocksure.

'Well, Bebon, have you had time to think?'

'About what?'

'Have you nothing to tell me about Kel the scribe?'

'Me? Nothing, honestly! I just want to get out of prison and get on with life.'

'Are you planning to travel?'

'That's my profession.'

'Failure to tell me the whole truth would be a serious crime.'

'I know, and I've told you everything.'

'Your arrest involved brutality. Do you wish to lodge a complaint about it?'

Bebon's eyes widened.

'Such a complaint would be acceptable,' continued Gem, 'and you would only be exercising the right of an innocent man.'

'I've had enough trouble already.'

'As you wish.'

'Are you . . . letting me go?'

'No charge has been made against you.'

'So there is justice in this country.'

Bebon was given a loaf of fresh bread, a jug of water and a new pair of new sandals. As soon as he emerged from the offices of the legal administration, he hailed the sun and the blue sky.

He went straight to a tavern. Strong beer at last – a vital aid to clarifying one's thoughts. How was he to find Kel, whose only friend he was? Where was the scribe hiding? A thread of a lead existed, but it was so fragile . . .

As he left the tavern, Bebon sensed that he was being watched. He walked randomly, changing direction several times, crossed a busy market-place and chatted with the traders, and spotted the man following him. So his release had merely been a deception. Suspecting complicity, Judge Gem was hoping that the actor would lead him to Kel.

Killing the inconvenient fellow trailing him would be an admission of guilt. So Bebon took a room on the second floor of an inn on the outskirts of the city, frequented by travelling pedlars. Almost as soon as he had settled in, he climbed up on to the roof and saw the soldier, who was having to pace up and down near the inn. Leaping from terrace to terrace, Bebon reached a working-class district, then set off along a side-street leading to the Temple of Neith.

Nitis, the priestess who had met Kel at the banquet, might know a good deal. She would talk, either willingly or by use of force.

According to a letter the messenger had just brought her, Nitis was to go urgently to her former house to resolve a practical problem. Although she was already overburdened with work, she decided to sort it out immediately.

Scarcely had she stepped over the threshold when a hand was clapped over her mouth and a voice hissed in her ear, 'Don't make a sound. And whatever you do, don't try to run away.'

The door closed behind her.

The attacker took the priestess into the bedchamber. 'My name is Bebon and I am Kel's only friend. Answer my questions or I'll strangle you.'

'Ask them.'

'Superior of the songstresses and weavers of Neith ... you were easy to track down. The pure priestesses talk of nothing but your promotion and your brilliant future. Do you admit that you know Kel?'

'Yes.'

'You trapped him at the banquet.'

'I had nothing to do with that trap.'

'Prove it.'

'What about you? Are you his friend, or one of the informers who've been ordered to find him?'

Bebon burst out laughing. 'Me, an informer? That really is funny! You might as well accuse me of being married with children!'

His sincerity seemed glaringly obvious.

'I believe that Kel is innocent,' declared Nitis, 'and I helped him to hide.'

Bebon let out a sigh of relief. 'An ally ... The gods be praised! Where is he?'

'He's gone to Naukratis. If Demos and Stubborn, who must be mixed up in the interpreters' murder, are living there he'll find them and question them.'

'And if they're guilty they'll kill him.'

'I tried to dissuade him, but I failed,' said Nitis sadly, 'for he could see no other solution. In the eyes of the authorities, Kel is a murderer and a fugitive.'

'I shall help him,' promised Bebon. He looked at her penitently. 'Forgive me for handling you so roughly, but I thought you were one of the conspirators.'

Nitis smiled. 'I would have done the same.'

'Helping Kel could cause serious trouble for you.'

'Seeking out the truth and fighting falsehood are the duties of a priestess.'

'Meeting you was an honour.'

'Bring Kel back safe and sound. Together, we shall prove his innocence.'

35

In a single day, Kel had got through more work than Zekeh's three secretaries got through in a week. Several administrative problems had been resolved, and he had established that the management of the lands would require profound reforms, after which they would bring in a noticeably larger income.

'Excellent,' she said. 'I was right about you. There are still other matters to be dealt with, but I shall keep my word. Since you are cooperating, you deserve to meet an important man who will obtain reliable information for you. There is only one condition: he will not speak to you except in my presence.'

'When can I meet him?'

'Tonight.'

The commander of the army in Naukratis devoured Zekeh with his eyes.

'This is a friend of mine,' she told him. 'He needs your services.'

'Unofficially, I assume?'

'I will stand guarantee for him; you can speak freely. And this conversation never took place.'

'What does your anonymous friend want to know?'

'Have you recently recruited a young Greek interpreter called Demos?' Kel asked.

The commander consulted his lists. 'Negative.'

'What if he took up an administrative post? Would you know about it?'

'Of course.'

'Then what about an older man called Stubborn?'

The commander frowned. 'A former officer who became a milk-seller in Sais?'

'That's him!'

'He enlisted last week.'

'I'd like to speak to him.'

'You can't.'

'But I must!'

'During his first training period, Stubborn had a fatal accident.'

'What happened?'

'He slipped on the wet ground and was impaled on the spear of the soldier he was attacking. During these kinds of accidents, we often suffer losses. It's the price you pay for training soldiers and not young girls.'

Kel couldn't concentrate on his work. Clearly, someone had given the order for Stubborn to be killed. With that trail cut, there was only Demos left. The Greek had gone to ground, unlike Stubborn who was too visible an accomplice, so he must be innocent. But how was Kel to find him?

Suddenly, he realized that document in front of him was astounding. Incredulously, he wondered if he still understood Greek. But he read it again and there was no doubt about it.

At that moment Zekeh appeared, wearing a broad collar formed of eight rows of cornelian and faience, lotus-flower earrings and a belt made of gold plates held together by five rows of faience beads. Jewellery like that must be worth a fortune.

But the spell did not work.

Kel brandished the document. 'I don't dare believe this!'

'Why are you so indignant?'

'You are really planning to buy . . . human beings?'

'In Greece we call them slaves, and it's a perfectly respectable trade.'

'In Egypt the Law of Maat explicitly forbids it.'

'Egypt will have to modernize, young scribe, and understand that slavery is part of the forces of production that are vital for economic development.'

'At that price, it is better not to have it! No pharaoh will accept such barbarity.'

'That's an idealistic dream, my boy. The larger the population becomes, the more the laws of economics will impose themselves. And your ancient spirituality, however beautiful it may be, will be swept away. In our democratic towns, there are more slaves than free men. That model will become the norm.'

'Kindly accept my resignation, Lady Zekeh.'

'Certainly not. Where would you go? Here, you are safe and you can continue your investigation.'

Her alluring smile did not charm Kel. Controlling his anger, he moved forward another piece in the dangerous game he was playing against the Greek woman.

'I refuse to handle the files that deal – directly or indirectly – with the setting up of slavery in Naukratis.'

'Very well. I shall respect your archaic morality, in the hope of seeing you develop.'

'But will you still help me find Demos?'

'If he is hiding in this city, I will find him.'

'I am seeking something else,' revealed the young man. 'A priceless treasure.'

Zekeh's curiosity was aroused. 'What is it?'

'Do you know how King Ahmose took power?'

'During a military insurrection, his men crowned him with a helmet. At the end of the civil war, he unseated the reigning pharaoh, Apries, and subsequently gained the support of both rich and poor.'

'The precious helmet has disappeared – someone has stolen

it. It was kept in the palace, and I am convinced that the theft is linked to the murder of my colleagues.'

'In other words,' concluded Zekeh, 'a new uprising is being prepared.'

'If I can take the helmet back to Pharaoh,' said Kel, 'he will recognize my innocence.'

'No doubt,' murmured the businesswoman, thinking of a somewhat different outcome. Such a matter went beyond the case of a young scribe, however charming he might be. He would serve to enable her to get her hands on the treasure, but she would not allow him to enjoy it.

She alone had sufficient standing to bargain with a king and extort from him honorary titles and wealth. Respected and extremely wealthy, Zekeh would become one of the leading figures at court and would introduce many reforms of which the king – who was so taken with Greek culture – was bound to approve.

Lady Zekeh's real career was just beginning.

36

Ahmose had not slept well. His wife consoled him and asked him to receive some trading delegates from Greek cities which wished to strengthen their links with Egypt still further. Although he detested this kind of obligatory duty, the king came round to Tanith's way of thinking. Seeing the pharaoh was an immeasurable favour, and this favour would have happy economic consequences.

After the audience, Ahmose received Menk. The king was counting on this faithful servant to keep watch on the High Priest and ensure that the construction and renovation of temples in Upper and Lower Egypt was proceeding correctly.

'Has our great project made progress, Menk?'

'The island of Philae will be adorned with a magnificent shrine dedicated to the goddess Isis, Majesty. She will be delighted with that isolated and splendid location, which up to now has been completely unoccupied.'

'We must never neglect the great sorceress,' said Ahmose, 'for she knows the true name of Ra, the Divine Light, and the secret of creative power. Philae is to be one of the greatest achievements of my reign. Ensure that the work is carried out properly.'

'I shall indeed, Majesty.'

'What of my house of eternity in the sacred enclosure of Neith? Is it finished?'

'The craftsmen have toiled according to your instructions. It is fronted by a portico with palm-shaped columns, and closed by two doors, behind which lies the sarcophagus. The great chamber is a marvel.'

The tombs of early rulers opened onto a courtyard which lay in front of the pillared hall of the ancient shrine of Neith, and Ahmose's house of eternity did not diverge from the rule. In this way, it was placed under the protection of the mysterious goddess who, at each moment, used seven words to recreate the world.

'Has the High Priest correctly attended to my house of eternity?'

'Every day and with great vigilance, Majesty. He has dismissed two sculptors he considered second-rate and has personally chosen the words of glorification to be engraved in the stone in order to ensure the survival of your soul.'

'Has he made any criticisms of our government?'

'None at all. The High Priest is cold, distant and reserved, and shows little inclination to confide in anyone. Nevertheless, I have not detected any hint that your authority has been questioned in any way. The Temple of Neith is operating marvellously well, and it will not be easy to find a successor to Wahibra.'

'Continue to watch,' ordered Ahmose, 'and if there are any incidents report to me at once.'

The king returned to his apartments, where he drank some wine from Bubastis. The vineyards of the cat-goddess, Bastet, produced exceptional wine, merry and light. Ahmose needed this reviving beverage before his private audience with Henat.

As a priest of Thoth, Henat would have the task of honouring the memory of Ahmose after the king's death, but he did not have the calibre of a pharaoh. He knew how to keep to his place, preferred the shadows and was content with his position; but ambition could unfurl like a destructive wave, whatever a person's age or titles. It was impossible to see inside

144

this self-effacing character, whose skills were praised by all.

The first thing Henat said was: 'General Phanes is organizing a grand military parade, Majesty. This will act as a highly effective deterrent.'

'Have you invited our friend Kroisos?'

'He is away, travelling, but our messages will reach him, and I am sure he will not miss the opportunity to see the full might of Egyptian military power.'

'What news of my helmet?'

'There are no leads for the moment, but I am carrying out many interrogations. The instigator of the theft is probably a chambermaid from Lesbos.'

'Why do you suspect her?'

'Because she had access to the palace wing where the helmet was kept, and she has disappeared. If she has taken a boat for Greece, we shall not find her.'

'She must have had accomplices.'

Henat was doubtful. 'One thing is certain, Majesty: not a single dignitary or senior officer would dare put on your helmet and proclaim himself pharaoh. I am dealing with the civilians, and Phanes would crush any military rebels.'

'And yet the theft was committed.'

'Either to the benefit of a madman determined to imitate you, in peril of his life, or by a brigand who wishes to earn a fortune by selling the helmet back to us.'

'A matter of pure villainy?'

'At this stage of the investigation, I am not ruling anything out.'

'What about the murderer of the interpreters?'

'Unfortunately, he is still at large. Sometimes, I wonder if he has been torn to bits by a crocodile or strangled by bandits on the open road. A hunted man never survives long.'

'Extend the search to include the whole of the country.'

'As far as Elephantine?'

'Kel could have fled south.'

'I very much doubt it, Majesty, but I shall take the necessary measures immediately.'

'Have you recruited any new interpreters?'

'Only three candidates both have the necessary skills and seem sufficiently trustworthy. Recreating the secretariat will take time.'

'In the meantime, deal with the diplomatic letters yourself and submit the important ones to me.'

As usual, the conspirators were in awe of their leader. Despite the risks they all ran, his calm demeanour was reassuring. Admittedly the annihilation of the Interpreters' Secretariat had not initially been part of their plan, and some had feared that the incident would lead to disaster. But destiny was continuing to smile on them.

'We are still a long way from our goal,' admitted the leader. 'Nevertheless, our underground work is already bearing fruit. And the current situation shows that we are right: it was vital to get rid of the interpreters and to throw the blame on to Kel.'

'We were hoping he would be arrested quickly,' said one doubter. 'And if he has the coded papyrus, he represents a major danger.'

'Not at all,' disagreed the leader, 'for he will never be able to decipher it.'

'Let us hope that he is dead and the document has been destroyed.'

'Taking this minor incident in account, are any of you thinking of giving up?'

No one spoke.

37

By the light of several oil lamps, Kel continued to study the coded papyrus, applying keys derived from Greek dialects he knew. Nothing worked. Before him he had the Egyptian signs, which refused to come together and form words. The author of the code was an absolute demon!

'Aren't you asleep yet?' asked the seductive voice of the lady Zekeh, whose alluring perfume wafted into the scribe's bedroom.

'I like to read late. Did you have a good evening?'

'Boring, but useful. The Naukratis harbourmaster was boasting all over the place about his decrepit wife's fidelity. She's a farmer's daughter and deadly boring. I proved to him that he was lying. From now on, he'll be crawling at my feet.'

'Did you speak to him about Demos?'

'To him and to other notables, on the pretext of recruiting a young interpreter-scribe.'

'Did you learn anything?'

'No. Your friend is certainly good at hiding himself. Well, I am obstinate and I never fail. Tomorrow, we shall meet a senior officer who cannot hide the truth from me. He will set us on the trail of the helmet, if that precious object is hidden in Naukratis. Tell me, young scribe, are you in love?'

Kel hesitated. 'Do I have to answer you?'

'You already have. Good night.'

Kel went back to work.

Zekeh visited the goldsmiths working for her, and Kel noted down the number of pieces produced in the last month. She was a demanding employer, who granted bonuses to the bravest and dismissed the lazy. Satisfied with production, she left the blacksmiths' quarter and headed for a poorly maintained two-storey building.

With a kick, she awoke a sick man who was sleeping on the doorstep.

The unfortunate man moaned and said, 'The gods have sent you, gracious lady. Some bread – have pity.'

'My bakery, in the next street, needs an apprentice. Work, and you shall eat.'

Fearing another kick, the invalid left.

Kel followed Lady Zekeh into the shabby house and up a flight of well-worn steps. At the top were bedchambers, in one of which a bearded man was snoring loudly.

Zekeh shook him awake. 'So, Aristotles, still as drunk as ever?'

'Always, my darling. Drunkenness is the pleasure of the gods.'

'If they resemble you, it's enough to make one stop believing in them. Didn't your captain take you on again?'

'Yes, though he didn't care for my last fit of anger. But I was in the right. We'd been served some vile beer, and I threw it in the face of the steward responsible for it. Dismissed for that, can you imagine? A soldier of my quality.'

Aristotles sat up. He was a muscular man, still very capable of fighting.

'In memory of our old friendship,' he told Zekeh, 'you must persuade my imbecile of a captain to take me back. Without me, the Greek army will collapse.'

'Your case is becoming difficult.'

'But you're so charming, darling. One word from you, and the matter will be resolved.'

'It is possible,' conceded Zekeh. 'What do you offer in exchange?'

Head pounding, Aristotles tried to think. 'Will a poem to your glory do?'

'Think of something better.'

'A night of love—'

'I detest warmed-up leftovers.'

'You have an idea yourself.'

'Your perspicacity surprises me, Aristotles.'

The soldier looked worried. 'I hope you're not going to ask the impossible?'

'Just a piece of information.'

'Military secrecy . . .'

'I also detest bad jokes,' added Zekeh. 'Either you answer, or I leave. And you can sort things out with your captain yourself.

'Stay, sweet friend, stay!

The soldier drew himself up straight. 'Aristotles is ready to answer.'

'On account of your frequent, assiduous visits to the taverns of Naukratis, your hear all the gossip.'

'Affirmative.'

'Has anyone recently spoken of a treasure which has arrived in the city and which has escaped from the authorities?'

Aristotles' eyes widenened. 'How do you know that?'

'I am waiting for an answer, my fine friend.'

'To tell the truth, it's rather vague.'

'Well, you must be rather clear.'

'Very well, very well. One of my acquaintances, a nice girl with reasonable prices, heard about it in confidence from a client who was in his cups.'

'What's his name?'

'I don't know. But I do know he's a dock-worker. He and

his colleagues apparently transported this fabulous treasure on the sly, without informing the customs scribes or the port authorities. And I don't advise you to approach the dock-workers. Those fellows are quick-tempered and violent, and wouldn't hesitate to inflict absolute outrages on you.'

'That's useful advice, Aristotles. Anything more?'

'Forget this story and don't take unnecessary risks – I need you too much. And the captain . . . will you deal with him?'

'Present yourself at the barracks tomorrow morning.'

38

'I must go alone,' decided Kel.

'Aristotles wasn't exaggerating,' said Zekeh. 'Even the soldiers fear the dock-workers because they know how to fight and don't hesitate to fight dirty. It is a very closed caste, and they detest strangers.'

'I speak Greek, and they have no reason to be suspicious of me. Especially if you allow me to offer them a large reward in exchange for the helmet.'

'An excellent idea.'

'Your presence would disrupt the negotiations, don't you think? Those men wouldn't hesitate to . . . attack you.'

She knew Kel was right. In the eyes of the Greek dock-workers, a woman was worth less than a bale of linen, and Zekeh's beauty would play to her disadvantage. One thing worried her, though: once he had the helmet, Kel might leave Naukratis immediately. Zekeh must obtain this fabulous treasure, even if it meant – in one way or another – getting rid of a scribe who had become an encumbrance.

'Only I can protect you,' she said tenderly. 'You're a criminal on the run, don't forget. You will be arrested before you can hand the helmet back to the pharaoh, and then your innocence will never be proven.'

'Would you be willing to negotiate in my name?'

'I only wish to save you, my boy.'

'How can I ever thank you?'

'Bring back the helmet, and don't haggle too much about the fee. Then we shall go to Sais.' She found Kel's naivety touching. Believing in other people's sincerity and promises would shorten his life.

Zekeh guided him to the port and showed him the customs building. Dock-workers were unloading trading-vessels from Greece.

'Wait for sunset,' she advised, 'and then go slowly towards the far end of the jetty. The dock-workers gather there to eat their evening meal. If a customs scribe confronts you, tell him that you're looking for work. The gods will help you, I'm sure, and you will be exonerated.'

As he walked along the jetty, panic gripped Kel. Nothing had prepared him for such a confrontation. He longed to be back at the Interpreters' Secretariat, translating a difficult text before going for supper with Bebon. Would he ever experience those small joys again? Would he ever see Nitis?

Their work done, the dock-workers were playing dice and took no interest in the passer-by. In the distance, a brazier glowed.

Kel felt a desire to run for his life. Persuading the dock-workers to sell him Ahmose's helmet seemed impossible, unless they were unaware of the true nature of the relic and its incalculable value.

About twenty sturdy fellows were cooking fish, which they had stuffed with salt, onions and raisins. Beer was flowing freely.

Kel gritted his teeth and went forward.

'Well, well, a visitor!' a coarse voice called out. 'Are you looking for someone, boy?'

'Officially, I've come to look for work.'

'You don't have the build for it. Well, what's the truth, then?'

'I'd like to make a trade with your leader.'

The men stopped eating and drinking. Only the crackling of the fire broke the thick silence.

'I am the leader,' said Coarse-Voice, 'and I don't much like it when a guard comes and disturbs my dinner.'

'I'm not a guard – quite the contrary.'

'Which means what?'

'That the men who wield the clubs would like very much to get their hands on me.'

'You're a criminal?'

'That's my concern. Is a small fortune of any interest to you?'

Stunned into silence, Coarse-Voice looked closely at the young man, who seemed serious and sure of himself.

'In exchange for what?'

'A treasure you have obtained which belongs to me. Name your price.'

'A treasure? Are you mad?'

'Lying is pointless.'

Suddenly Coarse Voice regretted having got involved with a suspicious but lucrative scheme. Then again, he had had no choice. Now, he was facing an envoy from the authorities and would have to get rid of him discreetly.

The solution was obvious.

'We are only go-betweens. You need to see our colleagues at Pe-guti, "The House of the Dock-workers", at the mouth of the most westerly branch of the Nile. They hold the treasure. They make the decisions.'

'I shall pay you for this information.'

'We'll see about that later. You can sleep here, and tomorrow morning we'll take you to Pe-guti. It's a question of security.'

The circle of dock-workers tightened.

Closely watched, Kel was obliged to stretch out on a grubby mat. Nobody offered him anything to eat or drink.

If he tried to escape, the men wouldn't hesitate to smash his head. He couldn't inform Zekeh, and nobody would come to help him. He would not return from this journey.

39

The wind was blowing hard, and the waves were angry. Inhospitable and dangerous, the coast marked the end of a marshy area which was difficult to cross.

Out at sea was a ship. Like most Egyptians, Kel knew that a fearsome demon inhabited the sea and was subject to outbursts of destructive anger. He did not envy the sailors who had to face it.

'Is this Pe-guti?' he asked in astonishment.

'I've changed my mind,' said Coarse-Voice. 'Getting rid of a guard requires taking precautions.'

'I told you, I'm not a guard, I—'

'I'm used to judging people, boy. Your chief did you a bad turn, entrusting you with this impossible mission. Ardys the pirate will pay a good price for you. If he's in a good mood, he'll tell you about the treasure you're looking for before reducing you to slavery. If not, he'll amuse himself by torturing you and then throw your remains to the fish. Ardys hates Egyptians.'

Even if he ran like the wind, Kel could not escape the dockworkers, who were armed with throwing-sticks and daggers made in Naukratis. Several of them began to laugh heartily at their prisoner's distress.

The ship was anchored a good distance from the shore. The

pirates launched a boat and headed towards the fire the dock-workers had lit.

'So Ardys has the treasure,' murmured Kel.

'Well, yes, boy. In a way, you've achieved your goal. But your success will be fatal, and the authorities will know nothing about it.'

The young man decided it was futile to beg Coarse-Voice for mercy. To him, Kel was just a piece of merchandise he must get rid of as quickly as possible, and for the best price.

Kel mused that he would never see Nitis again. At that moment, he realized that he loved her passionately. Death would prevent him from revealing his feelings to her and would deprive him of her gaze, her beauty and her radiance.

The boat reached the shore, and five pirates disembarked. They were led by a massive, bearded fellow dressed in a short tunic. Two swords hung at his belt.

'Greetings, Ardys,' said Coarse-Voice uneasily.

'What have you to offer me today?'

'This,' replied the dock-worker, pointing at Kel.

The two men spoke in an Ionian dialect which Kel knew.

'Where does he come from?' asked Ardys.

'He's a guard, sent to recover your treasure.'

The big man burst out laughing. 'You put me in a good mood, my friend. How much do you want for him?'

'A good price.'

'Three jars of old wine?'

'Five, and a precious vase.'

'Too dear.'

'A young guard . . . A fine distraction, don't you think?'

Ardys grumbled. 'Four jars and a small Cretan vase which the ladies of Sais will love.'

'Done.'

The exchange was agreed.

'You and your men, on your way now,' ordered the pirate. 'We're going to use your fire to grill some fish. We'll meet again at the new moon. Try to bring me some clothing and some weapons.'

'Very well.'

Two pirates gave Coarse-Voice the jars of wine and the Cretan vase, which had come from sacking a trading-vessel. Ardys had expected to pay more, and felt pleased with the transaction.

His gaze turned towards Kel. 'A guard doesn't make a good slave, and you have got much muscle. No time to teach you how to row for whole days at a time. You don't understand what I'm saying, do you, Egyptian? That's a pity. My men and I are going to amuse ourselves by roasting you while we eat. A guard's screams will make excellent music for the table.'

'You are a true foreigner,' said Kel, 'since you don't speak Egyptian. Why do you hate my country so much?'

'You . . . you're speaking my dialect!'

'I am not a guard, I am a scribe-interpreter, and I work in Naukratis, in the service of the lady Zekeh.'

Stunned, Ardys stood open-mouthed for a long time. 'The lady Zekeh,' he repeated eventually, as though talking of a fearsome goddess. 'What precisely are you looking for?'

'A treasure which the dock-workers transported recently, and which is apparently in your possession.'

The pirate brought his fist up to his forehead. 'This is complete madness! Why do I hate your damned country? Because of its customs scribes, its guards and its taxes. An honest trader can no longer manage to earn a decent living – not a single cargo escapes taxation. Well, I get by in a different way. From the boats coming from Asia Minor, I take wine, oil, wool, wood, metals, and the dock-workers sneak them in under the noses of the authorities. The buyers pay less, and everyone is happy.'

'The treasure I mentioned is no ordinary piece of merchandise.'

'There's no need to remind me of that!' Ardys thundered. 'Does somebody not trust me?'

'Certainly not,' declared Kel, surprised at the turn of the conversation.

The pirate's expression grew suspicious. 'You're carrying out a final check, aren't you? It is a war, after all! Before moving to the offensive, it's best to ensure the quality of one's troops.'

Ardys led Kel to one side. Kel wondered if the pirate, too, had changed his mind and was planning to stab Kel instead of roasting him.

From the pocket of his tunic, Ardys took a small circular silver object. Kel had never seen anything like it.

'Superb, isn't it? The chest hidden in my cabin contains a hundred identical pieces, struck in Greece. Soon, our coinage will circulate in Egypt, and that'll be the end of your barter system and your outdated economy. The reference ingots in the temples, which the state doesn't put into circulation, will be forgotten and outmoded in favour of these coins. Everyone will be able to have them, and they'll change the world.'

'Pharaoh will forbid it,' objected Kel.

'No, he won't – he loves Greece. As the first importer, I shall become a very rich man. A former pirate, can you imagine? Very well, we have to be cautious until the adoption of this formidable change, but then we shall reap the benefits. You've chosen the right path, boy. An intelligent Egyptian is a rare thing. Most important, you must tell our employer that she's not to worry. Ardys is looking after the treasure, and nobody will take it from him. And when the moment comes, Greek money will invade Egypt.'

'Our employer . . . ?'

The pirate gave a ribald laugh. 'She's a cunning little minx, that one. Even a fellow like me is willing to obey her. And they say that in bed . . . But maybe you know all about that, eh?'

'Haven't you got a helmet belonging to King Ahmose?' Kel asked.

Ardys's surprise was genuine. 'I always fight bare-headed, and my sword can cut through a bronze helmet. Go back to Naukratis, scribe, and reassure the lady Zekeh. Ardys won't betray her.'

40

He was still alive! Basically, Ardys the pirate cared nothing for the fate of the all-powerful Zekeh's envoy. If he died, she would easily find another one to run her errands.

In order to make use of what he'd learnt, Kel must cross a vast, marshy expanse where several forms of death lay in wait, beginning with crocodiles and other reptiles. However, the presence of many birds reassured him. Ibis, woodcock, herons, cranes and pelicans revelled in this vast domain, where food was abundant. He admired their flight and their games, so far from human baseness. Here, life was expressed with all the magnificence of the first morning of the world.

Kel picked a young papyrus stalk, cut off the upper end and ate the inside, which was about one cubit in length. It was simple nourishment, which would give him the energy necessary to walk for hours, keeping up a regular pace and never relaxing his vigilance.

Before nightfall, he had the good fortune to encounter some fishermen, who were content with their hard day's work. They took him to their village, shared their meal with him and offered him a sleeping-mat; they were tired, and not in the mood to chatter. The following morning, as dawn was breaking, they indicated the best route to a town from where a road led to Naukratis.

Kel's head was buzzing with questions, and Zekeh was

going to answer them, by force if need be. Had she sent him off to certain death, or did she really think the dock-workers had Ahmose's helmet? By killing him they would have admitted their guilt, so he had served as bait, without the least chance of reappearing.

'Halt and don't move!'

Three men armed with clubs emerged from a thicket of papyrus and surrounded the young man.

'Travelling customs guards,' declared the officer, a man aged around forty, with thin lips and a low forehead. 'Out for a little walk, my lad?'

'I'm going to Naukratis.'

'Where have you come from?'

'From the town of the Heron, two hours from here.'

'Do you live there?'

'I was visiting friends.'

'I know the place and I've never seen you there.'

'That's not surprising; it was my first visit.'

'Who are these friends of yours?'

'The owners of the bread oven.'

'We'll check. What are your name and your profession?'

'I'm a servant in Naukratis.'

'I didn't hear your name.'

'Bak.'

'Bak, "the servant" – that sounds good. Who is your employer?'

It seemed a bad idea to mention Zekeh.

'Why are you asking me all these questions?' Kel asked in a tone of astonishment. 'I'm not carrying any untaxed goods.'

'Exactly, and that's very strange,' replied the officer. 'We often catch travelling pedlars who are not entirely obeying the regulations, but not empty-handed walkers. Now, who is your employer?'

'A Greek soldier.'

'We'll check that, too, when we take you back to Naukratis.'

161

'I'd rather go on my own.'

'Don't you feel safe with us?'

'What are you accusing me of?'

A guard whispered a few words in the officer's ear.

'At the moment, we are not only looking for thieves and fraudsters. We're also hunting a murderer, a scribe called Kel, who goes from village to village and may be hiding in the marshes in the hope of escaping justice. My colleague, who is extremely good with faces, thinks he has recognized this dangerous criminal from the portrait sent to us by the authorities in Sais. So you are going to follow us without any fuss, and we shall check.'

The guards were all were thinking of the generous reward.

'You are mistaken,' protested Kel. 'I'm not a murderer.'

'Ah, but you certainly are Kel the scribe.'

'Will you hear me out?'

'No, we're content just to have caught you. You can talk to the judge.'

Head down, Kel dashed forward and butted the officer in the stomach. Caught off guard, his men were slow to react. Kel took to his heels and ran.

'Catch him!'

Used to this kind of exercise, they quickly gained ground. The first managed to get his arms round Kel's waist and flattened him face-down on the ground.

'Now, my lad, you're going to learn to obey and you're going to behave yourself.'

The prisoner stiffened and waited for the blows to rain down on him. Instead, the officer cried out in pain and collapsed beside him.

'Get up, Kel, and let's get away from here.'

That voice . . . It was Bebon!

'Is it you?' cried Kel. 'Is it really you?'

'Have I changed that much?'

'What about the other guards?'

'I finished off the officer with a punch to the back of the neck, grabbed his club and used it on his first henchman. I've just rid you of the other one.'

'Did the court find you innocent?'

'There were no charges, so they had to let me go free. The authorities arrest so many innocent people who look like you that Judge Gem no longer knows if he's coming or going!'

'How did you get here?'

'Your friend Nitis the priestess told me you'd gone to Naukratis. In a tavern near the customs post I pretended to be a guard, and a "colleague" told me about two teams which were about to leave to search for a dangerous criminal. As luck would have it, I followed the right one.'

'Nitis . . . So she trusts me?'

'She is a valuable ally – and so pretty. To hear her, I wouldn't say she's indifferent to you, either. Note well, a priestess and a murderer on the run – it won't be easy.'

'Stop talking nonsense!'

'Everybody has to relax a little bit. I don't knock out three customs guards every day, you know. When they wake up, they're probably going to be in a very bad mood. They didn't see me, but as for you, they know you're in the area.'

'We must go to Naukratis and question someone who knows a great deal.'

'Not a mercenary armed to the teeth, I hope?'

'A very beautiful Greek businesswoman.'

He's forgotten the pretty priestess already, thought Bebon.

'Don't let her seduce you,' Kel went on. 'The lady Zekeh is more fearsome than a horned viper. Come on, I'll explain on the way.'

41

As she removed linen fabrics from the room where the priestesses were working, Nitis thought of Kel. Would he come back alive from Naukratis with his friend Bebon? And would he bring back proof of his innocence?

His absence caused her profound sadness. Kel offered a new horizon, an ideal which only he embodied. Would Neith's magic turn away the attacks of destiny and recreate a path of light, which the priestess and the scribe could explore together?

'I have some bad news,' announced the High Priest.

Nitis felt a cold hand about her heart. 'Kel . . .'

'No, don't worry, Judge Gem's investigation is at a standstill. There is no trace of the murderer.'

'Kel didn't kill anyone!'

'I know that, but we must use the official words. The judge complains about the inefficiency of the guards and about Henat's silence. According to Gem, Henat is not playing an honest game, and does not pass on the information he has at his disposal.'

'Is that your opinion, too?'

'It would be better if the judge found Kel first. Henat will not bother with procedure and will have the so-called criminal executed. His men's reports will establish that they acted in legitimate self-defence, and the affair will be buried.'

'Gem wouldn't accept such a travesty!'

'Unless he is an accomplice of the murderers.'

'If that were the case, our country would be in great peril.'

'The bad news confirms that it is. The king has ordered us to set aside a part of our workshops to serve the outside world.'

Nitis was appalled. 'Is he trying to destroy the temples?'

'A new economy is being born, and we must adapt to it.'

'Since the age of the pyramids, it is the temples which have dictated the economy. It is up human beings to respect the Law of Maat, not for Maat to bend to the base failings of humanity.'

'Ahmose has decided to abolish the temples' privileges, which he considers excessive. From now on they will be subject to his government and, with the exception of the very ancient shrines of Iunu and Memphis, they will no longer receive income from their estates. Only the state will levy taxes, and it will also engage priests just like peasants and craftsmen, pay them a salary and maintain the buildings. Our workshops will produce fabrics for outsiders and thus contribute to the country's prosperity.'

'The Divine Worshipper will never accept this madness!'

'Thebes is a long way away,' the High Priest reminded her, 'and she rules only a small territory. Here, in the Delta, the future world is being born.'

'But you advocate a return to the values of the Old Kingdom, and you entrusted me with the task of reviving the rituals of ancient times. Our sculptors take their inspiration from the statuary produced by the pyramid-builders.'

'That is still my position. Ahmose is turning his gaze towards the Greeks and his caste of senior officials to whom he will grant the temples' lands.'

'Will you try to persuade him that he has chosen the wrong path?'

'He has made his decision, and my words are of no interest to him. Now, tell me, is Pythagoras correctly performing the ritual duties assigned to him?'

'He is behaving like a perfect *wab*.'

'He, being a Greek, might perhaps exercise some influence over the king. Let us continue to test him and, above all, prepare for the next festival of the goddess. She alone can protect us from the worst, and her service must not suffer delay or a lack of precision.'

'Menk and I arc working together well,' Nitis assured him. 'He's proud of his reputation as an excellent organizer, so he gives of himself unstintingly and does not tolerate failure.'

'But remain cautious,' advised Wahibra. 'He is a born courtier, and we do not know the true part he is playing.'

'Since I have not managed to decipher a single word of the code,' said Nitis, 'I must ask you for permission to write to the late head of the Interpreters' Secretariat and solicit his aid.'

'A letter to a dead man?'

'I hope that he will answer us.'

'Choose your words well, Nitis. And let us hope that your magic is persuasive.

Nitis went to the small shrine belonging to the head interpreter's tomb. On the offertory table, she placed a loaf of bread made from stone and poured some fresh water.

The soft light from the setting sun lit up the accessible part of the house of eternity. Here, the living could commune with the dead.

The priestess raised her hands to venerate the statuette of the *ka*, the vital power that escaped death after dwelling within a mineral, vegetable, animal or human being during its life.

'Be in peace,' she wished it, 'and join once again with the original Light.'

She hung a small papyrus round the statuette's neck. The text of her letter to the dead man begged him to help her and unmask the real criminals in order to save the life of an innocent man, Kel the scribe. When the soul, nourished by the sun, came to bring the statuette of the *ka* to life, would it bear an answer from the world beyond?

At dawn, Nitis returned to the door of the shrine. She read out a long hymn to the glory of the reborn light at the end of a fierce battle against the darkness, stepped across the threshold and halted in the middle of the modest shrine.

She had the feeling that a presence was there. Was it a dangerous demon or a friendly spirit?

The papyrus had unrolled, and lay at the foot of the statuette. Hesitantly, Nitis reached out and picked it up. In red ink, and in the dead man's handwriting, there was an answer: '*The ancestors have the code.*'

42

'You're back at last!' exclaimed Zekeh. 'What happened?'

'You made a complete fool of me me,' said Kel, 'and I've been desperately stupid. But fate has dismantled your plans.'

The Greek feigned astonishment. 'I don't understand anything of what you're saying.'

'Play-acting is pointless, my lady. I know about your role.

'What do you mean?'

'I believed you were sincere, and you sent me to my death.'

'Dock-workers are violent and dangerous – you knew that.'

'Ardys the pirate works for you, doesn't he?'

Zekeh smiled strangely. 'Did you meet him?'

'Did you order him to kill me?'

'You were supposed to find the treasure.'

'I did.'

'So we have Pharaoh Ahmose's helmet! Ardys really is the best of thieves. He deserves a good reward.'

'I am not so sure.'

'Did he refuse to sell us the helmet?'

'The treasure you entrusted to him is something very different.'

Lady Zekeh's expression darkened to one of ferocity. 'Has that second-rate pirate been loose-tongued?'

'By introducing Greek coinage into Egypt,' said Kel, 'you want to destroy our economy and our society. By seizing the helmet of Ahmose, you would gain a decisive weapon in the battle for power. No doubt you have already chosen the mercenary who will wear it and proclaim himself king. In this dangerous game I was nothing but a pawn, destined to die.'

'With your keen intelligence,' said Zekeh in a soft voice, 'you must surely understand that the old world will soon be snuffed out. The Egyptians look towards the past and ancestral values. Some even think of reviving the age of the pyramids, which inspires your sculptors. We Greeks represent the future.'

'A future I reject.'

'A young scribe, reactionary and in love with the past: a fine representative of a decadent elite. Look at Naukratis, Kel: this is the new world. Who defends your old Egypt, if not Greek soldiers? In exchange for their efforts, they demand better pay. Two bags of oats and five of wheat per month? It's not enough! They want proper coins, and I shall soon put thousands into circulation.'

'Coinage and slavery . . . Is that it, your progress?'

'Am unstoppable process.'

'You must have accomplices in the government. If not, you would have doubts about your success.'

'Do not get too curious, Kel. Only my husband will share my secrets. Either you marry me, or you run away. And if you choose the wrong answer, do not rely on me to protect you any more.'

Kel turned white. 'I'll never yield to this vile blackmail!'

'Don't be ridiculous. You desire me, I desire you. Together, we shall do excellent work. Without my help, you are condemned to death.'

'Death may be the best escape of all.'

'At your age, it is a horrible punishment. Be sensible, Kel. I'm the only one who enabled you to escape from the authorities. But first of all, tell me where Ahmose's helmet is hidden.'

'I don't know.'

'The pirate betrayed me, and you're his accomplice!'

'No, my lady.'

They glared at each other.

'I had hoped for more,' she admitted. 'So Ardys is loyal to me and the only treasure he holds is a stock of Greek coin?'

'That's right.'

'What is your decision, Kel?'

'I shall leave Naukratis.'

Zekeh turned her back on him. 'As you wish. I shall however do you one last service. Wait here for two or three hours. I shall go and find out where observation posts have been set up, and tell you how to get out of the city.'

'Thank you.'

'You are heading for disaster.'

'I shall prove my innocence.'

'Such a pity, Kel. Together, we would have renewed your outdated world.' Zekeh swept out of the vast reception hall, leaving behind a waft of overpowering perfume.

Kel paced up and down anxiously. Would Zekeh deliver him up to soldiers who would sell his remains to the authorities?'

Greedy for power, Zekeh was planning to take over the country. Was she suffering delusions of grandeur, or was it a realistic plan? Nothing proved that she was involved in the murder of the interpreters. However, she did not deny being acquainted with highly placed individuals.

Unable to sort the truth from falsehood, Kel was relieved to see her returning.

'The craftsmen's gateway isn't yet being watched,' she told him. 'Take what you need and go.'

'Thank you again for your help.'

'In losing me, you lose everything.'

Kel returned to his lodgings. He would collect his scribe's palette and equip himself with a mat, a water-container and a bag of food.

170

He tried to push the door open, but something heavy was blocking it. With immense effort, he managed to move the obstacle and squeeze into the room.

On the floor lay a dead body, the body of his friend and colleague Demos the Greek. Someone had cut his throat. Near his head lay the murder weapon: one of those Greek knives which Egyptians refused to use because they considered them impure. The Greeks re-use them after killing animals. Such objects were contaminated, and would sully human food.

Demos . . . Innocent or guilty, he would never speak again.

Rooted to the spot, Kel stared at the corpse, begging it to reveal the truth. But Demos was silent for ever, indifferent now to the fates of mortals.

'It's the murderer!' shouted a rough voice. 'Come on, let's catch him!'

A firm hand gripped Kel's shoulder. 'We must get out of here!' ordered Bebon.

'Look, that's the body—'

'It won't wake up. And we must escape.'

Kel allowed himself to be dragged along and started to run.

Bebon guided him away from the front hallway, where Zekeh's servants were waiting for them, armed with sticks, and they crossed the large kitchen, watched in alarm by the boys who minded the cooking-pots.

'We'll have to climb,' said Bebon.

An aged scribe tried to bar their way, but Bebon elbowed him out of the way. The two men jumped on to the roof below, reached a terrace, then clambered down a long ladder which took them into a side-street.

'We've lost them,' said Bebon.

43

Delegated by the central government, the accounting scribe met Nitis in the middle of the morning, after she had given her instructions to the priestesses.

The scribe seemed rather sympathetic. 'This temple is splendid,' he remarked, much impressed. 'I am sorry to inconvenience you, but orders are orders. I am going to check your accounts, reduce certain expenses and favour certain investments. The king is eager to develop your workshops and sell your products in the outside world.'

'That is not our vocation,' objected Nitis.

'I know, I know. Nevertheless, neither of us has a choice. Let us try to get along together.'

Free of of hostility and not at all happy with his mission, the scribe proved conciliatory and reduced the Temple of Neith's obligations to the minimum.

'One should apply the same law to everyone,' he grumbled. 'When I think of the fate that befell my unfortunate colleague in the Interpreters' Secretariat! If justice disappears, Egypt will be destroyed.'

'What happened to him?'

'All the interpreters were murdered, including my colleague,' whispered the scribe. 'It's out of the question to speak of that horror. The guards will arrest the murderer, and we will forget the tragedy. All the same, they ought to have listened to my colleague.'

'Did he notice irregularities in the management of the secretariat?'

'Indeed not, for the head scribe was the most meticulous of men – it was futile to ask for undeserved favours or benefits. But my colleague had handed him a document concerning apparent financial misappropriations in Naukratis, the Greek city. Down there people have a tendency to make their own laws.'

'What happened to the document?' Nitis asked, her curiosity aroused.

'After studying it, the head scribe passed it on to higher authorities.

'To whom, exactly?'

'My colleague did not know.'

'Was there any reaction?'

'Not to my knowledge. That is why we are hurtling towards disaster. Anyway, our lips must be sealed. This kind of affair is too big for us. Getting involved with it would only attract serious problems for the incautious. I shall see you again soon, Superior.'

Nitis went immediately to see the High Priest, who was drawing up a detailed table of the tasks to be accomplished before the goddess's next festival.

'Is our friend Pythagoras proving efficient?' he asked.

'Impeccable and discreet: I cannot criticize him in any way.'

'Continue to watch him.'

'I have just heard some astonishing information,' said Nitis.

Wahibra listened attentively to what she said.

Pefy was overburdened with work. He was enjoying a moment's rest in the shade of an age-old palm tree, beside a lake in his vast Sais villa. Because of the budgetary restrictions which had been imposed in order to benefit the army, he must reorganize the services of the Double House of Gold and Silver, whose officials were not at all fond of changes.

As 'Overseer of the Banks which Flood', he was also concerned with the proper farming of the fields and personally dealt with the officials in charge of the main agricultural areas. Fortunately, there was nothing worrying. Nevertheless, he must not authorize any laxity, for fear of leading to disaster. Pefy often thought of Osiris's holy city of Abydos, to which he would have loved to withdraw, worshipping the god of the reborn.

The minister closed his eyes and dozed, dreaming of a peaceful world without fraudsters or lazy people.

His steward dared to wake him. 'High Priest Wahibra wishes to see you.'

This nap had been a rather short one.

Pefy received his friend in one of the villa's airy rooms, away from indiscreet ears. They were served light beer and honey-cakes.

'In these difficult times, my friend,' said the minister, 'we must be sure to appreciate small pleasures. Shall we be able to do so tomorrow?'

'Are you becoming a pessimist, Pefy?'

'Age and fatigue do not incline one to a joyful outlook on life. And your visit is probably not going to give me back my smile.'

'Probably not,' admitted Wahibra.

'I hope you aren't going to talk to me about the interpreters' murder?'

'I have some new and disturbing information.'

'My friend, my very dear friend, don't get involved in that affair. Henat is reorganizing our diplomacy, with the king's agreement. And the guards will soon get their hands on the murderer. Forget this tragedy.'

'Do you refuse to hear me out?'

Pefy let out a sigh of exasperation. 'Knowing how obstinate you are, I surrender.'

'Among the many sensitive cases to be dealt with by the head of the Interpreters' Secretariat was an accounting document concerning the Greeks of Naukratis. It proved grave misappropriations, and it should have been passed on to the authorities.'

A heavy silence followed this declaration.

'That is correct,' admitted Pefy.

'You knew about it?'

'It was I whom the head of the secretariat approached.'

'What were your conclusions?' asked the High Priest.

'Obvious financial skulduggery! Naukratis observes its own rules, which are very different from those of the pharaonic state.'

'What were the punishments?'

'There were none.'

'What do you mean, none?'

'Naukratis is a protected territory, the direct responsibility of the king.'

'Does he know about the Greeks' actions?'

'I give him regular detailed reports. That one was part of a long list.'

'And Ahmose does nothing?'

'Yes, he does, by forbidding me to intervene. He alone deals with the Greek city.'

'A state within a state!'

'Either I obey or I resign. Now, I very much wish to guarantee the perennial survival of Abydos. My successor would neglect the city of Osiris.'

'That document might be one of the causes of the interpreters' murder,' said the High Priest.

'Surely not! I tell you again, there are many other reports of the same nature, and the facts have been established. Basically, the Greeks sort things out among themselves and they do not overflow into the world outside. Is it not wisest to let them continue?'

44

Judge Gem had just put an end to a shady affair, involving joint ownership, which had been going on for thirty years. Owing to the lack of proof, the opponents had finally accepted a compromise. Already excellent, the senior magistrate's reputation had been further enhanced by this case. Thanks to him, the legal system was resolving complex cases.

There was, however, one exception: Kel the scribe, a murderer who was still at large.

Angrily, Gem forced his way into Henat's office. He found Henat filing small papyri bearing names, dates and facts – he allowed no one else to do this, for his prodigious memory registered each detail.

'This situation cannot go on,' said the judge.

'Problems?'

'Despite the king's orders, you are not cooperating and are keeping to yourself information that would be useful to me.'

'You misjudge me.'

'Prove it.'

'Certainly, Judge Gem. I have just received a report from Naukratis and, after checking, I was planning to hand it directly to you.'

The judge was flattered. 'What have you learnt?'

'We have picked up the murderer's trail. Kel was hiding in the Delta marshes, near Naukratis. Customs guards spotted and intercepted him, but he managed to escape, with the aid of an accomplice.'

'Was the accomplice identified?'

'Unfortunately not. We don't know if it was a member of his network or just someone offering help on that occasion. But that's a mere detail, in view of the new facts.'

'What facts?'

'Kel went to Naukratis with the specific intention of killing Stubborn and Demos.'

'Are you serious?'

'Their bodies have been identified,' said Henat. 'As regards Stubborn, who had enlisted in the army, it was apparently an accident.'

'But you don't believe it was?'

'Not for one moment.'

'And Demos?'

'According to several witness reports, including that of the lady Zekeh, an important person in Naukratis, Kel slit his throat. Unaware of his true identity and crimes, Zekeh had employed Kel as a scribe, not suspecting that he was manipulating her. Through his connections, he found Demos and got rid of him.'

'Have depositions been taken?' asked the judge worriedly.

'Here they are.'

Dubiously, Gem read the texts, which were clear and consistent with each other.

Zekeh's servants had seen Demos enter Kel's room, then heard the sounds of a violent struggle. The scribe had emerged from the room with a bloody knife in his hand. Wild-eyed, he dropped his weapon and once again fled.

'That man Kel is a veritable wild animal!' exclaimed the judge.

'He killed his two accomplices, for fear that they might talk, and has declared himself head of the criminal network,' Henat concluded.

'A network serving whom?'

'That is for the investigation to establish. Perhaps it is all just a sordid series of murders.'

The judge buried his head in his hands. 'This tragedy is taking on terrifying proportions. And we still do not know the murderer's motives.'

'He will reveal them when you interrogate him,' Henat predicted.

'If it ever happens! He seems impossible to catch.'

'A hunted animal always ends up falling into a trap, and Kel will not escape that rule.'

'Given his murderous madness, I am obliged to take rigorous precautions. If he feels all is lost, he will react with increasing violence. So no soldier or guard should risk his life.'

'I don't quite understand you,' said Henat worriedly.

'I am going to give the order to kill him on sight,' said the judge. 'The forces of order will be acting in legitimate self-defence, and will not be punished.'

Henat turned purple. 'No! We must take Kel alive, and make him confess the motives for his crimes.'

'That may be impossible. And I think more of the lives of our men than that of this madman.'

'Don't make this mistake,' advised Henat, 'or the king will hold you personally responsible.'

'Are you his spokesman?'

'Indeed, Judge Gem.'

'If other incidents occur, do you undertake to cover me?'

'My official functions do not permit me to do so.'

'Then I shall conduct this investigation as I see fit.'

'Would you dare defy His Majesty?'

'If he gives me an official order, I shall respect it. Your voice is not enough for me, Henat.'

'Defying me will lead you nowhere, Judge. Your role consists of arresting a formidable killer, and arresting him alive so that he may talk. Then, and only then, will he be tried and sentenced.'

'There is no need to remind me of the duties of my office; I have been faithfully fulfilling them for many years.'

'Then do not begin to trample upon them now.'

'I dislike your tone of voice, Henat. As I said, I shall favour the lives of our men over that of a criminal madman. Unless information received from your spies enables me to arrest him safely.'

'His Majesty has asked me to cooperate.'

'Then obey him.'

45

Kel and Bebon hid in the middle of a palm-grove and tried to get their breath back.

Sensing that something bad was going to happen, the actor had studied an escape route in order to escape from any future attackers. And this precaution had proved decisive.

'You must alter your appearance,' he told Kel. 'If you change your haircut and grow a little clipped moustache, like some scribes in the Old Kingdom, you'll be unrecognizable.'

'We'll need a knife.'

'I have one.'

Kel couldn't believe his eyes. 'You didn't . . . ?'

'I picked up the murder weapon, this superb Greek knife. Look at the letters engraved on the hilt.'

'Zekeh!' the scribe deciphered.

'Your "protector" probably personally slit the throat of your colleague, whom she was hiding in her house or keeping prisoner. But we cannot prove anything.'

'Zekeh mixed up in the conspiracy . . . So nothing was down to chance.'

'Did you still think it was? Sit down, and keep your back nice and straight. I'll clean the knife and play at being a barber. Don't worry, I've got quite good it it through all my travelling.'

'Zekeh is the head of a network of murderers and traffickers

180

who want to turn the country's economy upside down and seize power,' said Kel, thinking out loud. 'I must write a report and send it to the palace. King Ahmose is in danger.'

'You've lost your mind,' remarked Bebon.

'Do you deny the evidence?'

'The Greek woman probably has one or several accomplices at the palace, and we don't know who they are. If you send your magnificent report to one of the conspirators, it will be a waste of time.'

Bebon had a point.

'We must return to Sais,' Kel decided. 'I shall talk to the High Priest of Neith, and he will warn Pharaoh.'

'And you will see the beautiful priestess again,' murmured the actor.

'We are caught in the middle of an affair of state,' Kel reminded him.

'That doesn't stop people having feelings. Good, you look quite different – I almost think you look better this way. Now, we must be able to move about without risks. There's only one solution: pass ourselves off as hawkers.'

'We have nothing to sell.'

'I shall solve that little problem.'

'How?'

'Not far from here there's an inn where many itinerant sellers stop. They're Greeks, who love playing dice for high stakes. And I know a few tricks myself. I shall put our entire fortune on the table.'

'Our fortune? All we have is a knife.'

'Exactly. We have nothing to lose, so we're invulnerable.'

Incredulous and anxious, Kel followed Bebon to the inn where the hawkers gathered; it was a good distance from Naukratis. Here, they drank beer and wine, ate fish and stew, slept, exchanged goods and conducted business deals, some more legitimate than others. Most especially, they played ferociously competitive dice games.

In the middle of the tavern there were four players, whom the excited spectators were watching. Kel and Bebon mingled with the audience.

Mad with rage, a loser stood up, shouting at the victor.

Bebon immediately took his place. 'I have a stock of ivory, pots and wine jars,' he said, 'and I only like playing serious folk, who can afford to pay me. Do we agree?'

His three opponents nodded.

'First stake,' announced Bebon, 'is a donkey, young and in good health. Three winning turns and you have it. I have one, what about you?'

'A fine, tireless animal,' said a bearded man from Samos.

Bebon lost the first two turns, and sneering smiles heralded his certain defeat. Then his luck changed. He won the next turn, lost again, and then won three times in succession.

'The donkey's mine. Shall we continue?'

'I will,' grunted one of the losers. 'Your ivory against my jars of oil. One turn only.'

The dice rolled.

'I win,' said Bebon, 'and you'd do better to give up.'

The bearded man fulminated. 'I'm not used to losing, especially to a lucky amateur. You're the one who wants to retire, I'm sure of it. You haven't the stomach for a real game.'

'We'll stake everything again, plus five jars of wine. Two winning turns.'

'Done.'

The first throw was a bad one for Bebon. Kel closed his eyes. If his friend lost, how would he pay his debts? The second throw favoured the actor. The third would determine the winner: the tension rose to a maximum.

It was the bearded man's turn to throw. And fate was against him.

He stood up, very stiffly, and glared at the winner. Kel feared it would end in violence, but the loser merely took Bebon outside and handed over his winnings.

'The donkey's name is North Wind,' he said, 'and my produce is excellent. If you'd cheated, I'd have broken your head. Since the gods granted you luck, you deserve this small fortune. But avoid crossing my path again.'

'You will win next time,' predicted Bebon.

The donkey headed for Kel and gave him a trusting look. Bebon filled two panniers with jars of oil and wine, and the donkey consented to carry them. Under a gentle sun and at a leisurely pace, the trio made their way towards Sais.

'We are perfect hawkers,' declared Bebon, 'and we have goods that will be easy to trade. For a while, our subsistence is assured. If the guards check us, they won't find anything amiss.'

'You took enormous risks!'

'Yes and no.'

'Did you . . . cheat?'

'Yes and no. I swapped the dice, becaue the ones belonging to my opponent were weighted.'

'And what about yours?'

'Very little. Not enough for them to notice. And besides, at certain moments I lost.'

'At the decisive moment, it was the bearded man who threw the dice. How could you be sure of winning?'

Bebon smiled. 'I put myself in the hands of chance. If I'd taken the last throw myself, it would have attracted suspicion.'

'Utter madness!'

'We won the game. Isn't that what matters?'

46

Kroisos, the wealthy former king of Lydia who now headed the Persian diplomatic service, bowed respectfully before the pharaoh.

Ahmose was wearing a sort of coat of mail and a helmet which resembled the one which had made him king. 'Get up, my friend, my great and dear friend,' he cried. 'What happiness it is to welcome you here!'

'Your invitation honours me, Pharaoh. And my wife Nitetis is happy to see her homeland again.'

'The queen and I are delighted that she is here. Some fine receptions lie ahead of us, but first we must attend a military parade organized by General Phanes, commander-in-chief of my armies.'

'His reputation has spread beyond the borders of Egypt.'

'Deservedly so, as you will see.'

Ahmose and Kroisos took their seats in a pavilion of light wood, which sheltered them from the sun.

On a vast plain, to the north of Sais, the foot-soldiers filed past, helmeted and with breastplates, spears and swords. Ever-disciplined, the Greek mercenaries marched impeccably, to the rhythm of heady music which would have stirred the most timid heart. After them came the cavalry, an elite force proud of its own superiority, mounted on magnificent horses, swift and high-strung.

184

Although accustomed to the exploits of the Persian cavalry, Kroisos could not conceal his admiration. 'The vigour of those animals stuns me, and their riders' control is unequalled.'

'Phanes is an exacting demanding commander,' said Ahmose. 'He constantly seeks excellence and will not tolerate any disobedience. At his signal, the entire army must move. And you have not yet seen the best.'

A chariot drawn by two white horses came to fetch the king and his guest, and took them to the military canal, where Kroisos found an impressive flotilla of war-boats.

Their number, size, weaponry and large crews amazed him. 'I had not expected such power,' he admitted.

'Control of the sea guarantees Egypt's security,' said Ahmose. 'Thanks to the constant efforts of Udja, who is responsible for the development of my fleet, our boatyards are constantly producing vessels which are both solid and fast.'

'May I go aboard the flagship?' asked Kroisos.

'Of course.'

Side by side, General Phanes and the head of the navy, Udja, welcomed the illustrious visitor and made no attempt to hide any of the remarkable equipment which the pharaoh's fleet enjoyed. Kroisos felt the ropes and the sails, noted the quality of the masts and size of the crews.

'Impressive,' he concluded. 'Are all the units like this one?'

'We are proud of them,' said Udja. 'Would you like to take part in a manoeuvre?'

Kroisos nodded. From his vantage-point at the bow of the flagship, he marvelled at the skills of Ahmose's sailors.

'The Mediterranean belongs to you,' he told the pharaoh.

'That is not my intention. These forces have only a defensive role to play. Egypt will not attack anyone, but is capable of defending herself against any predator.'

'Knowing its dissuasive power, who would dare to attack the land of the pharaohs?'

Pensively, Kroisos savoured the gentle north wind and the

peace of the sunset. The softness of the palm-groves, the silvery waters of the canal, the sky's orange hue: all these things charmed him so much that he quite forgot the warlike nature of this parade.

The banquet hosted by the King and Queen of Egypt would linger long in the memory. The thousand guests enjoyed varied dishes and excellent wines, and the servants were attentive to their smallest desires.

To the left of the royal couple sat Kroisos; to the right was Nitetis, daughter of Ahmose's predecessor.

Cold and tense, she barely touched her food.

'The past is the past,' Ahmose told her. 'I admired your father and had no intention of overthrowing him. Only a conjunction of circumstances brought me to power. Today, will you consent to forget the painful past?'

She looked hard at the pharaoh. 'You ask a great deal.'

'I am aware of that, but your presence is balm to my heart. So many years have gone by. Does it not ease your pain to see Egypt again?'

'My period of mourning has reached its end, Majesty.'

'Thank you for granting me that happiness.'

At the end of the banquet, the queen invited Nitetis to enjoy the services of her masseuse, who was an expert in the use of essential oils.

Ahmose and Kroisos went off alone to a terrace which looked out on to a garden filled with sycamores, jujube trees, oleanders and tamarisks.

'What a marvellous country,' said Kroisos. 'The fragrance of eternity is in the air.

'A very fragile eternity . . .'

'Why do you say that?'

'Does the Emperor Cambyses really not dream of conquests?'

Kroisos breathed in the warm night air. 'Let us forget

diplomacy and be honest with each other, Majesty. Yes, Cambyses dreams of invading this land with its inexhaustible wealth. As an alert ruler, you have perceived his intentions and built a war machine designed to resist him. And your invitation was designed to inform me of this, so that I would dissuade him from undertaking an adventure doomed to failure.'

'Have I succeeded, Kroisos?'

'Beyond your hopes. I have already tried to direct Cambyses towards a lasting peace, and he has consented to listen to me. On my return, I will report to him the precise facts, which will finally convince him. However powerful it may be, the Persian army has no chance of defeating you. Before my journey I had assumed so; now I am sure of it. Pharaoh has not slumbered in a false sense of security, and thanks to the enlargement of his armed forces, notably his navy, a bloody disaster will be averted.'

'Will Cambyses plan other conquests?'

'The management of the empire will require his full attention, and he will be inspired by his father's example. The time for battles is over, Majesty, and the time of tranquil diplomacy is beginning.'

'Your words warm my heart, Kroisos.'

'The most urgent need is to develop our trading relations, in order to increase our two countries' wealth. So I would like to meet the head of your famous Interpreters' Secretariat and provide him with the names and titles of his future correspondents.'

'Alas, he has died,' said Ahmose.

'Was he ill?'

'No, it was an unfortunate accident. The director of the palace, Henat, has taken his place. He is an experienced and trustworthy man who will place himself at your service and give you complete satisfaction.'

'Perfect, Majesty. This journey will without a doubt turn out to be the most important of my career.'

47

The previous evening, Pharaoh Ahmose had purified, decorated and crowned the black cow that was the embodiment
of Neith. Then, in the centre of the grand courtyard, he
had shot arrows towards the four points of the compass,
in order to prevent the forces of chaos from invading the Two
Lands.

The first procession of the Festival of Neith took place.
A ritual priest preceded the king, while another recited the
ritual texts celebrating the radiance of the Mother of mothers.
Priests and priestesses were posted around the sacred lake
and were present at the voyage across the water of the divine
boat, the symbol of the creative powers' community which
gave birth to the many forms of life.

Outside the sacred enclosure, the celebrations were
beginning. Dozens of families were arriving by boat from the
villages and towns around Sais, eager to celebrate the goddess
and ask for her protection. Flutes were played and the sound
of wooden clappers was used to drive away demons. Wine and
beer were abundant, both provided by the king. All over Sais
people were dancing, and under cover of darkness, they began
to pair off.

Bebon would gladly have done likewise, but he had a
delicate mission to fulfil. So he slipped through the crowd,
heading in the direction of the great temple. He walked along

the path lined with sphinxes and gazed upon Ahmose's two obelisks.

As this was a special occasion, a certain number of guests were permitted to enter the courtyard in front of the principal temple. Bebon mingled with a group of granary administrators, then detached himself and approached a shaven-headed priest dressed in a white robe.

'I have a message for the Superior of the songstresses and weavers of Neith. It is urgent and personal.'

'Wait here.'

Endless minutes crawled by.

On this night of celebration, would Nitis take the time to come herself? She was conducting rituals and could not leave the shrine. She would probably send a priestess, to whom he would refuse to speak.

Outside the enclosure, the celebrations were at their height. On each terrace and in front of every door in Sais, as in all the large Egyptian towns, lamps had been lit. Their light would enable Isis to find the scattered parts of the body of Osiris, who had been murdered by his brother Set. At the end of the quest, the sacred ship would transport the body of resurrection to the Temple of Neith, where the final words of transmutation would awaken the recreated god, victorious over death.

Nitis appeared. How could anyone not fall in love with such a beautiful woman?

'Bebon!' she exclaimed. 'Is Kel alive?'

'Yes, don't worry.'

'We must not stay here.'

She took him to a small shrine dedicated to the lion-goddess Sekhmet.

'Kel is unhurt and is here in Sais,' confirmed Bebon. 'He wants to speak to you.'

'During the festival it is impossible for me to be absent. Are you safe?'

'We're pretending to be street hawkers and managed to get through the security checks without difficulty.'

'Aren't you in danger of being spotted?'

'I have altered Kel's appearance and we behave exactly like real traders.'

'Do you have any wine to sell?'

'Excellent wine!'

'Come here tomorrow, at the first hour of the day, and report to the traders' gate. I shall receive the goods in person.'

Menk was very surprised as he approached the line of traders who were hurrying towards the temple gate, where verifiers and scribes were standing. They examined the produce, refused some that was of poor quality and wrote down the remuneration paid. Why was Nitis bothering with these formalities herself?

'Problems?' he asked her.

'No, no, everything is going well.'

'Could your assistants not have relieved you of this drudgery?'

'During the festival period, I trust only my own judgment.'

Menk nodded. 'I do exactly the same. Delegating more would ease my burden, but making good the consequent mistakes would take me for ever. Are you pleased with how the rituals are proceeding?'

'Remarkable work, as usual. You have lived up to your reputation, Menk.'

He quivered with pleasure. 'If I can help you . . . ?'

'I shall soon have finished. Would you be good enough to check the number of jars destined for the purifications?'

'I shall do it immediately.' At last, Menk went away.

Nitis dealt with a fruit-seller, who was delighted to be supplying his produce to the temple. After him there was nobody left except two hawkers and their donkey, a fine animal with an exceptionally calm temperament.

The young woman recognized Kel, and her heart beat faster. She would have loved to talk to him about her fear of never seeing him again, and about the profound joy she was experiencing at that moment.

'We have some best-quality wine to offer you,' said Bebon. 'Will you smell and taste it?'

Nitis did so.

'I have important information for you,' whispered Kel.

'You must speak to the High Priest.'

'How can I reach him without danger?'

'The clerk will register your delivery of wine and you will follow the other suppliers to the main storehouse. There Bebon will wait with the donkey, and I shall dress you in the white tunic of a pure priest. Then you will go to Wahibra's hall of records.'

The two men did as they were bidden.

At the storehouse, a simple meal was served to the suppliers chosen by the temple. Bebon had a discussion with a vegetable-seller, while Kel made himself scarce.

Bebon was uneasy and remained on his guard. Although he did not doubt Nitis's sincerity, he feared that she might be watched and, despite herself, lead them into a trap. And what if the High Priest had sold himself to the enemy? What if he was obeying the king and the guards, furthering his own career by delivering a fugitive criminal into the hands of the forces of law?

48

Nitis checked that nobody was watching them and pushed open the door. Usually kept locked, it led to the papyrus store belonging to High Priest Wahibra's hall of records.

The place was dark and silent.

Kel entered and froze. If this was an ambush, it was impossible to escape. But Nitis could not betray him, could she?

'What have you to tell me?' demanded the High Priest's stern voice.

'Both the men who could have cleared me are dead. Stubborn had a fatal accident while with the army at Naukratis, and someone slit the throat of my colleague Demos, whose body I found in my room; of course, I will be accused of his murder. With the aid of my friend Bebon, I managed to escape.'

'That is extremely bad news,' said the High Priest.

'I can see things more clearly now. True, I have not found King Ahmose's helmet, but nevertheless I have some solid information. A Greek businesswoman named Zekeh, wants to overthrow the Egyptian economy by introducing slavery and the circulation of coins.'

'Those acts of madness are contrary to the Law of Maat. The pharaoh will oppose such measures.'

'Might he not covertly encourage them?' Kel replied. 'As a great admirer of Greek culture, might he not consider it a form of progress which must be imposed upon the Two Lands?'

The question disturbed the High Priest. 'If that were so, the gods' vengeance would be terrifying!'

'The Interpreters' Secretariat probably intercepted documents relating to this conspiracy,' ventured Kel, 'and that is why it had to be eliminated. And the coded papyrus contains incendiary information destined for the conspirators.'

'These are hypotheses, Kel, mere hypotheses.'

'The new murders are facts. And the lady Zekeh does not hide her intentions. In other words, she has accomplices in the government.'

'I have not succeeded in deciphering the code,' said Nitis sadly. 'Only a high-ranking scribe could have perfected such a complex system.'

'Horkheb must be questioned,' said Kel.

'He is dead,' revealed the High Priest.

'Was it a natural death?'

'We do not know.'

'What a marvellous stroke of luck! More than ever, I am the ideal scapegoat. Nobody will find me innocent; all lines of investigation are cut off.'

'I wrote to the head of the Interpreters' Secretariat,' said Nitis, 'and his soul answered: "*The ancestors have the code.*"'

'That is no great help,' said the High Priest. 'In the absence of precise details, it is impossible to use that clue.'

'Perhaps we shall obtain those details.'

'Will they be sufficient?' Kel worried.

'Let us face the facts,' said Wahibra. 'Only Judge Gem can save Kel. You must give yourself up and reveal what you have discovered. Gem is an honest man. and even the pharaoh is not above the law. A thorough investigation will be carried out and your innocence will be glaringly obvious.'

'I don't trust Gem,' protested the young scribe.

'He is the head of Egyptian justice,' the High Priest reminded him. 'If he betrayed the Law of Maat, our civilization would soon crumble. From his point of view, with regard to your catastrophic record, you seem to be the worst of criminals. When he sees and hears you, he will change his mind.'

'Are you not sending me to my death?'

'I myself shall tell the judge what you are going to do and ask him for an important guarantee: no arrest before you have given your explanation. If he will not grant it to me, the conversation will not happen. You will be able to persuade him, I am sure of it.'

Shut away in the High Priest's hall of records, Kel tried one more time to break the code of the papyrus which lay at the root of his misfortunes. Had the hieroglyphs been reversed, the words mixed up? Did the direction in which it was to be read vary according to an idea or a group of signs?

All his attempts failed. The text merely sneered at him. It was indecipherable.

Tired and on the verge of despair, he thought of Nitis. Seeing her again had given him a moment of indescribable happiness, but he felt stupid, incapable of confessing the intensity of his feelings to her. So this was love, the certainty that someone so different from oneself, so far-off, so inaccessible, had become the main reason to go on living!

The door opened. Nitis walked forward slowly. 'Here is some water and a flat-cake filled with green beans and cheese.'

Kel stood up and thanked her. 'Will the High Priest succeed in his negotiatiations?'

'The judge will listen to you, and you will at last be able to defend yourself. Your friend Bebon has left the temple and is staying with his donkey in a stable near the sellers' entrance.'

'Nitis . . .'

'I must go to the weaving workshop, immediately.' She escaped, forever out of reach.

He had no means of holding her. She was a priestess of

194

Neith, destined for an exceptional career; he was a murderer on the run. Their destinies could merely meet briefly.

Kel ate his simple meal and tried to attack the papyrus again, but Nitis's face stopped him concentrating. The idea of giving her up filled him with unbearable pain. To see happiness and immediately deny it was torture. And to ask her for anything more than help in his hour of need seemed impossible. Already she was taking enormous risks.'

At nightfall, she reappeared.

'Why hasn't the High Priest come?' fretted Kel.

'The negotiations must be difficult.'

'What if the judge arrests him?'

'Gem will not do that. He wants the truth, and only you can give it to him.'

'Forgive me, Nitis, for disturbing the peace of your existence. I feel it is my fault and—'

'All that matters is the Law of Maat,' she interrupted him. 'Knowing that you were unjustly accused, I could not stand idly by.'

'Your trust touches me deeply, and I would so like to tell you . . .'

The dusk hid her face.

'I'm listening,' she murmured.

Wahibra's footsteps echoed on the stone floor. 'Judge Gem agrees to meet you,' he announced. 'He has granted me an exceptional favour, which will not be repeated. You must be very convincing, Kel.'

49

Unshaven, dressed in the worn-out tunic and cheap sandals of a hawker, Kel did not look much like a distinguished scribe from the Interpreters' Secretariat.

North Wind was delighted to see him again and rewarded him by braying with pleasure. The young man caressed the donkey for a long time, as he explained to Bebon that he was preparing to meet Judge Gem.

'That's insanity!' protested the actor. 'It's obviously an ambush. How can you believe for a single second that he will come alone? Scarcely will the conversation have started when a horde of guards come charging at you.'

'This is the only opportunity I have to convince him of my innocence.'

'He won't even listen to you.'

'The High Priest has promised me that he will.'

'And what if the High Priest is in the conspiracy, too?'

'That's impossible!'

'You've been accused of murder: wasn't that impossible? Wahibra wants to get rid of you and keep his reputation intact. So he sells you to the legal authorities – who have already judged and condemned you.'

'I shall turn the situation round.'

'Utter madness!'

'Didn't you win at dice by calling on destiny to help you?'

'At least I had a chance of winning. Stop dreaming, Kel. If you agree to this meeting, you will be throwing yourself into the jackal's mouth.'

'There is no other way. Judge Gem has agreed to meet me in private, at the place chosen by the High Priest, with no guards present, and promises that he will not arrest me before he has heard my arguments and my revelations. They will strike him so forcefully that he will change his mind, and then he will be obliged to open an investigation. Once that is under way, the truth will save me.'

Bebon was devastated. 'Your naivety worries me!'

'When the sun reaches its zenith, Judge Gem will await me inside a potters' workshop belonging to the Temple of Neith. At that time of day, the craftsmen will have gone for their lunch.'

'Don't do this, my friend.'

'I have to.'

Bebon sighed. 'I shall inspect the place. If I spot any guards, I shall start singing a merry little song, then I'll call out to some imaginary colleagues, in the hope that North Wind will join in with his braying. Then run for it. We will meet at the northern gate to the town.'

'If you don't launch into that terrible cacophony, I shall see Judge Gem.'

The craftsmen were eating their lunch together in the shade of a sycamore tree. They talked about the latest order from the temple, family matters, and the king's policies, which were increasingly favourable towards the Greeks. At least Egypt was well defended and people could live there safely, protected from invasion.

Bebon and North Wind roamed the district for a long time. The actor walked up and down every side-street, not forgetting to look up and scan the roofs and the terraces. Well accustomed to scenting any sign of guards' presence, he did not notice anything out of the ordinary.

He was astonished when he spotted a respectable, elderly man with a serious face and an authoritative stride.

Judge Gem stepped through the doorway and into the potters' workshop. Bebon became even more attentive. The guards could not be far away.

Several minutes went by, and still the place remained tranquil.

Kel went to the door of the workshop. Since Bebon had not sounded the alarm, there was nothing to fear. He stepped inside and found himself face to face with Judge Gem.

They stared at each other for a long time.

'Without the insistence of High Priest Wahibra, whose probity is known by all, I would have refused this absurd meeting,' declared the magistrate angrily.

'I am not a murderer,' declared Kel, 'but the victim of a plot.'

'I have often heard such words. You may have fooled the High Priest, but fine declarations do not impress me.'

'It is the truth!'

'I know the truth already.'

'It is an attempt to deceive you.'

'By whom?' demanded the judge.

'I don't know the name of the conspirators' leader, but I do know that they want to dethrone King Ahmose and seize power.'

'Your delirious ramblings do not interest me, boy. You killed your fellow interpreters and then fled. An innocent man would have gone to the authorities.'

'Circumstances prevented me, and—'

'Your murderous progress did not stop in Sais,' Gem cut in. 'You went to Naukratis to kill two accomplices who could have denounced you.'

'I am innocent!' Kel protested. 'Those murderers are part of the plot.'

'A judge pays no heed to the denials of the guilty and bases his words on irrefutable proof. I have properly registered testimonies in your file. Servants saw you cut the throat of your colleague Demos.'

'They lied!'

'In the face of the implacable reality, all you give me is a story of conspiracy, without the slightest proof or the name of a possible guilty party. Stop behaving like a child.'

'I swear to you—'

'Do not commit another crime. Inventing nonsense in order to minimize your responsibility only aggravates your case. Confess to your crimes and tell me why you committed them.'

'I have not killed anyone, and you must look for the real murderers. The Greeks—'

'Abandon this ridiculous and futile system of defence, and follow me to the prison. You will have the right to a trial in the proper manner.'

'Judge Gem, you promised to listen to me!'

'The proof is overwhelming, my boy. I only accepted this meeting in order to persuade you to be sensible. There are already too many victims, and I do not wish to risk any more lives. By giving yourself up, you may perhaps benefit from relative clemency, and you can explain yourself as you wish.'

'You are mistaken. I—'

'Let us end this little game and leave here.'

His face masked by a linen scarf, Bebon rushed into the workshop. 'A mass of guards are on the way!'

Kel regarded the judge with disgust. 'You have broken your word.'

'The time for talk is over. I am arresting you, you and your accomplice.'

Bebon caught the magistrate's throat in the crook of his

arm. 'Take the first street on the right and run like the wind,' he ordered Kel.

'What about you?'

'I'll catch up with you.'

The scribe ran.

Bebon faced the first of the guards. 'Get back, or I'll break the judge's neck.'

They realized by the tone of his voice that the hostage-taker was not joking.

'Go!' roared Bebon, tightening his grip.

An officer nodded. His men dispersed. As soon as they were a good distance away, Bebon let go of the judge and fled.

Gem was no longer in any doubt: Kel was a killer of the worst kind.

50

'I am sorry,' Pythagoras told Nitis, but the king has ordered me to go to Naukratis, and talk to the priests of Apollo and Aphrodite, so that they may benefit from the teaching I have received in the Egyptian temples. Ahmose wants to see deeper contacts between the different forms of thought and has entrusted me with this delicate mission before I return to Greece. I would have preferred to spend a long time listening to the voice of Neith, whose words have dazzled me. She, Father of fathers and Mother of mothers, Male who made the woman, Woman who made the male, the mysterious creator of beings, the sovereign of the divine stars, remains eternally hidden from outsiders, and no mortal can lift her veil.'

Nitis would dearly have loved to trust Pythagoras and ask him if he could help her to decipher the coded papyrus. As a Greek, would he not apply his own particular kind of reasoning? But she remained silent. Pythagoras was the friend and favourite of King Ahmose. He might be more of an adversary than an ally.

'I hope that we shall see each other again, Nitis. My stay in Sais was one of the most important stages in my journey.'

'This temple remains open to you.'

'I am thankful to you for that. We shall meet again soon, if the great goddess wills it.'

Nitis found the High Priest within earshot of the shrine. He looked devastated, and seemed to have aged suddenly.

'The meeting turned into a disaster,' he told her. 'Guards accompanied Judge Gem and tried to arrest Kel.'

Nitis felt her chest tighten. 'Was he injured?'

'No, and he escaped thanks to his friend Bebon, who took the judge hostage before fleeing himself. It is easy to imagine Gem's fury! From now on, the archers have orders to shoot on sight.'

'The judge betrayed you!'

'Not from his point of view. He believes only in the written evidence, and was granting me a favour by trying to take Kel alive. We must fulfil our ritual obligations, Nitis. We are powerless now.'

The young priestess went to the shrine housing a life-size wooden cow, an incarnation of Neith, 'the great swimmer'. In this form, she had travelled the primordial ocean, at the dawn of time, and formed the universe, where the soul-stars were born and regenerated.

On either side were lamps and incense-burners. With the exception of the gilded neck and head, a veil of purple covered the cow, which carried the sun's disc between its horns.

Nitis presented it with the seven holy oils, then poured water on to the offertory table, which was furnished with fresh bread, onions and figs. Each day the foods were renewed and the goddess absorbed their *ka*, the vital power.

'Nitis, over here.' It was Kel's voice.

Standing up, he emerged from the shadows. 'I could not find a better hiding-place.'

'Come, we must go to the High Priest.'

'Won't that place him in danger?'

'That is for him to decide. What about Bebon?'

'He is lodging near the market, with some hawkers – Judge Gem couldn't identify him. Before I join him and disappear, I wanted to see you again.'

'Since you are free and unharmed, we must not lay down our arms yet.'

'If you knew—'

'Hurry. The ritual priests will soon be bringing the offerings.'

The High Priest gave Kel a warm welcome and embraced him as if he were his son. 'Forgive me for leading you into that trap. By acting in that way, the judge has discredited himself. But he remains the principal investigator and his only thought is of killing you.'

'I did not have time to talk to him,' said Kel.

'We would need proof so firm that even that stubborn magistrate would be forced to face the facts.'

'Stubborn or manipulated,' said Nitis. 'If he is a servant of the conspirators, his attitude can be explained.'

'Whom can I contact at court?' Kel asked. 'I must talk to someone trustworthy and sufficiently influential to alert the king without fail.'

'The queen,' declared the High Priest. 'She will listen to you.'

Soberly dressed, with wigs worthy of the Old Kingdom, Wahibra and his assistant reported to the palace gate reserved for dignitaries. A Greek soldier checked that they were not armed and informed a steward.

'The High Priest of Neith wishes to see Her Majesty the Queen as a matter of urgency,' said Wahibra. 'I shall wait as long as is necessary.'

Wahibra feared that he might be seen by Henat or Udja, who were probably aware of the latest developments in the Kel affair. Fortunately, the wait was a brief one.

Although she had reached her middle years, Queen Tanith remained a charming and highly attractive woman, her face made up to perfection. She was seated on an ebony throne, wearing a gold collar, cornelian earrings and silver bracelets.

'What brings you here with such urgency?' she asked in a steady voice.

'Majesty, have you heard about the murder of the inter-preters?'

'The murderer has been identified, but has not yet been found.'

'This is he.'

Kel bowed.

Tanith started. 'Is this a joke?'

'Kel the scribe is innocent,' continued the High Priest, 'but no one will hear him. Judge Gem, who is in charge of the investigation, has already condemned him. In order to avert a grave legal error and to seek at last for the truth, will you consent to listen to this young man?'

The queen stood up, remaining a good distance from her visitors. 'I should call the guard and have this criminal arrested.'

'I am not guilty, Majesty,' said Kel.

'The evidence is all to the contrary, or so it seems.'

'A conspiracy has formed against the pharaoh, and the head of the Interpreters' Secretariat must have discovered it. My colleagues were killed to ensure total silence and I have been designated the author of the crimes in order to mislead the authorities.'

The queen looked straight at Kel. 'You seem sincere. Who are these conspirators?'

'The lady Zekeh, a businesswoman from Naukratis, is trying to introduce coinage and profoundly alter the economic structure of our country. She must receive orders from a senior dignitary who has stolen the king's helmet of power and who – when the moment comes – will don it and proclaim himself pharaoh.'

This seemed to have an impact on Tanith. 'The theft of the helmet – you know about it?'

'A document in my possession probably contains precise

details, but I have not succeeded in decoding it. In the king's name, Majesty, I swear to you that I have committed no crime.'

The queen sat down again, her face pensive.

'Will you consent to put the pharaoh on his guard,' asked the High Priest, 'and submit this young scribe's case to him?'

Tanith thought for a long time. 'I will.'

'Will you permit me to keep him under my protection and not send him to prison, for fear that he will not emerge alive?'

'I will.'

Wahibra and Kel bowed low to the queen. Hope was reborn.

51

Ahmose drank a cup of new, slightly acidic wine, then burst out laughing as he thought of the way he had handled the credulous or hypocritical priests who put all their trust in oracles.

Before becoming king, Ahmose had freely indulged in the pleasures of life and attracted thunderbolts from moralists. Wishing to ruin his reputation and have him dismissed, they had accused him of theft.

Faced with his vehement denials and the absence of proof, there was only one solution: consult the oracle. So Ahmose had stood before several divine statues, in different shrines. Their heads leant one way to condemn him, the other to declare him innocent.

As the accused was given the benefit of the doubt, Ahmose was acquitted. Once he became king, he had enjoyed summoning the priests and announcing his decision to them: he would endow with wealth the shrines housing the oracles that had been determined to condemn him and withdraw it from those who wished to absolve him, since the former had spoken the truth and the latter had lied. The true gods knew of his theft and deserved to be honoured, while the false ones would bear his contempt.

Ahmose still savoured that stroke of genius. No oracle now troubled him, and he ruled with an iron fist, pushing aside the religious zealots. The future lay with thinkers like Pythagoras, capable of gathering the important part of the old Egyptian wisdom and nourishing it with Greek philosophy. Other philosophers would come to Sais and would fashion the future world.

Far from the Delta, the Divine Worshipper continued to preserve the ancient traditions. Her domain, Thebes, the sacred city of Amun, played only a secondary role, devoid of economic importance. The old lady celebrated rites which made her the equivalent of a pharaoh, but fortunately lacked any real power. Devoting herself to the service of the gods, denying herself marriage and pleasures, she had no political ambition. So Ahmose allowed this outdated institution to exist, far distant as it was from reality.

As a great reformer of the legal and fiscal systems, high priest of a successful economy, creator of a military deterrent and an ally of the majority of Greek kingdoms, Ahmose was opening up the way to a new Egyptian society. The progress was taking place here, in the North, close to the Mediterranean. Sooner or later, they would shake the South out of its lethargy, too.

'Did the meeting of the Council of Ministers proceed satisfactorily?' asked the queen.

'Tanith, what a beautiful gown. The weavers of Sais have surpassed themselves.'

'In accordance with your instructions, this is the first non-religious garment to come out of the temple workshops.'

'So you see, I was entirely in the right. Why limit their talent merely to rituals?'

'Rumour has it,' said the queen, 'that the gods are angry.'

Ahmose scoffed. 'The priests will happily make them speak in order to defend their own interests. Believe me, I have scarcely begun to attack their privileges.'

'I have just had a meeting with the High Priest of Neith.'

'Wahibra?'

'In person, accompanied by a strange visitor: Kel the scribe.'

The king started violently. 'Kel? The one from the Interpreters' Secretariat, the murderer who is on the run?'

'Exactly.'

Ahmose sank down on a pile of cushions. 'My head is spinning. Are you teasing me?'

'The scribe proclaims his innocence. According to him, conspirators are seeking to seize your throne. A usurper, aided by a certain Zekeh, a businesswoman from Naukratis who wishes to introduce coinage into Egypt, will soon don your helmet. The interpreters noticed compromising documents, and were killed. And this young man Kel serves as an ideal scapegoat.'

'What proof does he have?'

'His good faith and a coded papyrus which he considers decisive.'

'What does it say?'

'He has not succeeded in deciphering it.'

Ahmose exploded with rage. 'And you did not summon the guard?'

'The young man seemed sincere to me. And the High Priest is a cautious man—'

'Wahibra has lost his mind! You do not know about your "innocent"'s latest exploit: after committing two more murders in Naukratis, one in the presence of witnesses, he took Judge Gem hostage.'

The queen paled. 'Is he hurt?'

'Fortunately, Kel and his accomplice let him go.'

'The businesswoman, Zekeh—'

'The murderer tricked her. And it was precisely the servants of this woman, who is well respected in Naukratis, who saw Kel slit the throat of his colleague Demos, who was also on the run. We are in the presence of a monster of the worst kind, and I have given the judge permission to kill him if, during the arrest, lives are threatened.'

'I don't understand. He did not seem criminal or inhuman to me.'

'Your soul is too tender, my dear wife. And this Kel fellow seems to possess a great deal of charm.'

'He knew about the theft of the helmet, and this conspiracy—'

'He's is probably mixed up in it. By obtaining your support, he was hoping for an audience, during which he would have slit my throat, too.'

Trembling, Tanith embraced her husband. 'And I would have been the cause of your death.'

'Calm yourself, the danger has been averted. Do you know where Kel is hiding?'

'No. The High Priest asked permission to keep him under his protection.'

'Wahibra . . . Is he naive, or an accomplice?'

'He has always been loyal.'

'Today he brought you a murderer who sought to manipulate you. A surprising way of serving his king!'

'The High Priest, mixed up in a conspiracy against you? I cannot believe it.'

'I say again, your soul is too tender. When power is at stake, men become capable of the worst things.'

'We must find the helmet,' Tanith declared, 'and punish the culprits.'

'They were wrong to attack me and one of the departments of the state,' said Ahmose, 'and they will pay dearly for it.'

52

'Queen Tanith listened attentively to us,' Kel told Nitis. 'The High Priest's moral caution was a decisive factor, and I hope that I have convinced her of my innocence. She has promised to speak to the king.'

'Then the investigation will begin again, on a new basis. Soon you will be proved innocent and set free.'

Her joy overwhelmed Kel. 'I dare not believe it, Nitis.'

'The strength of the truth will triumph in the end, and your future will open up before you. Would you like to . . . work in the temple?'

'I have so much still to learn.'

'One day, perhaps, you will have access to the archives in the House of Life. They contain such riches that an entire lifetime is insufficient in which to explore them.'

'Will you help me to make progress?'

The two young people were interrupted by the High Priest, who burst in and told them, 'I have just been informed that Henat is here and wishes to see me immediately.'

'The king has reacted very quickly!' exclaimed Kel.

'Not in the way we had hoped. He ought to have summoned me, not sent Henat to me. This course of action is worrying, and it would be best to take precautions. Nitis, hide Kel in the third crypt.'

She took him to the principal shrine, where everything was

in twilight. A few lamps lit the pillared chamber, the one in which the sacred ship lay and the mysterious corridor leading to the shrines that clustered around the innermost one, with its closed doors.

Several crypts were hidden within the enormous walls and the stone floor. Only the High Priest and his assistants knew their location and the means of access to them. He had revealed the secret of the third one only to Nitis, at her initiation into the mysteries of the House of Life.

She checked that no ritual priests were making offerings. By positioning her hands at two precise points on the flagged floor, she made a heavy stone pivot and revealed a narrow opening.

'Take a lamp and go down,' she told Kel. 'Don't worry, you won't be short of air. As soon as possible, I will come and fetch you.'

Kel found himself in a narrow, long room. It contained gold vases used during the rituals in honour of Neith. Its walls were covered with hieroglyphs and strange scenes evoking the creation of the world from the primordial waters that the goddess had brought to life using the radiant energy of the Word. Fascinated, the young man forgot his worries and tried to understand these extraordinary texts, which were capable of coming to life and passing on their power at the heart of silence and secrecy, far from human eyes.

The High Priest had granted him an incredible favour, and he must prove he was worthy of it by opening his heart to the words of the gods.

Compared to the vast apartments of the senior dignitaries at the royal palace, Wahibra's official quarters seemed modest and very austere. The furniture imitated that of the Old Kingdom, with its sober, uncluttered lines.

Henat chose a straight-backed chair without cushions.

'Given your position and your reputation,' he said

emphatically, 'the king wishes to avoid scandal, despite the extremely serious crime you have committed.'

'Of what am I accused?' enquired the High Priest.

'Of supporting the ramblings of a criminal, protecting him and hindering the course of justice. Only His Majesty's indulgence prevents you from suffering a severe punishment.'

'Something you regret, it seems.'

'I am merely carrying out orders.

'You are wrong, Henat. Kel has committed no crime, and there is indeed a conspiracy aimed at overthrowing Ahmose. By choosing Kel as the culprit, the rebels have diverted your attention and that of Judge Gem.'

'The proof accumulated against Kel is overwhelming, and his behaviour confirms it, if there was any need for confirmation. All you have are impressions and feelings. I know my profession, and Judge Gem knows his. We have thwarted more than a few conspiracies, and this one will fail, like the others. That murderous and treacherous scribe will be arrested, tried and executed.'

'Will the archers not kill him before he can defend himself?'

'Everything will depend on his attitude. There have already been too many deaths, and His Majesty does not wish to risk the lives of our men.'

'In other words, the affair is to be kept quiet.'

'You should change your tone and your attitude,' advised Henat.

Wahibra stood up. 'Get out of here,' he demanded in an icy voice.

'The accomplice of a murderer is in no position to give orders. From now on, you are confined to your residence and will no longer leave the temple.'

'I shall go immediately to the palace.'

'You do not properly appreciate your situation, High Priest. I speak for the king.'

'When he receives me—'

'He will not receive you. If you leave the temple enclosure you will be arrested. His Majesty orders you to devote yourself to your ritual activities, and nothing else. This is a special favour, I repeat. The celebration of the cult of Neith must be your sole preoccupation. If you disobey, do not hope for any clemency.'

Wahibra had become a prisoner of the temple.

'Where are you hiding the murderer?' Henat asked, his gaze becoming penetrating.

'Kel has refused to hide inside this sacred domain.'

'Another detailed search will be conducted first thing tomorrow.'

'As you wish.'

'Since you are protecting him, you know where to find him.'

'Kel has not told me the location of his refuge. He will contact me tomorrow at noon, at the small northern gate.'

Henat displayed a faint smile. 'You are beginning to co-operate ... So much the better. We know the murderer has the help of an accomplice. Do you know who that is?'

'I have never met him.'

'Do not make any more mistakes,' warned Henat, 'and be content with your religious offices.'

The two men did not take leave of each other.

Facing such a powerful opponent, and deprived of the king's support, Wahibra was shackled hand and foot. Why should he continue to support a man who was condemned to death?

Because he believed in Kel's innocence and could not tolerate injustice. Tolerating it would lead to chaos and to the destruction of a thousand-year-old civilization. Even muzzled, the High Priest would not give up. But how was Kel to avoid a terrible fate?

53

Bebon made a perfect hawker, and nothing worried him. Although well-liked by his new colleagues, the actor could not remain idle. So, at the end of a successful day's bartering, he went to the area around the barracks to speak to his friend Nedi, the only honest guard officer in Sais.

At sunset, Nedi emerged from his office and walked calmly towards his home.

Bebon and North Wind caught up with him.

'Leave me alone,' he snapped. 'I don't want to buy anything.'

'Don't you recognize me?'

Nedi stared at the hawker. 'Bebon? It's not possible! Have you changed your profession?'

'More or less. The Kel affair continues to get bigger, and I need your help.'

'Don't go anywhere near it. That's a domain reserved for Judge Gem. We've had orders to kill the murderer on sight.'

'Curious justice, don't you think?'

'I'd rather not think about it.'

'Don't be like the others, Nedi, This affair is rotten to the core, and I happen to know that Kel hasn't killed anybody.'

'Can you prove it?'

'Not yet.'

'Then forget about it and go off on a tour.'

'Abandon a friend who is unjustly accused? Certainly not.'

'Aren't you just deceiving yourself?'

'At court there's a conspiracy against the king, and Kel is serving as a distraction.'

'If you're right, he has no chance of getting out of it. He'd best surrender to the authorities and put forward his arguments.'

'Judge Gem has refused to listen to him. All he wants is for his archers to kill him. Go and see your superiors, Nedi. Tell them the authorities are preparing to execute an innocent man.'

'They won't listen to me any more than they will to him, and my career will be destroyed. I've already been told off for defending certain suspects, and as for this one . . .'

Bebon did not persist. 'At least get me some information. I'd like to know where guards are posted and have details of the plan to arrest Kel.'

'It might be possible.'

'Try to get access to the documents. They may contain other leads which haven't been explored up to now.'

'That will be difficult, very difficult.'

'Someone is making a mockery of justice and the truth, Nedi. Help me to defend them.'

At noon, a young man presented himself at the northern gate of the Temple of Neith.

Immediately, ten guards charged at him and flattened him to the ground. As he was struggling, one of them knocked him out with a blow from his staff.

Henat ordered the archers to lower their bows. Thanks to the High Priest's cooperation, the interception had passed off smoothly. After a muscular interrogation, Henat would hand over the murderer to Judge Gem, who would read him the list of charges before incarcerating him.

'Good work,' said Henat to his men. 'You will be paid a bonus.'

The guards stood aside. The face of the unconscious man bore no resemblance whatever to the portrait distributed to the forces of order.

'Wake him,' ordered Henat edgily.

A jar of cool water revived the young man.

'My head . . .' he moaned.

'Who are you?'

'One of the scribes working for Menk, organizer of festivals in Sais.'

'Why are you here?'

'I've come to check a list of ritual items . . . What is the meaning of this attack?'

'It's a regrettable mistake.'

The scribe rubbed a large lump on the back of his head. 'A mistake? You're joking! I'm going to lodge a complaint.'

'I have full powers within the framework of a criminal investigation,' stipulated Henat. 'Be content with my apologies and be off with you.'

Fearing a second beating, the young man decided to obey.

As for Henat, he marched through the northern gate and into the temple. Beside a colonnade stood High Priest Wahibra.

'Was the arrest successful?' he enquired.

Henat clenched his fists. 'Your sarcasm is misplaced.'

'I don't understand.'

'On the contrary, you understand very well indeed. It was not Kel who arrived, but one of Menk's assistants.'

'Your men were not discreet enough,' said the High Priest. 'A fugitive is constantly on his guard. He must have spotted your men and fled.'

'You would love to make me believe that fable. In reality, Kel is hiding inside the temple enclosure. This time, I demand a total search – including the House of Life.'

'Impossible,' objected Wahibra.

'I have a royal warrant. If you oppose it, you will be sent to prison.'

'In that case, you alone will enter the secret places of the temple with me.'

'Agreed.'

'Do you not fear the brutality of this murderer?'

'So, a confession!'

'Not at all, Henat. Perhaps he has succeeded in hiding there without my knowledge.'

'I am armed, and my men will keep watch at the entrance to each building. If I call out, they will come immediately to my aid. And besides, there will be two of us – for you will assist me, I assume?'

'Fighting a criminal does not frighten me, despite my age.'

The methodical search of the domain of Neith began. Around a hundred men explored every last cubit of it.

Henat explored the secret shrine of the House of Life, where the resurrection of Osiris was prepared, and the vast library, where the initiates worked on the mysteries.

He recoiled as he prepared to enter the shrine, which was accessible only to the pharaoh and his representative, the High Priest.

'Wahibra, do you swear to me that Kel is not hiding here?'

'I swear it. Nevertheless, walk along the mysterious corridor and look inside each of the shrines.'

Uneasy, fearing the anger of the gods, Henat did so. There was no trace of Kel.

54

Accompanied by ten admirals, Udja met the commander-in-chief of the Egyptian armies, General Phanes, north of Sais. The Greek was conducting large-scale infantry and cavalry manoeuvres.

This meeting of the general staff was designed to perfect a strategy which would prove effective in the event of an invasion.

One officer was astonished. 'General, why are these forces being deployed? Hasn't Ambassador Kroisos officially promised peace with the Persians?'

'Ambassadors don't inspire trust in me. And I am paid to defend Egypt. So we will train until each soldier can carry out orders to perfection. I want men who are swift, powerful and effective.'

'Two new warships have been launched in our boatyard,' said Udja, 'and three others will soon be finished.'

'Excellent,' said Phanes. 'I watched Kroisos carefully during his visit. He was stunned and impressed. He probably thought our system of defence still had weak points. Well, now he is convinced that the opposite is true. Nevertheless, I would advise against slackening our efforts.'

'That is not His Majesty's intention,' declared Udja. 'He requires an increase in the number of men and an improvement in weaponry.'

'New recruits will be welcome. And believe me, my lord, their training will be correctly carried out. In the Greek ranks, there is no place for laziness or indolence. There remains one delicate problem . . .'

'What is it?

'The men's pay. I feel that a small gesture is needed.'

Udja relaxed. 'The king has authorized me to increase the taxes on civilians, which will now all be properly recorded and strictly controlled. So the soldiers will be much better treated, and the officers will receive land free of taxes.'

'The army's morale will remain at a high level,' Phanes promised. 'Now, let us examine our defence strategy.'

On the ground, two scribes unrolled a large map of the Delta, Syria and Palestine.

'There are two possible attack routes: by sea and by land. The Mediterranean coast is dangerous and presents numerous dangers for a fleet which does not know it. If Persian boats succeed in getting through them, the superiority of your vessels will not allow them the smallest chance of reaching land. And if, by some extraordinary chance, a few reached one of our ports, they would be caught in a net and rapidly destroyed.'

Udja and the admirals nodded.

'Given his experience,' one of them commented, 'Kroisos cannot have failed to notice that. Any attempt to invade by sea would be suicidal.'

'But we must not drop our guard,' waraned Udja. 'And we must consolidate our positions.'

'The land route worries me more,' said Phanes, 'and I strive constantly to seal up the remaining breaches. Our foot-soldiers and our lines of fortification will be positioned in such a way that only one corridor remains open to the enemy. At its end, our cavalry will be waiting and will inflict severe damage while we cut off all possibility of retreat.'

Several officers insisted on one detail or another in order to improve further this plan, which promised to safeguard Egypt.

Their commander-in-chief listened attentively to suggestions and undertook to check their validity himself.

It was quite clear that even an army twice the size of Egypt's could not invade the Delta.

After purifying herself in the sacred lake, Nitis went to the covered temple, where she made offerings of milk, wine and water to the statues of Neith, who wore the Red Crown and held the Life and Power sceptres. Then she prayed to all the gods and goddesses who were present in the shrines and passed through the gate of the heavens, which gave access to the most secret part of the temple.

Initiated into the Mysteries of Isis and Osiris by the ritual priests of the House of Life, Nitis could represent the High Priest in presenting the ritual texts, which were alive for ever, existing beyond time.

She opened the hidden door of the third crypt.

'It is Nitis, Kel. You can come out.'

Very slowly, the scribe left the universe in which he had just experienced a profound transformation. Nourished by each hieroglyph, his heart filled with Neith's words of creation, and his mind opened to the universe of perpetually-renewed energies, in a few hours he had passed through territories of the soul which were accessible to very few people.

'Nitis . . . Am I still alive?'

'More so than before.'

'It wasn't a hiding-place, but a trial. Now do you trust me?'

'I have never doubted your innocence.'

'Is a mere interpreter-scribe, however skilled he may be, capable of feeling the power of the divine words, and re-emerging unharmed from the cave of metamorphoses? This is the question you asked yourselves, you and the High Priest.'

Nitis smiled. 'It was also a hiding-place, Kel. Henat's men searched the domain of Neith without finding you. On the other hand, you have found yourself.'

Their eyes met with a new intensity.

'I know I am doomed, Nitis. Nevertheless, I shall fight to the end. And you have opened my eyes by shattering the blinkers that blinded me. Although I am still unworthy of you, I now see the importance of your office more clearly.'

She held out her hands to him, and he dared to touch her.

'Your friend Bebon wishes to speak with you.'

55

Kel left the temple with the gardeners who cared for Neith's trees. Detaching himself from the group, he mingled with the passers-by as he waited for a sign from Bebon.

A donkey's muzzle nudged his hand.

'North Wind!'

Its ears pricked up, the donkey headed for a small square, from which several side-streets branched off. Kel followed it to a stable. There, North Wind drank fresh water and ate a tasty mixture of hay, vegetables and lucerne.

'Well, you look all right to me,' observed Bebon. 'Neith must be protecting you.'

'The High Priest has been confined to his residence, and the king refuses to see him. Henat has searched the goddess's domain, and only Nitis's help enabled me to escape.'

'I've noticed a lot of look-outs around the temple. Fortunately, they're relying on your portrait. And I have found a precious ally, my old friend Nedi, whom I've helped several times in the past.'

'How can he help us?'

'By telling us the real contents of your file. It must be full of forged items, false depositions and conveniently arranged witness reports. I would like to know who signed them. And then Nedi, the good fellow, will describe in detail to us the operation designed to intercept us. Anyway, we shall have one piece of advance information.'

'When are we to meet him?'

'Tonight, outside the workshop belonging to Sais's foremost seller of jars.'

The silvery light of the full moon bathed the constantly-growing city. Cats were on the prowl, hunting for prey; young couples talked of love; craftsmen and scribes toiled by the light of lamps.

North Wind strode along in front.

'Do you know, he found me and led me to you,' Kel marvelled.

'That donkey's intelligence passes understanding! There are three of us now, not two. And we would do well to pay heed to him.'

The place seemed quiet. Two enormous jars flanked the entrance to the workshop, in the heart of the potters' district.

North Wind stopped dead.

'Better watch out,' advised Bebon, suddenly on the alert. He turned round. Nobody was following them.

The donkey rushed towards one of the jars, charged at it and knocked it over. With a cry of pain, injured by the broken pieces, a guard tried to extricate himself.

The second jar suffered the same fate, and a second lookout was knocked unconscious.

'Follow North Wind!' ordered Bebon as three men armed with clubs emerged from the workshop.

He brought down one attacker with a kick to the face. His agility enabled him to dodge the weapon about to strike him, and he dealt a forceful blow to the back of his adversary's neck.

As he turned Bebon glimpsed a club. But it was too late. Blood spurted from his nose.

Mad with fury, he abandoned all restraint; and with a forearm blow to the throat, he knocked the guard's breath out of him. Then, with no one left to bar his way, he fled.

Nitis examined Bebon's injury. 'A broken nose,' she diagnosed. 'That is an illness I can cure.'

After cleaning the wound with two wads of linen, she soaked another two in grease, honey and vegetable extracts, and placed them on it.

'When the swelling goes down,' she said, I shall re-set the nose with two splints, covered in linen. Every day, until healing is complete, I shall change the dressing. There will be no further problems and, since the plants I have used have pain-killing properties, you will not suffer pain. You may eat normally and must rest.'

'Aren't you taking too many risks by hiding us in your official residence?' asked Kel worriedly.

'The domain of Neith has been completely searched,' Nitis reminded him, 'and Henat's lookouts are mainly keeping watch on the High Priest. If he tried to leave the enclosure, he would be arrested.'

'Be very careful,' urged the young scribe.

'Have no fear, I shall not relax my vigilance.'

'Your so-called friend sold us to the guards,' Kel said to Bebon.

'I don't believe so.'

'Then how do you explain that ambush?'

'I know Nedi well, and he wouldn't betray us. While he was searching for the information to pass on to us, he must have been spotted. It proves the seriousness of the situation – if any proof were needed! The hierarchy arrests one of its own officers and reduces him to silence.'

'Henat wouldn't dare—'

'We shall never see Nedi again,' declared the actor in a sombre voice. 'But perhaps he had time to leave us a message.'

'How?'

'By hiding a document in his home. I shall go there as soon as possible.'

'Do not leave this house without my permission,' demanded Nitis.

Bebon lay down on a mat. Like his friends, he was aware of the extent of the conspiracy. An inveterate optimist, he wondered if he and Kel would succeed in escaping from this wasps' nest.

'I sent Nedi to his death,' he lamented.

'He agreed to help you,' Kel reminded him.

'He had no idea of the level of danger. And I feel responsible for his death.'

'Aren't you making the situation worse than it really is?'

'Since an ambush was set for us, Nedi must have revealed the location of the meeting. And he would not have talked except under torture.'

56

Confronting Henat's cold anger was not a pleasant experience. The man responsible for the failed operation was in a sorry state.

'My men were severely beaten,' he confessed.

'Five experienced officers against one man!' Henat exclaimed. 'Is this some kind of joke?'

'Kel was not alone. According to the reports, which are rather confused, several accomplices are protecting him.'

'How many?'

'Two, three or four. Particularly vindictive fellows, well-schooled in the arts of fighting.'

'And they got away without a scratch?'

'Perhaps a minor injury.'

'And the whole lot of them managed to get away, when our ambush had been carefully prepared?'

'We weren't expecting such resistance. Besides, you ordered us to allow the murderer to enter the workshop and then arrest him without further ado. He and his band attacked us with unexpected violence, as if they knew we were there.'

Henat grimaced. How could Nedi have alerted Kel? Arrested on account of his suspicious investigations, he had been intensively interrogated. Fearful of pain, he had resolved to reveal the location of a mysterious meeting regarding the Kel affair, before succumbing to heart failure.

That little scribe was proving tough. He had a veritable network at his fingertips, enabling him to hide and to escape from the forces of order. Although patient and methodical, Henat was not taking his temporary defeat very well. It was up to him to learn a lesson from his failures and allow the fugitive to believe that he could escape. Once he began to feel confident, Kel would make the fatal mistake.

'You should not have come,' Wahibra told Pefy.

'I wanted to hear the truth from your own lips! Have you really been confined to your quarters?'

'The king forbids me to leave the temple enclosure, on pain of being thrown into prison.'

'What crime have you committed?

'I introduced Kel the scribe to the queen, so that she might plead his cause to Ahmose.'

'You are the High Priest of Neith! Have you gone mad?'

'That young man is innocent.'

'Do you possess irrefutable proof?'

'His sincerity has convinced me.'

'This is a nightmare! A dignitary of your age and experience, displaying such credulity!'

'And what if my age and experience help me to perceive the truth?'

This argument troubled Pefy for a moment. 'Gem is a meticulous and thoughtful judge. Now he declares that he has all the proof he needs.'

'Was the true killer's first task not to deceive the investigating magistrate?'

Pefy grunted. 'Apart from your intuition, do you have anything tangible?'

'In Naukratis, Kel made some disturbing discoveries, which nobody is willing to take account of. Contrary to your reassuring certitudes, the Greek traders and financiers do not intend to limit their activities to that one town.'

The minister frowned. 'Be more specific.'

'They want to introduce slavery into Egypt and impose their monetary system upon it, circulating their metal coinage throughout the entire land.

'That's completely out of the question!'

'The illegal traffic in coins has already begun, yet the royal palace does not seem worried by it. Are they bowing to a development they believe is unstoppable? And what about you, the head of public finances? You do not appear very well informed.'

Pefy remained silent for a long time. 'I do not see much connection with the murder of the interpreters.'

'Is it not the case that someone is in the process of selling our country?'

'You are losing your mind, Wahibra! Do not do anything unwise, no matter how minor, and keep yourself well away from this affair. I am leaving for Abydos, in order to check if the maintenance work on the temple is being correctly carried out.'

'In other words, you will not intervene with the king.'

'That would be futile. He listens only to himself and to Pythagoras, a Greek philosopher who fascinates him. I beg you, my friend: forget those horrible murders, let the storm pass, and the powers that be will forgive you your mistake.'

Despite renewed attempts, neither Kel nor Nitis could decipher the coded papyrus. And they did not know where to find the ancestors capable of providing them with crucial help.

Content with the quality of the wine and the rather frugal food, Bebon recited the text from the Mysteries of Horus in which the falcon-headed god, inspired by his mother Isis, harpooned the hippopotamus of Set and rendered evil helpless.

'May this divine magic protect us!' the actor prayed.

The arrival of Nitis gave him hope. Her very presence dispelled despair.

'According to the High Priest,' she said, 'only one man could talk at length to the king and plead in Kel's favour.'

'What is this saviour's name?' Bebon asked.

'Pythagoras, a Greek thinker who has come to seek wisdom in Egypt. He has spent time in numerous temples, including this very one, and we entrusted him with ritual tasks which he carried out with thoroughness. He is currently in Naukratis, at the house of the lady Zekeh.'

'Zekeh's servants provided Judge Gem with false statements accusing me of cutting Demos's throat,' Kel reminded her. 'Nevertheless, I must see Pythagoras and convince him of my innocence. I shall leave immediately for Naukratis.'

'I shall come with you,' decided Bebon.

'Out of the question,' decreed Nitis. 'You are not yet recovered, and the guards are bound to be looking for a man with a broken nose.'

'She is is right,' cut in Kel. 'Don't worry. I know Naukratis well, and can slip through the net.'

'Here is a document giving you the right to consult Pythagoras on behalf of the High Priest of Neith and ask him to provide him with answers regarding his view of the planets. It will enable you to present yourself as a Greek from Samos.'

'Pythagoras and Zekeh,' murmured Bebon anxiously. 'What if they are in this together, and this is a new trap? Kel emerges from his refuge and falls into the crocodile's open mouth. Why does the High Priest suggest this strategy?'

'Because he has received information in confidence from his friend Pefy, the minister of finance.'

'An official of the first rank, who may be mixed up in the conspiracy.'

'That is a risk I must take,' said Kel. 'I cannot remain idle.'

Neither can I, thought Bebon.

57

The short journey passed without incident. The guards posted on the Sais landing stage had intercepted a young man resembling Kel and, while he was being questioned, the scribe boarded the boat for Naukratis.

There were more checks on his arrival.

A soldier consulted the portrait of Kel, who was conversing in Greek with a seller of the coloured tunics much prized by mercenaries. Kel purchased a voluminous example.

The soldiers did not hinder them, and the two men ate lunch in a noisy inn where people were haggling over business deals.

Then Kel went to the Temple of Apollo, which stood between the Temple of the Dioscures, Castor and Pollux, and that of Hera, to the north of the town.

Beneath the esplanade that ran in front of the building, some priests were deep in discussion.

'Forgive me for interrupting you,' said Kel. 'I am looking for a philosopher named Pythagoras, in order to give him a letter.'

'We saw him yesterday,' said one priest. 'He is not planning to come back here.'

'Where might I find him?'

'He lives at the house of the lady Zekeh, the richest woman in Naukratis and our principal benefactress.'

The priest gave Kel directions to Zekeh's house. The scribe had hoped to contact Pythagoras a long way from that dwelling, but he had to face facts: he would have to step through the door of the sumptuous residence, at the risk of being recognized and arrested.

There were many soldiers in the streets and they turned round as free women walked past, their hair uncovered. Those who had recently arrived from Greece were astonished by such immodesty and independence. Shocked, they would have preferred to see these women cloistered and always ready to satisfy their desire. Thanks to a growing Greek presence, in Naukratis and other Delta towns, they were hoping to bring morals back to normal.

Kel presented himself to Zekeh's door-keeper, a thick-set man with a low forehead and a hard expression.

If he recognized him, the scribe would have to run away at top speed.

'I have come from Sais,' he said. 'The High Priest of the Temple of Neith has ordered me to hand a letter to Pythagoras in person.'

'Wait here.'

The first step was over. The second might be easy: Kel would ask Pythagoras to come for a stroll, so that he could talk to him in confidence. The third, on the other hand, promised to be difficult: convincing the philosopher of his innocence and asking him to intervene with Pharaoh Ahmose.

The door-keeper returned. 'Enter. A steward will take you to the reception room. Pythagoras will join you there.'

It was impossible to go back now.

'Follow me,' ordered the steward, who was every bit as disagreeable as the door-keeper. He too failed to recognize Kel. 'Sit down and wait.'

Nervously, Kel paced up and down. The beauty of the wall-paintings, which evoked Greek landscapes, did not distract him. Endless minutes passed.

At last, the door of the reception room opened.

And the lady Zekeh entered.

Never had she been so beautiful. A gold diadem on her shining black hair, a necklace composed of three beaded rows, silver bracelets, and a red gown with a plunging neckline. And an intoxicating perfume, based on jasmine.

'I knew you would come back,' she whispered.

'I have brought a message for Pythagoras and—'

'He left Naukratis this morning.'

'Where did he go?'

'To the Temple of Ptah, in Memphis. On the king's orders.'

'Allow me to leave. I must speak to him.'

'Forget him, Kel. Now you belong to me.'

'You murdered Demos and tried to have me killed!'

'Since destiny has spared you and brought you back to me, you're going to marry me.'

'Never!'

'So you would prefer to die?'

'I don't love you, Zekeh, and I cannot play the hypocrite.'

Sadness filled her eyes. 'The beauty and charm of my rival pass understanding, do they not? And the worst threats will not shake your fidelity.'

'No, they won't.'

'For the first time in my life, Kel, you force me to give up something I want. By humiliating me, you should have roused my fury, yet all I feel is admiration. You have a purity and rectitude which I thought were an illusion. I will spare you and give you back your freedom, but listen to me well, for we shall never see each other again. I am not involved in any way with the affair of state at whose centre you appear to be. If I am hoping to alter this country's economy by introducing slavery and the circulation of coinage, it is solely for my own benefit. Wealth fascinates me and, to my last breath, I shall never cease to increase my fortune.'

'Do you not have one or more accomplices at the palace?'

'I have no need of them. My kingdom is here, in Naukratis. I have bought the senior officials, the soldiers and even the priests. Every one of them eats out of my hand in order to get a share of the ever-growing cake. And my innovations will naturally win over minds, beyond the boundaries of this town. We Greeks call this progress. You Egyptians, turned towards the gods and the past, are incapable of it.'

'What about Ahmose's helmet?'

'You taught me a good lesson. Because of that story, I dreamt of political power. What a mistake! All that matters is the power of the economy. It will sweep away all regimes and make emperors, kings and princes bend the knee. I shall abandon them to their derisory games and busy myself with trade and business.'

'So you do not know who stole the helmet, the future usurper?'

'I know nothing about that conspiracy or about the crimes you are accused of, and I do not want to. Leave Naukratis, Kel, and never again try to impinge upon my life. If you do, I shall feel under attack and I will not spare you.'

58

With the aid of a fast boat, it took Kel less than four days to cover the distance from Naukratis to Egypt's largest city, ancient Memphis. Although it was not the official capital, it remained the economic centre of the country, at the junction between the Delta and the Nile valley.

The scribe paid for his journey by writing letters to the government on behalf of the captain and his mate. To obtain the desired result, it was important to use the right form of words and prove to the officials that the writers were aware of the laws. They were nervous, unwilling to take the risk of being punished, and gave satisfaction to the plaintiffs by hiding behind polite formalities.

The boat tied up at the port of Good Journey, with its impressively long dockside. Every day, cosmopolitan Memphis received large quantities of goods, from both the South and the North.

Anonymous amid the colourful crowd, Kel asked for directions from an old man who was entertained by the constantly changing spectacle. So he had no difficulty in finding the splendid Temple of Ptah, the god of the Word and of craftsmanship. It stood close to the white-walled citadel built by Djoser, whose brilliant master-builder, Imhotep, had erected the stepped pyramid at Saqqara.

A pathway lined with sphinxes led to the colossal entrance

gateway decorated with banners atop poles, proclaiming the divine presence. Kel followed a pure priest to a side door where overseers noted down his name on the register of arrivals.

'Here is my accreditation,' he said, producing the letter signed by the High Priest. 'I wish to see a Greek philosopher, Pythagoras, who has recently arrived.'

A security official examined the document. 'You may enter. I shall go and find out.'

The vast courtyard played host to processions and leading citizens, during festivals. Along with other visitors, he waited in the shade of a colonnade. The sounds of the outside world did not pass through the thick encircling wall. A ritual priest crossed the courtyard in the direction of the covered temple, bearing a platter laden with fresh fruit.

The overseer returned, together with a man of average height and a haughty expression.

'I am Pythagoras. Who asks to see me?'

'Wahibra has given me a confidential letter addressed to you. I must also explain it to you, away from indiscreet ears.'

Pythagoras contained his surprise. 'Let us go to the quarters allotted to me by the priests of Ptah. We can talk there in perfect peace.'

Pythagoras had the use of an austere bedroom, a small study and a washroom.

'Here,' he told his guest, 'I learnt to venerate the Ancestors and to respect Maat. The tradition of initiation does not belong to the past. On the contrary, it alone is the bearer of a harmonious future. In Sais, I very much appreciated the teachings of High Priest Wahibra, and practising the rites as shown to me by Nitis.'

'Neith wove the Word,' Kel recited, 'and her seven words created the world.'

Pythagoras regarded the messenger in a new light. 'So you have been initiated into her Mysteries.'

'Nitis and the High Priest have granted me their trust. Here is the document they asked me to show you.' He unrolled the coded papyrus.

Examining it attentively, Pythagoras seemed filled with consternation. 'My knowledge of hieroglyphs does not enable me to read this text,' he said. 'I recognize the signs, but I could swear that they do not form words.'

'Correct, and we cannot break the code. I was hoping to benefit from your insights. Might the key be a Greek dialect?'

'Let's see.'

'This papyrus came from the Interpreters' Secretariat, where I was one of the scribes,' said Kel. 'I have been wrongly accused of murdering them, whereas it was in fact part of a conspiracy against Ahmose. I do not know the name of the guilty party, but he is probably one of the senior figures in the government and, having stolen the pharaoh's helmet, will don it and proclaim himself king. Unfortunately, Ahmose refuses to listen to me because the judge in charge of the investigation has a file filled with overwhelming proof, all of it forged.'

Pythagoras appeared sceptical. 'Why should I believe you?'

'I have told you the truth. I shall add that I have discovered that the Greeks in Naukratis wish to overthrow the country's economy by introducing slavery and coinage. I do not know if these facts are linked to the murder of my colleagues, but I fear a disaster. Because he helped me by introducing me to the queen, High Priest Wahibra is now under house arrest. And this indecipherable document is the sole proof of my innocence, for it surely contains the conspirators' plan.'

'So it seems Egypt is in peril,' Pythagoras murmured, staring straight at the young scribe.

'Someone will not hesitate to kill anyone who gets in the way,' Kel reminded him. 'So much violence implies ferocious determination and ruthless cruelty.'

'What do you want from me?'

'The pharaoh likes you and listens to you. You are the only

one who can make him aware of the danger. My own destiny matters little. The investigation must be begun anew, on a different basis, and the monster hidden in the shadows must be identified.'

'We have conversed at length,' admitted Pythagoras. 'Ahmose hopes to preserve a lasting peace and is taking the measures necessary to avoid any conflict. For my part, I have decided to adapt Egyptian teachings to the Greek mentality and set up a school of thought which will distance us from a destructive rationalism and bring us closer to the mystery of life. At the end of this brief stay in Memphis, I shall say my farewells to the pharaoh in Sais, then return to Greece.'

'Will you report my words to him and try to convince him that he is not seeing things clearly?'

'I cannot promise you that I will succeed.'

'Be assured of my profound gratitude. Your intervention may save Egypt from a terrible fate.'

'While you await the results of my action, keep yourself safe. There is no worse crime than the murder of an innocent person. Shall we spend this evening decoding the papyrus?'

The two men rivalled each other in virtuosity as they applied many different decoding systems based on Greek dialects, but they failed. All the same, Kel remained hopeful. Ahmose would respond to Pythagoras's words.

59

Convinced that he had fully recovered, Bebon removed his latest dressings and begged Nitis to let him go out. He was unable to sit still, desperate to ensure that his friend Nedi had not died in vain.

The priestess was reluctant, and made him promise not to take any risks. To his own surprise, the actor replied honestly that he would be careful.

When night fell, Nitis guided Bebon to the little northern gate, which was closed at sunset. She had the key and entrusted it to him. On the way back, he would take the same route, being careful not to attract the attentions of a guard.

How delicious the night air felt! Living in a gilded cage really did not agree with him. Risk and danger: they were stirring and formative. He would leave boring family men to their cosy comforts and the boredom of their never-changing existence.

He, Bebon, was mixed up in an affair of state. Well, so much the better. The conspirators had better hold on tight. By attacking Kel, who was incapable of doing anything vile, they had trampled on vital values. And Bebon, although not much inclined towards morality, could not tolerate that. Justice was the basis of any civilization worthy of the name.

He reached the southern outskirts of Sais, which were edged by verdant countryside irrigated by countless canals. The district consisted of a few fine detached houses and some more modest ones, mingled with shops and workshops.

Nedi lived near a rich farmer who was proud of his property, which was surrounded by a garden planted with palms and jujube trees.

The place seemed tranquil. Fearing another trap, the actor looked around him. No lookouts on duty. Several times, Bebon walked past Nedi's house. Flat calm.

He walked round the house, forced the shutter of a window which looked out on to a vegetable garden, and slipped inside. There was a large living-room, a bedroom, a storeroom and a washroom. Nedi had been a widower, and lived comfortably.

A great lover of fine wines, he took pride in his cellar. Bebon went down into it. The moonlight filtered in through a skylight covered with a grille, enabling him to examine the jars, each marked with their place of origin and year. He soon spotted an anomaly: one of them had had its stopper removed and then replaced.

Bebon removed the linen and straw stopper. Inside there was no wine, but a rolled and sealed papyrus. A surprising message was written in fine handwriting.

Dear old scoundrel, Here's an initial discovery: the authorities have just arrested a trafficker in iron weapons stored in Naukratis. The fellow enjoyed support in high places, and was let off with a fine. I am continuing my investigation. If anything bad happens to me, you are bound to find this document. And don't forget to drink to my eternal good health. The jar from Imau, dating from Year 3 of Ahmose's reign, contains absolute nectar.

Bebon made sure that he paid homage to his friend. The red wine was strong, and made him slip into a heavy sleep from which he did not wake until the middle of the morning.

Satisfying his hunger with a piece of dried fish, he actor waited for dusk before leaving the house. Still flat calm.

Spotting the man who guarded the farmer's house, Bebon went over to him.

'My cousin Nedi isn't here,' he said. 'When should I come back?'

'Don't . . . don't you know?'

'What has happened?'

'He has died of a heart attack.'

'Here, at his home?'

'No, at the guard-post. He has already been buried and his house will soon be occupied by a colleague.'

'My poor cousin! And yet he seemed to be in excellent health.'

'No one knows the day or the hour. He was a fine man.'

'The situation seems clear,' Bebon told Nitis and Wahibra. 'A Greek faction in Naukratis is trying to arm itself in order to attack the king. He must be warned at once.'

'I am confined to quarters,' the High Priest reminded him. 'And even if I did succeed in seeing Ahmose, he would not believe me.'

'There may be a solution,' ventured Nitis.

'I need your help,' Nitis told Menk.

He quivered with pleasure. At last, she was taking a step towards him!

'You know that the king refuses to see the High Priest.'

'I much regret it, dear Nitis, and I hope that this regrettable situation will soon improve.'

'Wahibra has some information which is vital for the kingdom's security. Since he cannot leave the temple, he is seeking a messenger he can trust.'

Menk's joy was abruptly tarnished. 'Affairs of state are not my strong point, and—'

'The king listens to you, for he knows that you are honest and thorough. We are all involved, since this concerns the future of Egypt. Not to pass on this information would be a serious crime.'

'This is an extremely delicate course of action. I don't know if—'

'The High Priest has granted you his trust. As do I. We two are powerless, but you can save the Two Lands.'

On one hand, taking the initiative in this way and displeasing the king would destroy his career at a stroke; on the other, refusing Nitis's request would put an end to their relationship.

'This information . . . How did I obtain it?'

'From a soldier, who wished to remain anonymous but confided in you. Even though you found it hard to believe, you thought it best to alert His Majesty.'

'You are asking a great deal.'

The young woman smiled. 'I don't doubt your courage, Menk. This deed will prove your absolute loyalty to the king, and he will not prove ungrateful.'

The prospect reassured Menk. 'I am to have a private audience with His Majesty in four days. Will that suffice?'

'Wonderfully. That way, you won't attract attention.'

'Don't tell me that some of the palace dignitaries have been compromised!'

'The information concerns an illegal traffic in weapons.'

Anxious but attentive, Menk listened to Nitis.

60

Pythagoras was now regarded as an official personage, and benefited from royal largesse. Consequently he was using a private boat, together with his secretary, whom he had engaged in Memphis. Avoiding all checkpoints, Kel enjoyed a pleasant voyage to Sais.

Soon he would see Nitis again. And if Pythagoras succeeded in convincing the king, the young scribe would once again be a free man with a future.

Seated on the deck, sheltered from the sun by a white cloth stretched between four poles, the two men enjoyed the calm of a landscape composed of palm-groves and well-watered fields. A black ibis soared overhead.

'The bird of Thoth,' remarked Pythagoras, 'the repository of sacred knowledge and the patron god of scribes. In Greece, we call him Hermes. Through his teachings, I realized that our world is merely a small island which emerged in the middle of the ocean of primordial energy. When the Creator gazed upon his own Light, he gave birth to the life which came forth from Life. And initiation into the Mysteries of Isis and Osiris renders that Life self-aware. For true birth is not our mediocre, profane existence but access to the Light.'

Kel nodded. 'The head of the Interpreters' Secretariat talked to me about the *ka* of the universe, which is precisely what that generous Light symbolizes. Each morning, I worship the rising sun, bearer of resurrection.'

'Trust in Neith, young scribe. Masculine which made feminine, Feminine which made masculine, eternal stretch of creative water, living ancestor, blazing star, father and mother: she will open the gates of the heavens to you.'

The boat arrived at the main quay in Sais. Pythagoras headed for the palace, while Kel remained on board. The day crept by, seemingly endless.

Shortly before sunset, Pythagoras slowly climbed the gangplank. 'Total failure,' he said. 'Ahmose thinks I have fallen victim to an unfounded rumour.'

'Did you persist?'

'So much that I angered the king.'

'Then he will hear nothing?'

'He alone governs. And he has ordered me to return to Greece.'

'I am sorry to have placed you in an awkward position.'

'The date of my departure was already decreed. Shouldn't you come with me, Kel? Here, the situation seems heavily compromised. Together, we shall found a brotherhood and try to make the Greeks less materialistic.'

'Leaving Egypt would destroy me. And I want to prove my innocence.'

'May the gods protect you.'

Henat bowed before the king, who was visibly furious.

'I demand explanations.'

'Regarding what, Majesty?'

'Can you not guess?'

'We have not yet arrested that damned scribe, and I am the first to lament the fact. But Judge Gem and I are not relaxing our efforts. The killer is proving to be tougher than expected.'

Ahmose waved this away with a gesture of disdain. 'I was thinking of another, equally grave scandal.'

Henat seemed surprised. 'Enlighten me, Majesty.'

'Pythagoras has heard rumours of a conspiracy fomented by Greeks from Naukratis, and Menk has provided me with an additional detail: traders from Naukratis have allegedly been fraudulently importing iron weapons! If you, the head of my spy service, are unaware of this, where is the country headed? Tomorrow, a usurper will don my helmet, and the Two Lands will be delivered up to chaos.'

'I am aware of it.'

The king stared at Henat. 'What did you say?'

'It was I who organized those imports.'

Stunned, Ahmose drank a cup of white wine. 'So you lie to me and you betray me.'

'In no way, Majesty.'

'Explain yourself!'

'For several months now, Commander Phanes has been demanding improvements in the army's equipment, notably the weaponry used by the elite troops. When Cambyses came to power, this emphasized the threat of a Persian invasion. That is why I set up a new trading link between Greece and Egypt, reserved for the delivery of high-quality iron weapons. Our equipment will soon be considerably superior to that of the Persians. Since it concerns our defence, this operation remains confidential.'

'I, the pharaoh, ought to have been kept informed!'

Henat appeared astonished. 'You were, Majesty.'

'In what way?'

'I specified the details of the transaction and its secret nature in two reports.'

'Reports, always more reports! I do not have time to read everything, and all this documentation exasperates me. At my age, excessive work is absolutely forbidden, and if I do not take time to enjoy myself I cannot think straight.' He drank another cup of white wine. 'I prefer this, Henat. For a moment, I feared that a faction of Greeks in Naukratis was conspiring against me. People to whom I accord many privileges, because they embody the future.'

'My deliveries of weapons are under close supervision, Majesty,' said Henat. 'Not a single sword will fail to reach its proper destination.'

'I know who fabricated this rumour. The High Priest of Neith, of course. Powerful Wahibra cannot bear the humiliation and wants to continue to play a political role by provoking trouble. That man is going to get the punishment he deserves.'

'Majesty, his moral standing—'

'I know what remains for me to do, Henat. Continue to produce accurate, detailed reports.'

61

'You seem vexed,' observed Queen Tanith. 'Does this food or wine displease you?'

'No, I have no appetite,' replied Ahmose.

'Are there serious problems?'

'Just one: that damned High Priest Wahibra! This time he has gone too far. I have decided to rid myself of him. He will be arrested and deported for high treason.'

The queen delicately dabbed her lips with a linen cloth. 'The trial is likely to be a spectacular one. Do you have the necessary proof?'

'There will be no trial.'

'Wahibra is a highly respected spiritual and moral authority,' Tanith reminded him. 'If his sentence is not fully justified, you will be criticized for it. And if you set all the temples in Egypt against you, you run the risk of being weakened.'

'They do not represent the future.'

'True, but the Egyptians are very attached to them, and the temples link people to the gods. The Greeks themselves recognize that the Two Lands are the homeland of the gods and the spiritual centre of the world.'

'Wahibra detests me.'

'What does that matter?'

'He is conspiring against me.'

'Are you certain of that? And can you make the accusation stand up before a court?'

Ahmose hesitated.

'Having the High Priest of Neith killed would cause serious disturbances,' predicted the queen. 'The rites and festivals would no longer be celebrated in Sais, and the movement would extend throughout Egypt.'

The king laid his hand on his wife's. 'I do not want things to go that far. My dear, you have prevented me making a fatal mistake.'

'I have learnt to love and understand this country. Since Wahibra fights you, bind him hand and foot and prevent him from doing harm without affecting his religious offices. His age should incline him towards caution. And if he sets foot outside his own territory, the law will enable you to intervene.'

The head steward begged leave to interrupt their meal. 'Majesty, the lord Henat wishes to see you urgently.'

'Work, yet more work!'

Tanith smiled. 'Go, my friend. Duty calls you.'

Still grumbling, the king received Henat.

'Excellent news, Majesty. We have just received a long letter signed by Emperor Cambyses. I used the services of three translators so as not to miss a single nuance. Our strategy is a total success! The emperor declares himself impressed by our military power, and presents himself as a man of peace who wishes to develop the diplomatic and trading relations between our two countries.'

'In other words, he has decided not to attack us.'

'Exactly. Nevertheless, I advise against lowering our guard and believe we should pursue our military efforts. A Persian is still a Persian and he still dreams of conquest. At the first sign of weakness, Cambyses might change his attitude.'

'Fear not, I have no intention of reducing the military

budget. An increase in taxes will guarantee the development of our army.'

Ahmose had listened attentively to Menk before thanking him for his intervention. As a faithful servant of the state, he had supplied the king with an important piece of information. He was an excellent organizer of the many festivals in Sais, and would soon merit further responsibilities.

So it was with a light heart that Menk answered Henat's summons. The director of the palace was doubtless going to endow him with even more prestigious offices.

But the attitude and expression of the powerful man made Menk uneasy. He made it seem as though every person he spoke to had committed some kind of crime.

'His Majesty has informed me of the nature of your declarations,' declared Henat in a tone of veiled hostility.

'I was only doing my duty.'

'I consider spreading rumours and false information to be a crime.'

Menk's blood ran cold. 'I don't understand.'

'You have been manipulated. And I want to know the name of the manipulator.'

'It was just an anonymous rumour. I thought—'

'Do not take me for an imbecile, Menk. You may have thought you were serving the king, but you have become involved in machinations which may cost you dearly. What is the name of your informant?'

Menk swayed. How could he resist this merciless predator? Clearly Nitis, too, had been manipulated. Accusing the High Priest would worsen the case against that honest man.

'Kel the scribe.'

Henat froze. 'Where did you meet him?'

'He was waiting for me near my house, brandishing a knife – he threatened me. He forced me to listen to him, and I found him convincing. He declares that he is innocent and is the plaything of arms traffickers. Kel begged me to alert His Majesty.'

During the long silence that followed, Menk's back dripped sweat.

'There is no arms traffic,' revealed Henat. 'The confidential deliveries which arrive in Naukratis are destined for our soldiers, whose weaponry will dissuade any attacker. That murderous scribe lied to you. He leads a band of conspirators and criminals, determined to bring down Pharaoh's throne. You now know a great deal about this, Menk. Can you hold your tongue?'

'I swear it!'

'Do you know where Kel is hiding?'

'No, I do not!'

'You have committed a grave error by granting him your trust, and it must be made good.'

Menk felt almost ill.

'High Priest Wahibra committed the same offence,' said Henat, 'and he has lost His Majesty's esteem. I dare not imagine that he continues to help a fugitive killer, in one way or another. Nevertheless, it would be best to make sure. Don't you agree?'

'Yes, yes, of course!'

'In that case, since you frequently go to the temple, you will become my eyes and ears there. Inform me immediately of the smallest incident or remark pertaining to Kel, and denounce any accomplices to me.'

'The task will be a delicate one and—'

'You will fulfil it to perfection. And consequently I shall forget the mistake you have made.'

62

Judge Gem's mood was darkening. Despite all the men working on the case, the investigation was treading water, and the murderous scribe was continuing to mock him!

At least the judge was now certain about some things.

Kel's guilt was in no doubt whatsoever. Nor was his membership of a conspiracy designed to overthrow the king. Perhaps the scribe even led a pack of rebels, whose most ardent members were providing him with the help he needed to escape from the authorities.

The judge's dignity and credibility were at stake. This failure would soon provoke Ahmose's anger, and the king would reproach Gem for his ineffectiveness. And that accusation would be well deserved.

Why were there so many difficulties, if not because of the gravity of this affair? Kel was no ordinary murderer, but a formidable leader of men, ready to kill anyone who stood in his way. Such ferocity surprised the old judge, even though he was accustomed to human turpitude.

Sometimes Gem thought of the last words of the murdered head of the Interpreters' Secretariat: '*Decipher the coded document and . . .*' But the document could not be found. Had Kel got it, and would he use it against the authorities?

As the pensive judge was emerging from his office, Henat stopped him. 'You seem full of care.'

'Do I have any reasons to rejoice?'

'His Majesty's trust ought to reassure you.'

'Will it not soon be withdrawn from me?'

'Certainly not! The king appreciates your efforts and has no intention of replacing you.'

'You surprise me, Henat.'

'Order reigns and justice is respected: that is what matters. And you are playing a major part by applying the law.'

Judge Gem did not hide his dejection. 'I am floundering lamentably. This man Kel is no ordinary adversary.'

'We must not lose heart. You know very well that the worst of criminals always ends up making a mistake. Besides, we have a new ally: Menk, the organizer of festivals in Sais.'

'Does he possess important information?'

'I have instructed him to inform me about any incidents which may arise within the domain of Neith.

'A spy at the heart of the temple?'

'Menk is serving justice.'

'Do you suppose the High Priest would dare hide a criminal on the run?'

'A detailed search of the premises revealed nothing. Given his situation, Wahibra would not run such a risk, but he might use those loyal to him in order to help the scribe to escape from us.'

'In other words, the High Priest is one of the conspirators.'

'Not necessarily. Perhaps he believes in Kel's innocence. Whatever the case, Menk will be on hand to gather useful information. Of course, I shall keep you informed.'

The leader of the conspirators summed up the situation. 'Things are developing satisfactorily. It is true that we had not envisaged such resistance on the part of the petty scribe, but basically he is serving our cause by drawing all the attention to himself. However, you must continue to behave with extreme caution and keep your lips sealed tight, for victory is still a long way away.'

'Won't the king discover the truth?'

'That disaster is not impossible, which is why it is a good idea to weaken his *ka*, and make it the plaything of events.'

'A difficult task! Despite his laziness and his penchant for drink, Ahmose holds the reins of power. He has the instincts of a wild animal, capable of sensing danger.'

'We shall not attack his person directly,' decided the leader, 'but its embodiment, worshipped by all.'

One of the rebels protested, 'The shock among the populace at large will be enormous!'

'That is the effect we are seeking.'

Menk was dazzled by Nitis's beauty. With each new encounter, her attraction grew. One day she would belong to him. So he must protect her.

'Did the king listen to you?' she asked.

'Attentively. You have been deceived by a false rumour. In reality, there is no arms traffic.'

'Are you certain of that?'

'His Majesty himself gave me the proof,' declared Menk, disguising the truth a little. It was impossible to allude to the delicate mission Henat had given him. 'Be careful, Nitis, I beg you. Kel's case and the military problems derive from an affair of state which is far bigger than you and me. To become involved in it, even indirectly, would condemn us to destruction.'

'Thank you for your advice, Menk.'

'Do you promise me to heed it?'

'I promise.'

'You give me great comfort, Nitis. And yet one thought fills me with anguish: do you not think that the High Priest's natural goodness might have led him to help Kel, for example by recommending him to a friend?'

'Whatever are you imagining? For the High Priest, all that matters is the Law of Maat. He would never help a murderer.'

The opening of a new workshop, equipped with superb weaving-looms, led to the closure of an old building, which would remain unused for a time. An ideal hiding-place for Kel.

Bebon moved about as he pleased, playing to perfection his role as a supplier of foodstuffs, which were transported at a leisurely pace by the sturdy North Wind.

Nitis signalled to him to follow her, and she, Kel and Bebon went into the disused workshop. In the event of danger, the donkey would sound the alert.

In the half-light of the silent workshop, Kel gazed at Nitis. She was like the first glimmer of dawn's light, the embodiment of hope. So close, and yet out of reach!

'What progress have we made?' asked Bebon, shattering this delicious yet painful moment.

'Pythagoras failed to convince the king,' said Kel. 'He has been obliged to return to Greece.'

'Menk suffered the same failure,' said Nitis. 'According to the king himself, there is no traffic in weapons.'

'In other words,' said Bebon, 'Ahmose is behind all the crimes that have been committed.'

'I refuse to believe that!' protested Kel. 'Never has a pharaoh betrayed his country and his people.'

'Times are changing.'

63

As she did every week, Nitis paid a visit to the sacred cow, the earthly incarnation of Neith and mother of the Apis bull, the living symbol of the royal *ka*. Ordinarily, the calm cow with the soft gaze would come to lick the priestess's hand, and they would spend happy moments together.

This time the mother of Apis remained prostrate. Anxiously, Nitis summoned the animal-doctor.

His diagnosis was pessimistic. 'The mother of Apis is living through her final hours.'

Nitis went immediately to see the High Priest, who was affected by her distress.

'Is Kel in danger?' he asked.

'No, I have found him a safe hiding-place.'

'Then why are you distressed?'

'The great goddess's cow is in her death throes.'

The news caused Wahibra great consternation. 'I must go immediately to Memphis to check the state of health of the Apis bull, her son, guarantor of Ahmose's vitality.'

'You are confined to the temple,' Nitis reminded him. 'Do you authorize me to take your place?'

'Leave immediately. In the present circumstances, the death of Apis would be a catastrophe.'

*

On board the official boat belonging to the Superior of the songstresses and weavers of Neith, no one paid any attention to the presence of a scribe, a cup-bearer and a donkey. Kel, Bebon and North Wind travelled in complete safety.

Kel kept the boat's journal, Bebon filled cups with cool beer and North Wind, fed on thistles, lucerne and dates, enjoyed this delicious outing on the Nile, during which he did not have to do any work at all.

When they arrived at Memphis, the priestess announced to the captain that she would make do with a reduced escort of only two servants and a donkey, which would carry the clothing.

To the north of the fortified district of the largest city in Egypt, the temple of 'Neith Who Opens the Pathways' occupied a large area.

Nitis's counterpart, a stern-faced woman of forty, greeted her warmly. 'This visit honours us.'

'It is a joy to meet you. Alas, anxiety guides my steps, for Apis's mother has just passed away, and the High Priest fears that her son may weaken.'

The Memphis priestess stood stock still. 'Ought the worshipful Wahibra not to have come himself?'

'Grave difficulties prevent him doing so. He has given me the power to represent him.'

'We must go to the bull's enclosure.'

The cult of the Apis bull dated from the time of the unification of Upper and Lower Egypt. Herald and interpreter of the royal power,* the bull provided the table of the gods and goddesses with countless riches. The incarnation of creation, light and resurrection,† the giant bull was born to a

---

* *Ka*, 'creative power', is synonymous with *ka*, 'bull'.

† Apis renewed (*ouhem*) the creative act of Ptah, Ra's fertilizing Light and Osiris's capacity for resurrection.

cow illuminated by a bolt of lightning which flashed forth from the clouds. The symbol of the sky-goddess, united with the first radiance at the dawn of time, she never gave birth again. Her only son, Apis, guaranteed the pharaoh's vitality.

The sacred bull was like no other. Black, with a white triangle on its brow and the scarab of metamorphoses outlined upon his tongue, he occupied an enclosure to the south of the Temple of Ptah, near the royal palace. Care and attention were lavished upon him, and he lived for many long and happy years in the service of the kingdom's prosperity.

When he died, it fell to the temple of Sais to provide an Osiran shroud, vital for the burial. But the religious authorities in Memphis had not sent any alarming messages to those in Sais.

Apis's vast and comfortable domain testified to the importance attributed to the sacred bull.

The enclosure was empty.

'Where is he?' asked Nitis.

Astonished, her Memphis counterpart alerted the chief keeper.

'This morning he did not come out of his quarters.'

'Is he ill?'

'All I do is feed him.'

'Open the gate,' ordered Nitis.

It was better not to argue with women like that. If you angered them, they would make your life a misery.

The priestess crossed the enclosure and entered Apis's dwelling. The powerful animal was lying on his side, his eyes running. Nitis went to him. There was immediate trust between them. She touched his forehead: it was burning hot.

'We shall take care of you,' she promised him.

The young woman ran outside. 'Apis is gravely ill,' she told her colleague. 'We must inform the animal-healer immediately.'

As the healer was ill in bed, his assistant took his place.

After a brief examination, he gave his diagnosis: 'Nothing alarming. Just a passing fever.'

'Permit me to disagree,' said Nitis.

The healer was furious. 'No one has ever questioned my competence.'

'Ought the bull not to be rubbed with plants and made to sweat, in order to drive out the poisons?'

'Completely unnecessary. A little rest will suffice. Soon he will be completely recovered.'

'But—'

'I am the specialist, not you.' Flashing a look of disdain at Nitis, the healer walked away.

64

First thing the next morning, Nitis returned to the enclosure.

A guard barred the way. 'No one may pass. Healer's orders.'

'Not even the delegate of the High Priest of Neith?'

The visitor's title impressed the guard. She could have him transferred to some forgotten corner of the province.

'Very well. But don't stay too long.'

Apis was getting worse and worse. He was short of breath, his temples were burning, and the roots of his teeth were inflamed. He had not touched his food, whose smell intrigued the priestess. She took a sample to the workshop at the Temple of Ptah, and instructed a specialist to analyse it.

His examination was conclusive: poisoned food.

The young woman immediately requested an audience with the High Priest, who received her late in the morning.

'Someone is trying to murder Apis,' she revealed, outlining the facts.

'Impossible! Our healer is a remarkable practitioner. He would never have allowed such a crime to be committed.'

'He is ill. His assistant has taken his place and refuses to treat the bull.'

'I shall summon him immediately.'

After a long wait, the High Priest was informed that the assistant had disappeared, while the healer himself was very ill and incapable of intervening. So another healer was called in, and his diagnosis was pessimistic: the bull was living through his final hours.

Kel and Bebon were staying with the servants, and their lives were very different. The scribe seldom went out and, despite his repeated failures, kept trying to break the papyrus's code. As for the actor, he went out walking with North Wind and stopped to talk with passers-by.

At last Nitis reappeared. 'Apis is dying,' she told them.

'That doesn't surprise me,' said Bebon.

'How did you find out? It is still a state secret.'

'That depends on who you are. According to a ritual priest, Apis's tomb has been in preparation for more than a week.'

'So Apis's death was planned,' concluded Kel.

'In plain language, this is murder.'

'The death of the sacred bull weakens the king's power,' said Nitis. 'During the funeral period and until the consecration of a new Apis, Ahmose will be in danger.'

'Does that prove his innocence?' wondered the scribe.

'I remain sceptical,' declared Bebon. 'Let's have no hasty deductions.'

'What if the key to the enigma is at the tomb complex where the Apis bulls are buried? Perhaps they are the Ancestors who have the code!'

'Ordinarily,' said Nitis, 'access to it is forbidden.'

'The ritual priests must prepare for the funeral ceremonies. And Bebon will find a way to slip past the guards' watchful eyes.'

'We shall see. Am I to become the saviour of humanity?'

'Let's begin with just us two. Then we shall see.'

The Apis bull died at dawn. The High Priest of Ptah meditated before the body and entrusted it to the embalmers, whose task was to transform it into an Osiran body. Then he summoned the ritual priests who took part in the ceremony. Only they would be authorized to enter the tomb complex.

'Nitis, Superior of the songstresses and weavers of Neith, will assist us,' he decided. 'This moment marks the start of the official mourning period, which His Majesty wishes to be as short as possible. As the Apis bull's sarcophagus is already prepared, we shall ensure that it is swiftly moved into place.'

So the young woman officially had access to the complex. The king's haste proved how anxious he was, fearing that the conspirators would take advantage of this unsettling period to seize power.

Apis's body was transported to the embalming chamber, which stood at the south-western corner of the enclosure of the Temple of Ptah, and was laid on a bed of alabaster. Then the funerary vigils began, accompanied by a four-day fast, during which nothing was consumed except water, bread and vegetables.

With foresight, Bebon had hidden two jars of good wine. 'I'm very fond of bulls,' he said, 'but I prefer a good wine. It will help us to bear the privations.'

Kel refused the cup.

'Surely you aren't going to act like a bigot?'

'I wish to respect the demands of the ritual.'

'You're not a priest of Apis.'

'The power he embodies deserves to be venerated.'

'Away with your theological speculations! Me, I'm going to drink, and thank the gods for creating the vine.'

King Ahmose drained yet another cup.

'Should you not avoid such excess?' Queen Tanith asked anxiously.

'The death of the Apis bull makes me vulnerable. In the eyes of the people, my power is diminished. And the thief who stole my helmet is preparing to usurp power.'

'Has Judge Gem's investigation made any progress?'

'Not one bit! The murderous scribe has disappeared. It makes one wonder if he's dead and buried. And there is no trace of the helmet. As for Henat, he is floundering lamentably but at least he does not try to make excuses. He has just offered me his resignation, and I have refused it. Up to now, he has always been remarkably effective, and his experience is irreplaceable. We are in the presence of a particularly skilful adversary, Tanith. By murdering the Apis bull he damages my *ka*.'

'How can we fight him?'

'In two ways: by swiftly finding Apis's successor and by reducing the mourning period to the absolute minimum. That is why I have sent out emissaries throughout the land and given the High Priest of Ptah strict instructions.'

Tanith blocked her husband's path to the wine jar. 'Keep a clear head, I beg you. You will need it if you are to win this battle.'

65

The procession, made up of priests and priestesses, soldiers
and Pharaoh's delegates, came to fetch the Apis bull's mummy
and escort it to the purification tent, which had been set up
beside the king's lake. The High Priest of Ptah poured
fresh water which had come from the sky on to the Osiran
body, and spoke words of resurrection. Then the transfigured
body was placed in a boat and crossed the lake, the symbol
of the primordial ocean in which all forms of life were born
and reborn.

The route leading to the tomb complex presented serious
difficulties. Recently buried in sand because of violent winds, it
ended in a rocky ramp which demanded considerable efforts
on the part of the soldiers hauling the sled bearing the heavy
mummy.

Equipped with a small chest containing amulets, Kel
followed Nitis, who was at the head of the procession. Bebon
and North Wind were at the rear, bearing flasks. Professional
mourning-women chanted incantations in honour of the
deceased.

The funeral journey lasted about ten hours. At last the
sphinx-lined pathway appeared, leading inside the complex.
The procession halted.

'This is the Beautiful West, open to the Apis who is of
righteous voice,' announced the High Priest of Ptah. 'The king

offers him a sarcophagus of pink and black granite, his never-changing, indestructible boat of resurrection. Never before has a pharaoh done such a thing.'

Kel presented the little chest to Nitis, who opened it, took out the amulets and arranged them upon the mummy.

The most senior ritual priests and their assistants passed through the doorway of the bulls' burial place, laden with funerary offerings.

Two galleries served the Apis bulls' resurrection chambers. The first, dating from the New Kingdom, was some hundred and twenty-five cubits long. The second, dug out during the reign of Psamtek I, was almost four hundred cubits long and cut across the previous one at right angles. The ritual priests who had taken part in the funeral ceremonies enjoyed a remarkable privilege: they were allowed to place steles there in their own names, and thus be associated with Apis's eternal life.

The cavern belonging to the dead bull impressed Nitis: it was sixteen cubits down, and the sarcophagus weighed more than a boatload of grain.

The High Priest of Ptah proceeded to open Apis's mouth, endowing him once again with creative speech. He ordered the soldiers to place the mummy inside the sarcophagus and slide the stone lid into place. Fortunately, this difficult manoeuvre was accomplished without any mishaps.

While the chamber of eternity was being walled up, Kel explored the place. Swiftly deciphering the votive stelae, he hoped to discover a message from the Ancestors. Disappointed, he emerged from the great gallery and tried to approach the caverns which were plunged in darkness.

A soldier barred his way. 'Halt! Where do you want to go?'

'I was told to leave an offering.'

'This way is barred.'

'But my offering . . .'

'You have the wrong place. Go back.'

The scribe obeyed.

At the end of the ceremony, stelae in the names of the dignitaries were put in place before the walled-up doorway, and the ritual priests left the place of burial in silence.

'A soldier stopped me going to the end of a gallery,' Kel whispered in Nitis's ear. 'I've just seen him leave, so now there is nobody left inside. I must continue my investigations.'

'It's too dangerous. The guards will arrest you.'

'Bebon will cause a diversion. If I don't act immediately, we will never discover the truth. Tomorrow the site will be inaccessible.'

'I have to return to Memphis with the High Priest. Be careful, I beg you.'

'I want too much to see you again, Nitis.'

A priest called to her, and Kel moved away.

Bebon was chewing a flat-cake, and North Wind was dozing.

'I fear you have some mad plan in your head,' said the actor worriedly.

'You get the guards away, I go back into the Serapeum, I explore, and then we run away.'

'Admirable! Pointless to argue, I suppose?'

'Get ready.'

At dead of night, five of the ten guards were sound asleep. Three others were dozing, and the last two were talking about their marital problems. Often away on missions, they were beginning to doubt their wives' fidelity.

As clouds blotted out the feeble light of the crescent moon, Kel crawled towards the entrance to the underground chambers. Tomorrow it would be blocked off until the burial of Apis's successor. He slipped inside, stood up and ran towards the forbidden area.

With little time available before Bebon took action, Kel

used one of the lamps which had been left lit, and examined the stelae. Simple texts of worship, addressed to the Apis bull; not a single strange element derived from a coded language.

At the far end of the gallery was a small, open cavern. Inside lay a wooden sarcophagus without a lid. Surprised, Kel dared to look inside. And he stood there, flabbergasted, for a long time.

Distant shouts jolted him back to the urgency of the situation. Seizing the treasure, he left the complex.

The fire lit by Bebon had attracted the guards. They would soon find nothing but a simple pile of twigs and dry grass, posing no danger to the safety of the burial-ground.

'We must follow North Wind,' advised Bebon. 'He knows a good way. But what . . . ? Isn't that . . .?'

Kel brandished the precious object. 'I have found Pharaoh Ahmose's helmet!'

66

Udja was visibly furious. Tiredness had no hold on him, and his powerful frame loomed menacingly.

'You are not men to run away from your responsibilities,' he said to Judge Gem and Henat. 'And I was expecting a somewhat different account of your progress.'

'No leads regarding the king's helmet,' admitted Henat. 'The thief has hidden it well, and is not making any mistakes. Fortunately, my agents have not informed me of any attempts at sedition. The soldiers remain calm, and no one has spoken out against Pharaoh Ahmose. Because of my pitiful failure, I offered my resignation to His Majesty.'

'He was right to refuse it,' retorted Udja. 'Nobody else has your skills, and one does not abandon ship in the middle of a storm. Your difficulties show how extensive the conspiracy is, but the situation is not desperate. The enemy fears failure, and dares not launch the great offensive for which he is preparing in the shadows. And we do not know the identities of the ringleaders, apart from that of their probable leader, the scribe Kel.'

The judge seemed utterly downcast. 'This affair is too big for me. Neither the guards nor the informers have managed to track him down. I, too, offered to resign.'

'And the king was once again correct in keeping you in your post,' declared Udja. 'Kel is no ordinary criminal, and we must unite our efforts in order to save the pharaoh and the state. We must forget any quarrels and fight together.'

Henat and Gem nodded.

'Why is Kel impossible to find?' wondered Udja. 'Has he died a natural death? No, that would be too fortunate! Has he been murdered by his own accomplices, who wanted to get rid of a man who had become a hindrance? Possibly. If that were true, all our problems would be solved. Nobody would try to proclaim himself king, and the helmet would remain hidden for ever. If the rebels have panicked, they may even have destroyed it.'

'I don't believe so,' said Henat. 'The extent of the crimes committed demonstrates that Kel is the head of the network, a pitiless, cunning tyrant, capable of ridding himself of his rivals. He would undoubtedly love to see us lower our guard. After searching for him in vain, we conclude that he is dead and the investigation is broken off. Then Kel calmly emerges from his lair and is free to act. We must not lift a single security measure, and we must continue to hunt him down.'

Udja and Gem agreed.

'One detail puzzles me,' said Gem. 'Given the number of portraits distributed to the forces of order and to informants, it is impossible that Kel could have slipped through the net. Either he has taken refuge in the South, even in Nubia, and can therefore not count on elite troops. Or else he has changed his appearance. A different hairstyle, a shaven head, wigs, moustache, a workman's kilt, a trader's tunic, the garish clothing of a Libyan or a Syrian, Greek robes . . . There are so many different disguises open to him.'

'A good but disturbing thought,' said Henat. 'Alas, it rings horribly true. In other words, our portraits are useless and this killer will remain beyond our grasp.'

'It is here, and not in the South, that a usurper would try to take power,' Udja assured him. 'Nevertheless, we should place the Elephantine garrison under close surveillance. True, his rebellion would be doomed to failure and would not threaten the throne, but we must be prudent.'

'I shall strengthen the forces already there,' promised Henat.

'I fear that Judge Gem may well have found the correct explanation,' Udja went on. 'One deduction is clear: the killer has the aid of highly effective accomplices. Alone, despite his sinister talents, he would not succeed in escaping from us.'

'I am sorry to utter the name of High Priest Wahibra,' said Henat in a neutral tone of voice. 'I see the naivety of a generous and credulous man. Convinced of the innocence of this scribe, a man of formidable charm, he might have helped him in all good faith.'

'The detailed search of the temple revealed nothing,' the judge reminded him. 'Must we repeat it?'

'It would be futile,' said Henat. 'Confined to the enclosure, denied audiences with the king, the High Priest would not be mad enough to hide the criminal. And we have a man on the ground there: Menk.'

'Wahibra is stubborn,' said Udja. 'If he still trusts Kel, he won't abandon him.'

'Then he risks being imprisoned,' pointed out the judge.

'He won't act himself, he will leave it to one or more of those close to him. It is up to us to identify them.'

'Wahibra is neither worldly nor sociable, and has few friends. Indeed . . .' Gem hesitated, and thought for a moment. At this stage of the investigation, he must not neglect anything. 'His sole confidant is Pefy, the minister of finance.'

'He is clearly out of the question,' cut in Udja. 'He is a faithful servant of the state and would never betray Ahmose.'

'Pefy displays a great attachment to the sacred city of Abydos,' said Henat, 'and attempts in vain to obtain funds for restoration work. His persistence irritates His Majesty, which Pefy certainly resents.'

'Not to the extent of turning into a conspirator,' Udja protested.

'Where is he at the moment?' asked the judge.

'In Abydos,' replied Henat, 'celebrating the Mysteries of Osiris.'

'I shall question him on his return,' decided Gem, 'and I hope I shall not have any unpleasant surprises.'

'I am sure you will not,' said Udja. 'Pefy has no personal ambition and implements His Majesty's policies scrupulously. Egypt's prosperity proves the quality of his work.'

'The High Priest's closest colleague is a young woman,' said Henat. 'He appointed Nitis Superior of the songstresses and weavers of Neith, and she owes him everything. Intelligent and determined, she will be called upon to succeed him. She is not unaware of Wahibra's thoughts, and would not disagree with him.'

'Would she go so far as to become his accomplice?' asked the judge worriedly.

'I cannot rule it out.'

'A woman concerned about her own career does not make that kind of mistake,' objected Udja. 'Why would a future high priestess defend a criminal to whom she has no attachment? More likely she gives Wahibra useful advice and urges him to obey the king and confine himself to his religious duties.'

'If Nitis follows the wrong path, our friend Menk will inform me,' said Henat. 'Following his lamentable error, he is anxious to be forgiven.'

'I shall also question the priestess,' decided Gem.

'She has left Sais to take part in Apis's funeral rites,' said Henat, 'but she will soon be back.'

'Udja, have you identified a new sacred bull?' asked Gem.

'Not yet. All Egypt's large temples have been alerted, and the ritual priests are scouring the countryside to find him as quickly as possible.'

'May the gods favour us! This death weakens the king, and the people are beginning to whisper. Without the protection of the Apis bull's vital energy, can he vanquish adversity and the forces of darkness?'

Henat's expression darkened. 'Favourable circumstances for whoever stole the helmet.'

'What if he takes advantage of the funeral ceremonies to proclaim himself king?' asked Udja in alarm.

'The soldiers in Memphis are confined to barracks until the arrival of the new Apis, and elite soldiers are keeping watch over the ceremony. In theory, the situation is under control.'

67

Nitis, Kel and Bebon contemplated the helmet.

'So,' commented the actor, 'all I have to do is put it on my head and I'm Pharaoh.'

'I wouldn't advise it,' said Nitis. 'According to the High Priest of Ptah, elite troops loyal to King Ahmose are patrolling Memphis. Any usurper would immediately be executed.'

'What if the soldiers acclaim him, as they did in the past?'

'Those men had come to seek Ahmose. Today the pretender to the throne will have to win their support. Memphis does not seem the ideal place to me.'

'And yet,' Kel objected, 'this is where the conspirators hid the helmet. At the end of the funeral ceremonies, they could have tried their forcible takeover of power.'

Bebon handled the helmet gingerly. 'On reflection, I'm giving up supreme power. It's too dangerous and too tiring. Commanding, deciding, being responsible for people's happiness, getting to the bottom of intrigues – I'd rather not bother. It would be impossible to sleep at night.'

'And yet here you are, at the centre of an affair of state.'

'Let's try to forget that by getting rid of this damned treasure. Ahmose will continue to reign, and the usurper will agonize over his murderous plans before finally giving them up. And everything will return to normal, thanks to us.'

'This helmet is the only proof of Kel's innocence,' said Nitis.

'I don't follow.'

'Destroying it will effectively save Ahmose, but Kel will still be regarded as a fugitive criminal.'

'Are you advising him to proclaim himself king?'

'I advise him to take the helmet back to Pharaoh and thus prove his perfect loyalty. He, accused of conspiracy, will put an end to it in a brilliant way. Who would dare continue to accuse him?'

Bebon stared at her, open-mouthed. 'We're heading for disaster. Kel will never get near the king.'

'Nitis is right,' cut in the scribe. 'This is my only chance to prove my innocence.'

'Do you have a positive wish to die?'

'I would rather run this risk than continue to run away and hide. Sooner or later someone will spot me, and Nitis and you will be investigated. I'll be condemned to death, and you to many years in prison. Good fortune has allowed us to retrieve Ahmose's helmet. Let's use this powerful weapon.'

'I say it again: you will be killed before you can hand it back to the king.'

'We have no choice, Bebon. We must return to Sais and try to find an opportunity to approach him.'

'This is complete madness!'

'I understand your reservations, and I don't blame you for giving up.'

The actor turned purple. '*What?*'

'I'm sorry I dragged you into this adventure, and I apologize to you. Don't ruin your life because of me.'

'Bebon makes his own decisions. Bebon does not allow himself to be "dragged" by anybody. And Bebon does as he pleases. I am not a moralizing scribe and I don't think on behalf of other people. If I go back to Sais with you and help you meet the king, it is solely because I want to. Is that clear?'

'We bow to your decision,' said Nitis with a smile. 'However, there is one delicate problem still to be resolved: finding a safe hiding-place. Hiding you in the temple is impossible. The High Priest can't help us, and I shall probably be watched.'

'Don't worry about it,' the actor said proudly. 'Bebon has no lack of contacts. And we shall resume our roles as itinerant traders so that we can move about easily. On the other hand, finding out how the king spends his days is likely to be rather difficult.'

'I hope to be able to find that out,' said Nitis.

Her calm determination reassured Kel. Alone, he would have given up long ago. Thanks to her, he sometimes believed that their mad enterprise might succeed. Nitis seemed capable of moving mountains and changing the course of the Nile.

'The helmet, the helmet,' muttered Bebon. 'I don't see the link with the murder of the interpreters.'

The same question troubled the scribe and the priestess.

'The coded papyrus probably contains the answer,' said Kel. 'Alas, it resists our attempts to decode it, and the stelae dedicated to the ancestors of the Apis bull did not provide me with any clues.'

King Ahmose was standing on the terrace of his private apartments, gazing out over his capital, when Udja requested an audience.

'Excellent news, Majesty. The successor to the Apis bull has been identified, near Bubastis. Several ritual priests have examined him, and their judgment is unanimous: he bears the marks of his predestination. The new Apis is already on the way to Memphis, where he will be presented to the High Priest of Ptah.'

'I demand that three animal healers examine him daily, and sign a joint report. In the event of any mistakes, they will all be dismissed instantly.'

'Your instructions will be applied to the letter. The period of mourning will end when the bull arrives, and his vitality will strengthen your *ka*.'

'Anything to report in the garrisons?'

'Nothing at all, Majesty. This difficult period is coming to an end, and no agitator will disturb the public peace. In the eyes of the population, you remain protected by the gods.'

'Why has the thief who stole the helmet not taken advantage of such favourable circumstances?'

'Probably because he finds himself too isolated and lacks the necessary support. Nevertheless, neither Henat nor Judge Gem is relaxing his efforts. If we believe in the failure of Kel and his allies, we may perhaps become their victims.'

'I want that rebel, dead or alive.'

'You shall have him, Majesty.'

'In the meantime, Udja, let us celebrate. My cook has prepared a surprise for us and my cup-bearer has selected some exceptional wines. Have it announced everywhere that the Apis bull and Pharaoh Ahmose are very much alive.'

68

On his return from Abydos, where he had taken part in the ritual of the Mysteries of Osiris, Pefy was astonished to see Judge Gem entering his office without even consulting his secretary.

'Is there an emergency?' asked the minister.

'Your interrogation.'

'Regarding what?'

'You are the closest friend of High Priest Wahibra, are you not?'

'That's right.'

'Irksome, very irksome.'

'Why?'

'Because he is suspected of having helped the murderous scribe Kel. Kel benefits from powerful protection, vital for his survival. As the High Priest is confined to the temple enclosure, he cannot act directly, but he has no doubt confided in you, his friend.'

'You are talking nonsense, Judge.'

'I command you to answer my questions. I would not like to inculpate a minister and force him to appear in a high court of law, but I will not hesitate to begin the procedure.'

Pefy did not take the threat lightly. Like a hunting-dog, Judge Gem never let go of his prey.

'Wahibra may have believed in Kel the scribe's innocence,'

he confessed. 'He thought that there was a sort of conspiracy, organized by the Greeks in Naukratis, who wished to introduce slavery and coinage into Egypt. That would mean profoundly altering our society, trampling on the Rule of Maat, and would lead our nation to disaster. My ability to act is limited, for only the king himself deals with Greek matters.'

'Do you dare accuse His Majesty of incompetence and laxity?'

'Not at all. He is the guardian of the Testament of the Gods and guarantor of Maat's presence on earth; by his very nature he will act for the best.'

'Are you helping Kel escape from us?'

'I regard that question as an insult. If I did not respect your office, I would strike you!'

'I had to ask you, Pefy. We are hunting a savage beast, guilty of horrible crimes and determined to seize power at the head of his band of rebels. They went so far as to murder the Apis bull in order to weaken the royal *ka* and sow the seeds of doubt among Egyptians.'

Pefy was shocked. 'Has the new Apis been identified?'

'He will soon be in Memphis, under close protection. His Majesty's throne will be strengthened thereby.'

'Thanks be to the gods.'

'Does the High Priest have any other close friends?' asked the judge.

'Not to my knowledge. Wahibra is a solitary man, who has little trust in the human race.'

'Yet he furthers the career of the priestess Nitis, his closest colleague.'

'Wahibra takes account only of her spiritual qualities.'

'Could he have ordered her to hide the murderer?'

'Inconceivable! How can you imagine that a High Priest of Neith approves of violence and crime?'

'So you know nothing about Kel and his accomplices?'

'Nothing at all.'

'Good day, Pefy. If you remember any significant details, inform me immediately.'

'You have my word.'

Judge Gem would give the meagre results of this series of questions to Udja and Henat. One element troubled him: the barely veiled criticism of the king's Greek policy. Pefy did not approve of the development of Naukratis and its inhabitants' plans.

Did he confine himself to disagreeing with Ahmose, or had he decided to act by becoming the head of a faction? And would that faction use violence, securing the services of fanatics like Kel? A complacent High Priest, a minister who was hostile to his king, a scribe carrying out base tasks . . . The hypothesis was beginning to take shape.

But if the theory of the conspiracy was growing stronger, the destruction of the Interpreters' Secretariat still remained an enigma. Unless Kel's colleagues had got wind of his intentions, or had refused to participate in an attempt to bring down the king – *all* his colleagues, including the head of the secretariat: and that was hard to believe.

The judge must not form hasty conclusions.

Now he must have Pefy closely watched. A delicate task for, after this interrogation, he would be suspicious – if it was made an official operation, it would fail. Gem could not state precisely his motives on a properly constituted document, of which the minister was bound to be aware. Pefy was sure to counter-attack and lodge a complaint.

Despite his doubts, the judge had only one solution: to ask Henat to have his men watch Pefy. His spies knew how to be discreet, and Pefy would not know.

It was a truly unpleasant solution – and a risky one. Henat was not accustomed to passing on the information he obtained. If he sniffed out the right lead, he would follow it on his own and might act in a brutal manner, removing the guilty parties from the proper legal procedures.

On reflection, the judge preferred to play for time. The usurper had not taken advantage of Apis's death to don Ahmose's helmet, and the new sacred bull returned vigour to the king. So the conspirators did not consider themselves ready to act, and no other crime had been committed.

Assuming that he was guilty, would Pefy not give up his insane plans? And would he not order the elimination of the scribe, who had become a liability?

The judge would inform Henat that questioning Pefy had not produced anything. And he would continue his investigation in his own way, closely respecting the letter of the law.

69

Parting from Nitis had torn Kel apart. Even if he had not dared declare his feelings to her, which were more and more intense, he had just spent enchanting hours in her presence. Her gaze, her voice, her smile, her perfume, her supremely elegant bearing . . . all these were priceless gifts.

'Are you day-dreaming?' Bebon asked.

'A dream . . . You're right, it was only a dream.'

'Well, now it's broad daylight. Come back to reality, and move forward.'

Nitis had returned to the Temple of Neith, and Kel might never see her again.

Putting on their pedlars' outfits again, the scribe and the actor followed North Wind, who had been told of their destination by Bebon. With perfect calm, the donkey took the shortest route.

'Where are we going?' asked Kel

The actor seemed embarrassed. 'Just don't worry. I'm very confident.'

'You're not going to play dice again, are you?'

'Certainly not. Well, not like that. You know, friends are friends until the day when you have too many problems.'

'No, I don't know.'

'You and I, we're more like brothers. A friend has his own life, and—'

'Could you explain more clearly?'

'Your moral intransigence and your prim and proper scribe's way of thinking bore me a little. Well, it had to reach that point! My profession does not bring in much, so I have to be inventive. As the state levies a maximum of duties and taxes, my first priority is to evade them.'

'Are you talking about illegal activities?'

'Those are very big words. Just resourcefulness and nimble fingers, nothing more. Otherwise, I'd be poverty-stricken.'

'What kind of illegality are you involved in?'

'The king likes fine wines, and the storehouses of Sais house the very best. Each jar is labelled, listed and stored. The man in charge owes me a very big favour, because I told his wife that he and I were having dinner together when she suspected him of sleeping with a serving-girl from the palace.'

'Was it true?'

'It wasn't completely untrue. I saved a marriage, and we drank a full-bodied red from Bubastis to celebrate our collaboration. You can imagine my surprise: how would he cover up misappropriating that jar? Simple: a labelling error. And that's how the idea came: the king's table would hardly miss one little jar out of a hundred. On the other hand, it would help my friend and me survive.'

'You take wine from the royal storehouses?'

'Very, very little.'

'That is stealing, Bebon.'

'You have a very rigid attitude, Kel. In my opinion, it's merely a reduction in taxes. And our buyers are delighted.'

'I thoroughly disapprove of this crime.'

'Anybody would think you were Judge Gem! In your situation, it's better to forget conventions. The royal wine storehouse will be our best hiding-place.'

'On condition that your friend agrees.'

'He is very fond of his wife. She's the one who owns the house and a little farm south of Sais.'

Some guards were watching the donkey and the two traders. This would be a decisive test. If they were stopped, should they try and talk their way out of trouble or take to their heels?

North Wind kept up a steady pace, and his two companions followed him in silence.

'Success!' Bebon concluded. 'Those officers there are the best, the ones in charge of protecting the palace. So we must make perfect traders.'

Kel's breathing returned to normal.

'The cellarman is a foul-tempered Syrian,' said Bebon. 'Don't be surprised by the way he greets us.'

At the entrance to the storehouses many suppliers were milling about, along with around a hundred donkeys, their panniers laden with a variety of goods.

North Wind and the two friends set off along the path leading to the royal cellars. Outside the main entrance stood a large number of jars, which were being examined by a tall, balding man with a moustache.

'Greetings, Syrian.'

'Well, well, Bebon! Wherever did you get to?'

'I've been on tour in the South.'

'Was it a success?'

'So-so.'

'Feel like doing some business again?' asked the Syrian with a greedy smile.

'I might.'

'That's good; the situation looks promising. I've just received a nice little consignment from the oases, and there's plenty of demand.'

'I'm ready to deliver.'

The Syrian cast a suspicious eye over Kel. 'Who's that?'

'My assistant.'

'The serious type, is he?'

'An obedient simpleton. He understands absolutely nothing about anything, and won't cause any problems.'

'I like your donkey. It looks good and strong, ideal for making deliveries.'

'We can start whenever you like.'

'How about this evening?'

'Agreed.'

The Syrian patted Bebon on the shoulder. 'You're a real friend, you are.'

'The thing is, I just have one small favour to ask you.'

The Syrian's expression darkened. 'You're not in any trouble, I hope?'

'Not in the least. My assistant and I would like to spend a few nights inside the storehouses. Since you carry out the last inspection in the evening, and open the door in the morning, we could sleep undisturbed.'

'Is there a girl after you?'

Bebon hung his head.

'A married woman, and a well-to-do one at that? Is that it?' asked the cellarman.

The actor mumbled something.

'I despair of you, Bebon, You're going to end up getting yourself into all kinds of trouble. Very well then, agreed. But only for a few nights.'

'The beauty will soon forget me.'

'Come in, then.'

The cellar was remarkably clean, and lined with shelves strong enough to bear any load. There were three rows of clay-stoppered jars with handles, all lined up with impeccable precision. A label specified each wine's origin, year and quality. There were sweet wines, sugary wines, dry whites, light and full-bodied reds, and some exceptional varieties, notably River of the West. This was a true paradise!

'I'll feed the donkey at the stable next door,' said the Syrian. 'Before the door is closed, you can wash yourselves and eat. After that, total silence. And don't touch anything.'

'Have no fear, my friend. In exchange for this service, I shall leave you part of my legacy.'

The Syrian embraced the actor vigorously. 'I'm happy to know you, my lad.'

70

Seeing the Temple of Neith again gave Nitis renewed hope. She moved slowly along the sphinx-lined pathway named after Pharaoh Ahmose, gazed upon his obelisk, then walked along the monumental façade and went to the sacred lake, where dozens of swallows were flying overhead. The warm light of the setting sun suffused the surrounding area with a serenity that dispelled all torments and anguish.

How she would have loved to forget the outside world, dedicating herself to the practice of the rituals and to consulting the archives in the House of Life. But an innocent man had been unjustly accused, and she must contribute to establishing the truth, preventing him from suffering a horrible fate.

Nitis meditated, listening to the voices of the gods.

Soon the final form of the sun, the old man Atum, aided by the staff of righteousness, would leave the dying light and board the boat of metamorphoses, to confront the demons of the darkness. Guided by creative intuition and the nourishing Word, he would cross perilous regions, pacifying the terrifying guards at the gates, whose names he knew.

Once again, the fate of the world would be played out. If the gigantic serpent of nothingness succeeded in drinking the water of the celestial Nile and preventing the boat from travelling, the earth would vanish, and this little islet of existence would return to the original ocean. By celebrating the rites, those initiated into the Mysteries helped the Light to overcome obstacles, to vanquish the serpent and, following a fierce battle, to be reborn at dawn, in the form of a scarab beetle.

Kel was passing through terrifying darkness, too, and monsters with human faces were seeking his destruction.

Nitis went to the High Priest's residence. She crossed the threshold leading to the small courtyard in front of the dwelling. A servant was sweeping it.

'You are back, Superior! Was your journey a good one?'

'Excellent. May I see the High Priest?'

'His health has recently worsened, but he is expecting you.'

Wahibra had taken to his bed. Although thinner, he retained an impressive dignity. 'Did they really dare to murder Apis?' he asked.

'I am afraid so,' replied Nitis. 'But his successor is re-affirming the power of the royal *ka*, and Kel has found King Ahmose's helmet. The usurper has been reduced to helplessness.'

'That news revives my strength!'

'Kel is going to hand over the helmet to Pharaoh and thus proclaim his innocence.'

'That will mean taking an enormous risk.'

'Do you advise a different course of action?'

Wahibra pondered. 'You have chosen the best solution.'

'We have still to recognize a favourable opportunity and take advantage of it.'

'Formerly,' said the High Priest, 'I could have found out Ahmose's daily routine. But I am now confined here, and not a single dignitary will speak to me.'

'I shall manage,' Nitis assured him. 'You must concentrate on regaining your health.'

'This is just a temporary bout of fatigue. My robust constitution will enable me to overcome it.'

'Have you consulted the temple doctor?'

'There's no point. Rest will cure me.'

'Permit me to insist.'

His gaze was that of a father, at once stern and affectionate. 'Are you going to force me to pay attention to my insignificant self?'

'We need you so much. Without your help, we cannot emerge triumphant from this ordeal.'

'Go and fetch the doctor.'

The follower of the scorpion-goddess Serket and the lion-goddess Sekhmet, who propagated illnesses and also provided the means to cure them, spent more than an hour at the High Priest's bedside and carried out a variety of examinations.

'The voice of the heart remains clear,' he concluded, 'and energies are flowing through the channels. Nevertheless, age is gnawing away at their walls, and several remedies must be taken each day. Will the High Priest accept this servitude?'

'I will persuade him,' promised Nitis, 'and his servant will keep a stern eye on him.' Reassured, she went back to her official residence.

Outside the door stood Menk.

'I was worried,' he said. 'Did Apis's funeral ceremonies proceed smoothly?'

'He was buried according to the proper rites, and his *ka* will live on within his successor. So there will be no interruption in the flow.'

'That is wonderful news. Then we can prepare for the next festival in Sais. I need some special fabrics for the processional statue and I would like some new chants in its honour. Time is short; will your workshops and your musicians be able to satisfy my requirements?'

'We shall work day and night.'

'Many thanks, Nitis. His Majesty will be delighted to see the people rejoicing and forgetting these difficult times.'

'Will the king be present at the festivities?'

'He will celebrate the beginning of the public ceremony, surrounded by many dignitaries, then he will leave us to organize the rest while he hosts a banquet for at least twenty Greek ambassadors. It will be a very busy week of official receptions.'

'What other obligations does the king have?'

'Opening some new royal stables, presenting Commander Phanes with the gold award for bravery, appointing senior officers, solemnly celebrating the treaties of alliance with Greek towns, not forgetting an appearance at Judge Gem's court. The supreme court will meet the day after tomorrow, in front of the temple entrance, and Gem will once again declare that the Law of Maat must be pre-eminent. On this occasion, the pharaoh should remind the judges that he is its guarantor on this earth and will not permit anyone to violate it.'

'Why do you say "should"?'

Menk lowered his voice. 'Because King Ahmose is sometimes unpredictable. If this formality bores him, he will delegate his powers to Judge Gem and order him to make a speech in his place. Nevertheless, his entourage will beg him to be present, for respecting Maat remains the foundation of our society.'

This was it, the opportunity they had hoped for!

In front of the pharaoh and the judges of the highest court in the land, Kel would produce the proof of his loyalty and his innocence.

'Your mind seems elsewhere,' observed Menk.

'It is just a little tiredness. And the High Priest's health worries me.'

'What does the doctor say?'

'It is an illness which he knows and can cure.'

'He is an excellent doctor and is not in the habit of boasting. Wahibra will live many long years yet, I am sure.'

'May the gods preserve him.'

'And you, too, Nitis. Above all, don't forget my advice.'

'How could I?'

'Will you permit me to ask you an indiscreet question?'

'By all means.'

'Have you really forgotten Kel, that murderous scribe?'

'Today I would not even recognize him. I am tired, Menk, and I would like to sleep.'

'Forgive me for troubling you. Rest well, and first thing tomorrow we shall prepare for this new festival together.'

Reassured, he walked away. Nobody was prowling around Nitis's house, the High Priest was powerless to act, and the ritual priests were attending to their usual occupations. Having noted nothing unusual, Menk would submit a reassuring report to Henat.

It was clear that Kel was not hiding in the domain of Neith, and Menk would never tell Henat about Nitis's unwise acts. The beautiful priestess had seen reason, and was devoting herself to her duties and nothing else.

71

Bebon and Nitis had agreed to meet every day at the gateway used by the temple's suppliers. If the actor detected anything abnormal he would not speak to her, and she would do likewise.

North Wind, who was allergic to law officers of any kind, would be there to provide valuable assistance.

The priestess examined a piece of fabric. 'Tomorrow,' she whispered, 'the supreme court is meeting before the main gateway in the enclosure wall. The king should be there.'

'This is excellent quality,' said Bebon loudly. 'You won't find better.'

'I'll take it. Go to the steward and he will pay you.'

This formality completed, the actor wandered for a while around the place where the ceremony would take place. Then he returned to the royal storehouses.

To the Syrian's great satisfaction, Kel had agreed to arrange the jars and sweep the floor, in exchange for a modest meal. The scribe kept himself to himself, and was careful to remain quiet.

'Your friend may not say much,' the Syrian said to Bebon, 'but he doesn't cost much and he's quite a good worker.'

'The trick is knowing how to train a simpleton.'

During the meal break, the actor and the scribe sat on their own.

'Did you contact Nitis?' Kel asked.

'Tomorrow the supreme court judges are meeting in front of the Temple of Neith. Ahmose may be there.'

'Wonderful! We couldn't hope for a better opportunity.'

'I don't like it.'

'Why not?'

'Imagine how many guards and soldiers there will be. You won't be able to get anywhere near the king.'

'Unless I have a fine legal document with me. I shall write a letter to Judge Gem in carefully chosen words which will prove the seriousness of my actions. He will summon me to appear, and I will hand the helmet to the king as I explain.'

'More madness! I can't see it working.'

'On the contrary, we are really fortunate. When I justify myself before the king, Gem and the judges of the supreme court will put an end to this nightmare.'

'I'm more inclined to see it as the perfect occasion for an ambush.'

'That's impossible, Bebon.'

'All the same, we must plan an escape route, so we will need a diversion.'

North Wind nudged Bebon's elbow.

'Ah, so you have an idea.'

In the donkey's eyes, the actor did indeed perceive a solution. It would take him all afternoon at least to perfect his fall-back strategy.

As for Kel, he was already writing his letter to Judge Gem.

Nitis was pleased with the weavers' work. Menk would be delighted, and the next festival would be as sumptuous as the previous ones. By offering their masterpieces to the gods, human beings maintained harmony on earth.

'Judge Gem is asking for you,' a pure priest informed her. 'I have shown him to your official residence.'

Nities showed no trace of emotion.

Gem was waiting for her in the small anteroom.

'Please remain seated, Judge. How can I be of service to you?'

'I have a few questions to ask you. Will you answer them here, without formalities?'

'Of course.'

'We are still looking for Kel the scribe. Despite the scope of our investigations, we have not had the slightest success. We have to wonder if he is perhaps dead.'

'In that case, he will not harm anyone else, and the divine court will punish him.'

'That would be too beautiful. The truth seems to me to be rather less satisfactory. Not only must this criminal have changed his physical appearance, but he must also be receiving some very effective help from accomplices.'

'A worrying prospect.'

'Indeed,' agreed the judge. 'That is why, because of the higher interest of our country, I am asking you to be absolutely honest with me.'

Nitis withstood his suspicious gaze.

'Wahibra has confessed his sympathy with the murderer,' Gem reminded her. 'Let us attribute that grave error to kindness and naivety. But does that sympathy continue? You know him.'

'These events have so wounded the High Priest that his health has been damaged. He has taken to his bed and must follow an intensive course of treatment.'

'As you can see, that saddens me. Nevertheless, I repeat my question.'

'The High Priest would never help a criminal.'

'Not directly, I am sure. But does he have close friends or faithful followers whom he might have asked to hide Kel?'

'The High Priest's sole preoccupation is to fulfil his office properly. As the first servant of Neith, he passes on her message each day through the practice of the rites and by bringing the symbols to life.'

'I do not doubt that, Nitis. However, Wahibra has adopted positions which—'

'Have you not searched the domain of Neith from top to bottom, at the risk of displeasing the goddess and disturbing the peace of the shrine? Harassing a High Priest who is old and sick will achieve nothing and will merely tarnish the greatness of justice.'

'You, Superior, are his closest colleague. Did he order you to protect Kel and provide him with allies?'

The young woman's gaze did not falter. 'In no way. And I must point out to you that, in recent weeks, I have been in Memphis to take part in Apis's funeral ceremonies. Many witnesses will confirm that. Now I must take on some of the High Priest's responsibilities, while hoping for his swift recovery.'

'If you knew facts that were vital to justice, would you speak?'

'I would not hesitate for a moment.'

The young woman's assurance troubled the judge. To question her for hours on end would be futile. And he had no evidence which might enable him to establish her guilt. Perhaps Menk would obtain results from observing her movements.

Why would this sublime woman aid a fearsome assassin sought by every guard and soldier in the kingdom?

72

As one body, all the judges of the supreme court moved towards the door of the temple where, according to tradition, plaintiffs' demands were read out in order to distinguish justice from iniquity and protect the weak from the supremacy of the strong. This was where the truth of Maat was declared, and falsehood banished.

A troop of donkeys brought the scrolls of the law, the judges chairs and flasks of water.

When everyone was seated, Judge Gem hung a small figurine of Maat on the gold chain he wore round his neck. Before him, lay forty-two leather rolls containing the legislative texts applied in the forty-two provinces of Egypt.

Mingling with the large crowd attending this special event, Kel bit his lip nervously. Pharaoh Ahmose had not deigned to appear at this proclamation of the omnipotence of justice, despite the fact that it was vital in the eyes of the people. So his plan had failed. He would have to find another opportunity to restore the helmet to its rightful owner.

The scribe was about to move away when a murmur ran through the crowd.

'The king,' said an old man. 'The king is here!'

Preceded and followed by the soldiers of his personal bodyguard, Ahmose showed that the new Apis had passed on strength and vigour to him. Soberly dressed in the kilt worn by the pharaohs of the Old Kingdom, upon his head he wore the Blue Crown, which linked his thoughts to the celestial powers.

He took his place on a modest throne of gilded wood, outside the circle of judges. No intervention by the monarch would disturb their deliberations or influence their decisions. It was evident that he did not intend to deliver an opening speech.

The audience was reassured. Pharaoh reigned and justice was being handed down, the foundations of prosperity and happiness.

'In the name of Maat and of the king,' announced Gem in a firm voice, 'I declare open this session of the Court of the Thirty. Here is the first complaint.'

It was a sombre case involving boundaries which had been moved, leading to a farmer contesting the size of his lands, and consequently the level of his taxes. Refusing to listen to his protests, the taxation authorities were demanding payment, plus a penalty for the delay.

The Thirty unanimously condemned the administration, which ought to have requested the intervention of a surveyor and called upon the services of the land registry. Although the king was eager to impose his new fiscal measures, the judges rejected their arbitrary nature. And the tyrannical tax-collector was sentenced to compensate the plaintiff himself.

Gem then read the contradictory letters in a dispute between a craftsman and his former wife, who had just got divorced. Accusing her of infidelity, the craftsman demanded all of the possessions and custody of the children. The woman had produced written witness statements, proving her innocence. The husband had responded with insults and an attempt at physical violence in the presence of two colleagues.

Striking a woman was a serious crime, and the craftsman had his case dismissed and was sentenced to two years in prison. Not only would his wife keep the children, but she would also receive all of the couple's possessions.

The third complaint astounded Judge Gem. He hesitated to make it public. Seeing that he was troubled, one of the Thirty asked to speak.

'All voices must be heard. If this one seems impossible, we shall specify our reasons. To exclude it from the outset would be contrary to good justice.'

'The author of this document believes he is capable of resolving a serious problem which could damage state security and asks to appear in person before this court. He is aware of the unusual nature of this procedure, but insists that his request is a serious one and humbly begs us to listen to him.'

Ahmose's curiosity was aroused. Nevertheless, he refrained from intervening. It was the Thirty, and only the Thirty, who must pronounce a decision.

A legal debate began between those who held to the letter of the law and those who were more attached to its spirit. At the end of courteous exchanges, Judge Gem delivered his decision. The state's higher interest demanded that the writer of the alarming missive should be heard, but if his actions made a mockery of the court he would be severely punished.

'Let the plaintiff come forward and explain himself,' Gem declared.

A heavy silence fell. Everyone looked at the person next to them. Who would emerge from the crowd?

A young man came forward. He wore an old-fashioned wig and sported a neatly clipped moustache. His arms were held out at chest-level, and he was carrying something wrapped in a linen cloth.

Judge Gem could not see his face. 'Who are you and what have you to declare?'

'I have been wrongly accused of abominable crimes. Now I bring the proof of my innocence and my absolute loyalty to the pharaoh. Through my intervention, the conspirators will be reduced to silence.'

Judge Gem and the king froze. Neither of them dared guess what would happen.

Gem asked the burning question. 'Are you Kel the scribe?'

'I am indeed.'

The archers drew their bows; the guards gripped their clubs.

The judge raised his hand. 'No violence within this court! Wait for the judgment and my orders.'

Kel turned towards the king. 'I have not murdered anyone, Majesty, and I am the victim of a plot to overthrow you and plunge our country into misfortune. The real criminals have displayed unbelievable cruelty, and I feared even worse. But I have thwarted their evil plans. May I approach?'

The commander of Ahmose's bodyguard drew his sword from its scabbard.

'Approach, Kel the scribe. For the moment, you have nothing to fear.'

The young man slowly covered the distance which separated him from the throne. Kneeling, he removed the linen cloth.

'Majesty, here is the helmet that was stolen from the palace. Now no usurper can wear it.' He offered the precious relic to the king.

Ahmose contemplated it for a long time. 'Kel the scribe, you are not only a murderer but a liar. That helmet is not mine.'

73

'Arrest the murderer!' ordered Judge Gem.

A sudden movement of the crowd obstructed the guards, and Kel quickly crossed the court and mingled with the passers-by. The archers could not fire without injuring or killing innocent people.

And this was the moment Bebon chose to unleash the stampede of donkeys, all responding to the braying of North Wind, who was their respected leader. The animals caused total confusion, and one of them bumped into a judge, who was knocked unconscious by an over-eager guard. staff. The judges' indignant protests added still more to the chaos.

By the time the archers could at last see their way clear, Kel, Bebon and North Wind had vanished.

'The king is unharmed,' said Henat. 'That is the main thing.'

'That murderous scribe made the legal institution look ridiculous,' raged Judge Gem.

'Did you identify his accomplices?'

'I did not even manage that! He used the situation to his best advantage.'

'At least we know that he is alive and has changed his appearance.'

'It will be impossible to draw an accurate likeness of him.

The numerous witness reports all differ considerably, describing everything from a short, round-faced man to a bearded giant. I myself am unable to describe him with any precision. He kept his face hidden behind the helmet.'

'A strange course of action,' commented Henat.

'Pure provocation! He has proved his absolute contempt for justice and the law.'

'Strange,' repeated Henat. 'From the quality of his letter and his obvious intelligence, he does not seem insane. What if he really believed that the helmet was genuine?'

The question placed the judge in an awkward position. 'Kel is an enraged madman, a killer who is capable of the most repellent crimes. He does not reason like a normal man.'

'He did not even try to kill the king,' observed Henat.

'He thought His Majesty would not examine the helmet, and then Kel would have benefited from the king's graciousness. Cleansed of his crimes, he could simply have resumed a peaceful existence.'

'A clever plan,' agreed Udja, 'and one which might well have succeeded.'

'Who has Ahmose's real helmet?' Henat asked.

'Kel himself,' answered the judge. 'Having lost for ever any hope of establishing his innocence, only one solution remains open to him: to enable a usurper to set himself against the king. Here we are, facing a resolute and ferocious criminal. And his all-powerful reputation will spread among the population.'

'He cannot win,' said Udja.

'After such a show of strength, I am beginning to wonder!'

'The scribe used the advantage of surprise to perfect effect,' said Henat. 'If he had had the benefit of enough armed men, battle would have been joined.'

'It has only been postponed.'

'We control the army and the guards, Judge, and His Majesty continues to lead the country unfalteringly. This criminal matter has taken an extraordinary turn, I concede, but does it really involve more than a small faction?'

'Whether it does or not,' replied Udja, we must maintain extreme vigilance.'

'I suggest another search of the Temple of Neith,' said the judge.

'Surely that's the last place Kel would hide?'

'Precisely! He won't dream of another search. Assured of perfect safety, he could not find a better refuge.'

'That assumes the existence of accomplices,' pointed out Henat.

'Of course. A recent fact has alerted me: the sudden illness of the High Priest. It would be cruel to importune him in these painful moments, and his closest colleague, the priestess Nitis, is careful to emphasize the difficult nature of the situation, without answering my questions in a satisfactory manner. The murderous scribe will not make fools of us for ever. And this time he may have made a fatal mistake.'

Nitis was meditating on the seven words of Neith which created the world in seven stages. At night, when the scattered parts of the divine eye were gathered together in order to recreate divine sight, the goddess's words brought the golden scales of judgment. Thus the Word brought freedom from death and restored life, unity and prosperity. And these seven words cut off the heads of liars and enemies of the Light.

A new theory was going through the priestess's mind: what if the number seven was the key to the code used in the papyrus? Only the first hieroglyph, then the seventh, then the fourteenth and so on would have meaning. And that would mean that the author was an initiate into the Mysteries of Neith.

Desperately anxious, Nitis studied the document again. Total failure. But a reassuring failure.

One of the scribes from the House of Life dared to interrupt her work.

'Superior, come quickly! Judge Gem is here with a hundred soldiers, and he is demanding access to the temple!'

Nitis hurried out.

The judge seemed annoyed.

'What is going on?' she asked.

'You don't know?'

'Indeed.'

'Kel has defied the authorities and the magistrature. Unfortunately he fled, but I have good reason to think that he is hiding here.'

'You are wrong.'

'I am going to check. Two places interest me particularly: your official quarters and those of High Priest Wahibra.'

'I cannot agree. The High Priest is ill, and no one must disturb him.'

'Justice demands it. We shall begin with your quarters, while my men surround the dwellings belonging to the priests and priestesses. They will all be inspected.'

The judge knew he was right when he saw the anxiety in Nitis's face. The scribe had slipped into the net.

Ten soldiers rushed into Nitis's quarters. Fearing Kel's capacity for violence, they would not hold back.

'Nobody,' one of them told the judge.

'Search the High Priest's house,' ordered the judge.

'I cannot consent to this,' repeated Nitis.

'Stand aside, or I shall arrest you for obstructing my investigation.'

Two soldiers flanked the young woman, while several others forced open the door of Wahibra's house.

The sick man was was still confined to his bed. 'What are you looking for?' he asked the judge.

'Kel the murderer. Hand him over to us, and we will accept that there are extenuating circumstances.'

'You are losing your mind.'

'Proceed!'

Nothing escaped the forces of order, and even the smallest chest was emptied of its contents. In an extremely bad temper, the judge had to admit that he was beaten.

'I offer you my apologies,' he told Wahibra. 'You must recognize the difficulty of my work.'

The High Priest did not reply. He turned his head away and closed his eyes.

Outside, Nitis stood motionless between the two soldiers.

'The Superior is free to go,' said Gem, avoiding her gaze.

74

It was impossible to go back to the royal storehouses, And there was no question of asking Nitis for shelter inside the domain of Neith. Kel was convinced that Judge Gem would carry out further searches, especially of the official dwellings.

'All the ways out of Sais will be watched for several days,' said Bebon, 'and even itinerant pedlars will be stopped. What's more, soldiers will patrol the river and the roads. Shaving off your moustache won't be enough. We'll have to hide in the city, contact Nitis and wait for the storm to pass.'

'Do you have another reliable friend?'

'I have an idea, but it involves a few risks.'

'In other words, he might sell us to the authorities.'

'In my opinion, that's not his style.'

'But you aren't certain.'

'We've worked together for many years and get on extremely well, but bringing him a criminal on the run might catch him by surprise. Besides, the events at the Court of the Thirty won't improve your reputation! By scorning the king and the senior judge you have closed all doors against yourself.'

'The time has come for us to part, Bebon.'

'Oh, I see, you're going to abandon me, are you?'

'No, but—'

'Then stop treating me with such contempt. It's true that I haven't got many morals, and I haven't got the skills of a scribe. But surely you're not going to criticize me for that every minute of the day?'

'No, I—'

'Come on. I shall try to persuade my friend that you haven't killed anybody.'

North Wind led the way.

'How is it that this donkey always knows the right direction?' marvelled the actor.

In rage, Ahmose had trampled the false helmet underfoot before sinking into such a depression that he was obliged to keep to his bedchamber. Udja contented himself with handling current matters, declaring that the king was suffering from a fleeting indisposition.

Only the presence of Queen Tanith had any positive effect. With a mixture of gentleness and firmness, she reminded the monarch of his duties and managed to coax him out of his torpor.

'Why did the murderer mock me like that?' he asked, finding his voice again at last.

'It was a stratagem to have his innocence recognized, or so it seems.'

'A pitiful stratagem! How could he imagine that I would not closely examine the helmet that made me king?'

'Fortunately, he makes mistakes.'

'But he is still running. Summon my Great Council and give me something to drink.'

'Is that really a good idea?'

'Excellent.'

The queen yielded.

Ahmose took her in his arms. 'Thank you for your help. Those who believe my strength is exhausted are sorely mistaken. This incident tested me, I admit. Now I am taking up the reins again. Send for my barber and my dresser.'

*

Udja, Henat and Phanes were greeted by a king who had recovered completely and was in a combative mood.

'Has Kel's trail been picked up?'

'Unfortunately not,' said Udja. 'Once again, he has slipped between our fingers.'

'Have his accomplices been identified?'

'Alas, no. They created such confusion that we have no reliable witness statements. And the suspects we arrested have given us nothing. Judge Gem has ordered strict controls at every exit from the city, and all our informers have been placed on the alert. Only one thing is certain: the killer is not hiding inside the domain of Neith. The High Priest is bedridden and cannot provide him with any help at all.'

'Why have we not succeeded in arresting this man?' asked the king angrily.

'Because he works alone,' said Henat. 'That apparent weakness has become his main strength.'

'But he must have a network of supporters,' objected Udja.

'I am not so sure. I am more inclined to think in terms of brief stops and naive people, whom he exploits to best advantage. Perpetually alert, this highly unusual killer keeps moving all the time. Little by little, though, he will exhaust himself.'

'Judge Gem's ineffectiveness displeases me,' said Ahmose. 'I intend to remove him from the investigation.'

'To my mind, Majesty,' cut in Henat, 'that would be a mistake. Not only is he an excellent judge, keen and meticulous, but his professional pride has been wounded. He has made it a point of honour to resolve this affair.'

Ahmose nodded. 'In your opinion, has the scribe got the real helmet?'

'If so, a usurper would have taken advantage of the Apis bull's death. Even if he does have it, Kel seems incapable of using it.'

'Is all well among the Greek soldiers?' the king asked Phanes.

'Nothing to report, Majesty. They greatly appreciated their

increase in salary and speak of you in glowing terms. The elite troops continue to work hard, I hold a meeting of the senior officers every week, and I inspect the principal garrisons in order to hear any complaints. Sais, Memphis, Bubastis and Daphnai have remarkable installations. The men are well housed and fed, and the weaponry is improving day by day.'

'Our war-fleet continues to grow,' added Udja, 'and our admirals have perfect mastery of this weapon of dissuasion.'

'Something to discourage any spies,' said Henat. 'When they report back to the Persian emperor, they must feel quite sick. Attacking us would be suicidal.'

'Are you rebuilding the Interpreters' Secretariat?'

'Little by little, Majesty. It is still functioning at a slow pace, under close surveillance, but diplomatic correspondence has recommenced. Consequently, the assassin has failed completely. No one has benefited from the destruction of the secretariat, and we shall emerge from this crisis stronger and more vigilant.'

'Is there any news from Kroisos?'

'An official letter this very day. After requesting news of Your Majesty and the Great Royal Wife, he informs us that Emperor Cambyses is in excellent health, and determined to build a lasting peace by developing diplomatic and trading links with Egypt. A conventional form of words, it is true, but the letter does bear witness to Cambyses' realism.'

'Any reports from our spies?'

'The emperor rules with a firm hand, and is preoccupied with economic development. The diversity of his subjects and the numerous factions pose him serious problems. The desire for independence on the part of certain provinces will probably force him into military intervention.'

'Excellent!' Ahmose declared. 'While he is busy maintaining the unity of his empire, he will forget all about his dreams of conquest.'

75

North Wind stopped abruptly. His ears pricked up, and he pawed the ground with his left foreleg.

'Guards,' whispered Bebon. 'Back the way we came.'

The donkey refused to move. He lay down on his side and panted, his tongue protruding. Kel knelt down and stroked his head.

Ten armed guards appeared, and surrounded the two men and the animal. 'What is going on here?'

'Our donkey is sick,' said Bebon, looking woebegone. 'We were supposed to deliver our goods to the royal storehouses, and here we are, stuck.'

'Get that animal back on its feet and clear off. I won't have slowcoaches clogging up the streets.'

'Have you seen the weight of him? Help us.'

Making himself very heavy and feigning intense pain, North Wind required the assistance of four soldiers. And he walked away slowly, limping.

'Well acted,' Bebon whispered in his ear.

The trio were careful to take a large detour. Resuming his normal pace, the donkey showed no further signs of anxiety and halted before the door of a workshop in the heart of the craftsmen's quarter. North Wind had pinpointed the right address, and stood guard outside it.

Bebon pushed open the wooden door, and Kel almost jumped out of his skin: he was confronted by the face of Anubis, the god whose task was to guide the righteous dead along the roads of the afterlife.

'My friend makes masks,' Bebon explained. 'They're used at the celebration of the Mysteries and in rituals.'

Anubis, Horus, Hathor, Sekhmet, Thoth, Seth ... all the gods inhabited this dark place.

'Go on,' said Bebon. 'They won't bite you.'

Recovering his composure, Kel contemplated each mask as if it expressed a divine reality which demanded respect.

'Are you there, Lupin?' called Bebon.

'Right at the back,' answered a hoarse voice.

The craftsman was finishing off a mask of the hippopotamus-goddess Tawaret, protector of births. He was a thin fellow, with a domed forehead and bony shoulders; and a perfectionist who never kept track of the hours he worked, ensuring that not a single detail was left out.

'How are you, Lupin?'

'Got problems again, have you, Bebon?'

'More or less.'

'Rather more or rather less?'

'Things could be better.'

'The authorities?'

'You know how it is: suspicions, always suspicions.'

'Is this about a woman or a petty theft?'

'It's not about me, it concerns a friend.'

The craftsman did not pause in his work. 'And you've brought him to me?'

'He's been wrongly accused.'

'Of what?'

'Do you really want to know?'

'I'd prefer it.'

'Sometimes, not knowing—'

'What's your friend accused of, Bebon?'

'Murder.'

With infinite delicacy and a rock-steady hand, the craftsman painted in the outline of the goddess's eyes. 'One murder or several?'

'All the scribes of the Interpreters' Secretariat.'

'Ah!' Lupin's stifled exclamation betrayed genuine emotion.

If he flew into a rage, they would have to beat a hasty retreat.

'Helping a criminal like that takes courage,' he commented.

'I am convinced of his innocence. Kel is the victim of a conspiracy.'

At last abandoning the goddess's mask, the craftsman stood up. 'Show him to me, this scribe who's on the run.'

Kel stepped forward.

Lupin gave him a long, hard look. 'I suppose you're hoping to sleep here?'

'As long as it does not inconvenience you.'

'There are two mats behind my workshop. And you must be hungry.'

'If you have a little bread left . . .'

'I've boiled some lupin seeds which I soaked in water-baths renewed every six hours, so there won't be any bitterness. It's my favourite dish. And the beer isn't bad. How long are you planning to stay?'

'That depends on you – and on another favour we need to ask.'

'Ah.'

'Don't worry, it's nothing dangerous,' Bebon assured him.

'Go on.'

'Would you please contact Nitis, Superior of the song-stresses and weavers of Neith? She also believes that Kel is innocent, and her help is vital to us. By now, she must be wondering if he's still alive. Perhaps she'll find us somewhere safe to hide.'

'I don't know her.'

'Our donkey, North Wind, will lead you to her. Officially, you will be delivering the mask of a god to her.'

Lupin did not protest. 'We'll eat and sleep. Tomorrow I'll go to the temple.'

Would Kel escape from the net? Would he ever see Nitis again? Surrounded by so many divine faces, he was able to experience a moment's respite before the next storm broke.

After Lupin had left, guided by North Wind, Kel did not hide his anxiety from Bebon.

'Will Lupin sell us to the authorities?'

'He might.'

'How well do you really know him?'

'Pretty well.'

'My capture would be worth a sizeable reward.'

'Assuredly.'

'Then let's leave.'

'Outside we're at great risk of being arrested. And perhaps Lupin believed me. If he meets Nitis, she will persuade him.'

'And if he goes straight to the nearest barracks, we will soon be besieged and we won't have the faintest chance of escape.'

76

In the middle of the night, King Ahmose awoke with a start. Immediately he opened the door of his bedchamber.

The startled guards bowed low.

'Go and fetch Lord Udja,' he ordered.

The imposing Udja soon arrived. Such an unusual summons implied that something extremely serious had happened.

'I had a dream,' said the king, 'and I must learn from it immediately. We do not venerate our ancestors enough, Udja. True, our craftsmen imitate those of the golden age of the pyramids, but we have omitted to restore the monuments of that glorious era. That omission must be made good without delay. We shall begin with the temple of the Great Pyramid of Khufu, where my soul was transported during the night in order to witness the state of dereliction of certain shrines. Such negligence could cause us to suffer the curse of the dead pharaohs. At dawn you will requisition the best ritual priests and stone-cutters in Sais, and they will leave for Memphis that very evening. There, they will be assisted by their colleagues at the Temple of Ptah. I want as many men as possible to be put to work and I want the restoration to be swift. And then we shall deal with other ancient monuments.'

Despite his astonishment, Udja felt it would be futile to

protest. All he could do was rouse his colleagues and obey the king's orders.

Kel was so worried abut Lupin's attitude that he could not get to sleep. Had the mask-maker been too quiet and docile? His friend Bebon's revelations ought surely to have had a marked effect upon him.

According to the actor, Lupin never reacted in a rough or savage way. He took the time to mull over events, then acted as he saw fit. And nobody could influence him. Indeed, he had not uttered any opinion, just agreed to help Bebon as if this were an ordinary situation.

Faced with a criminal as fearsome as Kel, sought by half the kingdom, there was only one solution: to bend to his will and pretend to help him. Once he was outside, safe and sound, Lupin would alert the authorities and receive a fine reward.

Kel tried yet again to decipher the coded papyrus. Since the masks of the gods were gazing at him, he used their names. This enabled him to apply a system based on three hieroglyphs making up 'Anubis', opener of the paths of the afterlife.*

It was a pathetic failure. The names of the other gods produced the same result. And so the hours passed until dawn.

Lupin had not come back.

Kel shook Bebon. 'Wake up!'

The actor grunted. 'I'm sleepy.'

'The sun's up and Lupin is not back.'

'He must have been delayed.'

'Don't you understand? He's sold us.'

This loathsome thought woke Bebon up. 'But that's not his style.'

---

* I+N+P=Anubis. The hieroglyphs do not include vowels, a perishable aspect of language, and the vocalization of Egyptian words depends on diverse traditions.

'You aren't in the habit of presenting him with fugitive criminals. There is another, even more sinister, possibility: that he and Nitis have been arrested, and your friend has revealed that we're hiding in his workshop. Nobody can withstand a harsh interrogation.'

'That would mean that Nitis has been permanently watched . . . Unlikely. And besides, North Wind would have detected the danger.'

'In that case, Lupin should already be back.'

A dog barked. The two men's hair stood on end.

'Someone's coming,' whispered Kel, 'and I'm sure it isn't him.'

Although optimistic by nature, Bebon was beginning to experience a few fears.

'We'll fight,' he decided.

'It would be no use,' said Kel. 'They must have come in substantial numbers, and we have no chance of escape.'

'I won't let myself be caught like a chicken.'

'I'm the only one they're looking for. Hide at the back of the workshop. They may be so overjoyed at my capture that they don't search it.'

'Out of the question.'

'Please, Bebon. Please don't sacrifice yourself pointlessly.'

'Me, die a coward?'

'Simply survive, and you can drink to my health.'

'I tell you again, that's out of the question! Can you really see me crouched in the corner, watching you being arrested? We mustn't assume that all is lost in advance; we must take advantage of the effect of surprise. We'll stand on either side of the door, let the first ones come in, and then attack. With a bit of luck, we'll fight our way through them.'

Kel didn't argue. Bebon didn't believe for a moment that his plan would succeed, but it had a certain style. And it was better to die fighting.

'Sorry to have caused you so many problems.'

'Bah!' retorted Bebon. 'At least you aren't boring, unlike the average scribe. Nothing scares me more than old age. Thanks to you, I shall escape that torture.'

The dog stopped barking.

The guards must have killed it and be preparing to mount their attack. The two friends exchanged a final look and took up their positions. A heavy silence fell.

The guards must be discussing whether they should order their quarry to open the workshop door. Or should they simply break it down and charge inside?

Armed with a wooden mallet, Bebon prepared to strike hard. Kel preferred to dodge and weave. The silence grew still heavier. There was not a single sound; it was as if life had stopped in mid-flow.

Very slowly, the door edged open a little way.

The first guard must be wary, hesitant to rush in. Finally, a dark shadow crossed the threshold.

A perfume . . . A perfume that enchanted Kel.

'Nitis!' he exclaimed.

77

Kel and Bebon emerged from their hiding-places.

'You're safe and sound!' said Nitis in relief. 'Right up to now I wondered if this was a trap. Only North Wind reassured me. He is watching the area, with your friend.'

'A dog barked,' Bebon recalled.

'A good guard-dog, signalling my presence. I calmed him, and he went back to sleep. Come quickly, we are leaving for Memphis, on board an official boat.'

'You're coming with us?' Kel was astounded.

'The pharaoh has decided to restore the temple of the pyramid of Khufu, and has requisitioned ritual priests and craftsmen. Bebon will make an excellent sculptor's assistant, and you will make a perfect *ka* priest. As delegates from the Temple of Neith, we shall benefit from the protection of the army.'

'A new role to play,' declared Bebon appreciatively. 'Fortunately, I once worked on a building-site.'

'As soon as we reach Memphis,' announced Kel, 'we shall run away.'

'Absolutely not,' objected the priestess. 'Ahmose took his decision because of a dream which ordered him to venerate the ancestors and to restore their cult places.'

'The ancestors,' repeated Kel thoughtfully. Could this be

the hoped-for sign? Would they at last discover the key to the code?

The gods won't abandon us,' said Nitis.

The overseer of the sculptors' workshop was a rough and unpleasant man. However, with his own constant good humour and the efficiency of North Wind, who brought food and drink to the craftsmen, Bebon managed to soothe his employer.

'Humans are twisted staves,' said the overseer. 'All they think of is being idle and enjoying themselves. If I didn't impose strict discipline, the work would never get done. And the pharaoh is in a hurry. He demands that we create several dozen statues in the old style, in hard stone. I am rather pleased to be returning to the rigorous approach of ancient times, but my sculptors' hands sometimes falter, and I must rectify their mistakes. Basalt, serpentine and breccia demand a great deal of precision. And I insist on perfect polishing.'

Statues of gods and of important people who had been initiated into the mysteries took shape before Bebon's eyes. His job was to look after the workshop, clean the tools and put them away every evening. He had time to copy the texts that were being engraved, and passed them on to Kel and Nitis. But none of them provided a key to the code.

While Nitis and the House of Life's initiates were rewriting very ancient rituals, designed to revive the power of Pharaoh Khufu, Kel carried out his modest tasks as a servant of the *ka*, under the direction of an austere ritual priest who coordinated the various priests' activities on the plateau where the pyramids stood.

By restoring the temple to its original condition and shaping its statues, the priests and craftsmen were carrying out a vital process: reuniting the gods with their *ka*, their never-changing creative power. It was embodied in their sacred dwelling and their bodies of stone, thus escaping the vicissitudes of time and humanity.

By associating himself with the giants of the Old Kingdom like Khufu, Ahmose was strengthening his own power and declaring his respect for traditional values. Was he – the herald of Greek culture, which was beginning to take root in Egypt to the detriment of Maat – really going to change direction?

Kel and Nitis doubted it.

Since the dream urgently warning him that his actions were courting disaster, the king had tried to make good his mistakes by calling upon the protection of the ancestors. Would this course of action be enough?'

Kel performed his duties scrupulously, bringing vases and dishes containing offerings. The soul of the reborn king absorbed their subtle energy, restoring it in the form of creative radiance.

Pleased with Kel's work, the senior ritual priest gave him greater responsibilities. He would now choose the offerings himself, according to symbolic requirements, make sure that items were maintained, and would have access to a few shrines in the secret part of the temple, where the voices of the ancestors spoke.

The senior priest's deputy did not care much for this promotion. A man who ate too well, with plump hands and feet and black hair which lay flat on his moon-shaped head, he hoped soon to take over from his superior, who suffered from arthritis.

As he was filling an alabaster vase with wine, Kel sensed hostile eyes upon him.

The deputy senior priest was watching him. 'Be careful. That object dates from ancient times. If you were to damage it, you would be instantly dismissed.'

Kel bent down.

'Here in Memphis, we have a long and brilliant tradition of *ka* priests. And you, my boy, are not from around here.'

'Indeed.'

'Where are you from?'

'The North.'

'A big city?'

'No, a small village.'

The deputy sneered disdainfully. 'Well, don't have any illusions, my boy. Don't have hopes of making a career in Memphis. Only the heirs of good families accede to senior posts. How did you come to be taken on?'

'I was requisitioned.'

'Ah, a temporary. Keep to your place and be discreet.'

'I obey my superior's orders.'

'Illness sometimes prevents him thinking clearly. My role is to tell him about schemers like you, so that he isn't caught in their traps. So you won't be getting any more promotion. Be content with this one – it's your last.'

Certain that he had struck a definitive blow, the sour-tempered priest walked away.

Kel would have to be wary of him, and not go beyond the strict framework of his duties. Up to now, he had not come across a single clue that might enable him to decipher the code. And he avoided contact with Bebon. Whenever they encountered each other, a simple shake of the head expressed their current failure. Equally, it was impossible to spend a few moments with Nitis. What agony it was, to be so close to her and not be able to talk to her. At least she had not pushed him away, but she remained a dream, an unreachable horizon.

Each day Kel enjoyed his work as a *ka* priest even more. Directing his thoughts towards offerings, venerating the ancestors and trying to perceive the Invisible were exciting tasks. Why should he not be content with them and stop trying to hunt down an impossible truth?

Sooner or later someone would identify him. He would be arrested, sentenced and executed for crimes he had not committed. So destiny left him no choice: he could not rest until he had proved his innocence.

78

Kel began work at dawn. Carrying a dish of food offerings, he slowly entered the temple of Pharaoh Khufu's pyramid. The power of the architecture, the expression of the reign of giants, fascinated him. The gigantic blocks, arranged according to complex geometry, bore witness to the builders' knowledge. The Saites were unable to create such a work, and were content merely to restore it so that the magic of the age of gold would not disappear.

Inside the pyramid, inaccessible to mortals, the process of resurrection took place permanently. At his own modest level, a *ka* priest contributed towards nourishing it.

Kel laid the offerings on a stone table shaped like the hieroglyph *hotep*, meaning 'peace, plenitude, completion'. At that moment, this world and the world beyond entered each other. The scribe felt the presence of the royal *ka*, the founding ancestor, foundation stone of the edifice.

On either side of the central shrine, two small rooms served as storerooms for the ritual items. Kel knew the first, but had not yet explored the second.

As he crossed the threshold, he had a strange sensation. No, this was not just a storeroom.

In the middle stood two alabaster chests, bare of inscriptions. Judging from the quality of the polishing and the particular brightness of the material, they dated from the time of the pyramids. They were waiting for him.

With a hesitant hand, he lifted the first lid and found four gold amulets: Djed, the stability pillar, symbol of the resurrection of Osiris; Tit, the magic knot of the goddess Isis; Mut, the vulture of the goddess Mut, both 'mother and dead'; and Usekh, the broad collar embodying the Ennead, the brotherhood of the creative powers.

Without touching these masterpieces of the goldsmith's art, Kel raised the second lid. It contained a papyrus, whose seal had been broken. With painstaking care, Kel unrolled it. The quality was exceptional, the writing fine and precise. But the words were indecipherable. This was another coded document.

Could the amulets be the key to it, either if one were used on its own, or if all four were used at the same time?

The second solution turned out to be the correct one. Incredibly complex, it provided Kel with the breaks in the text, the words to be disregarded, the ones to be turned round and the ones to complete. Without stability, magic, death and breadth, there was no possibility of reading.

Kel proceeded to read the words of a prophet who was describing the times to come:

That which the ancestors predicted has come to pass. Crime is everywhere, the thief has become rich, people turn away from spirituality in order to amass material possessions, the words of the sage have fled, the land has been abandoned to its weakness, the hearts of all the animals weep, the writings of the sacred chamber have been stolen from it, the secrets held there have been betrayed, the magical incantations have been divulged and are in circulation, rendered ineffective now that the profane have memorized them. The laws of the hall of judgment are cast out, people trample them in the

*streets. Those who foment strife have not been driven away,
no office is in its proper place any more. Messages are no
longer being passed on.* *

Kel could not wait to find out if this code would at last enable
him to decipher the accursed papyrus that had caused so
many deaths.

An aggressive voice behind him barked, 'What are you
doing here?'

Kel kept calm. 'I am putting things away.'

'This shrine is being restored,' said the deputy senior ritual
priest. 'No one is permitted to enter.'

'I did not know that.'

'Stand aside.'

Kel obeyed.

'Anyone would think you were examining the contents of
the chests.'

Kel said nothing.

'Gold amulets, an ancient papyrus ... a nice little store
of treasure. You were stealing these precious items, weren't
you?'

'Certainly not!'

'You are lying.'

'You are wrongfully accusing me.'

'The facts are clear, boy, and this matter is particularly
serious. I shall lodge a complaint against you, and my testimony will carry a great deal of weight. In the meantime, you
will accompany me to the guard-post. Then I shall inform
my superior.'

'You are mistaken. I did indeed open the chests, but when
I saw what was inside I was going to put the lids back and
leave the shrine.'

* From the prophecies of Ipu-ur.

'A likely story! No doubt the guards will find stolen items in your room. And you will be severely punished.'

'You refuse to accept the truth and all you seek to do is get rid of me.'

'The truth is perfectly clear.'

'I have absolutely no intention of taking your place,' declared Kel. 'Let me close the chests, leave the shrine, and fulfil my ritual obligations.'

'That's enough talk. Consider yourself under arrest. Go on, walk in front of me.'

Although opposed to violence, Kel had to push the deputy away, and the man slipped and fell on to his back. Being a heavy fellow, he was dazed and winded, and it would take him a few seconds to get up and sound the alert.

Kel hurried out of the temple and across the forecourt, then took the path to the craftsmen's village. The guards would first rush to his quarters and question his colleagues. Nobody knew of his links with Bebon.

Fortunately, the actor was in the workshop. He was alone, sharpening copper chisels.

'Quickly, we have to run away!'

'Have you been spotted?'

'I'll explain. Where can we hide?'

'Fortunately I foresaw this happening, so you haven't caught me entirely unprepared.'

The two friends hurried to a disused storehouse where bricks had been kept. There, Bebon had hidden mats, some clothing, and jars of water and food.

'According to my superior,' he said, 'the building is in danger of falling down and will be demolished soon. Nobody comes here.'

'I may have found the key to the code,' said Kel, and told how he had discovered it. 'Go and fetch Nitis, and tell her to bring her copy of the papyrus here. Mine is still in my room, under my palette, and I can't get to it – the guards must be searching the place already.'

'Whatever you do, don't move and don't get impatient,' urged Bebon. 'Complications could delay us.'

79

Don't get impatient? That was easy to say! Kel could not wait
to apply his new system to the coded papyrus. By speaking
to him within the shrine dating from the time of the pyramids,
the voice of the ancestors had provided him with the right
key.

He heard voices, laughter. Someone was coming. It could
not be Nitis and Bebon.

Kel hid at the back of the building, behind some disused
brick-moulds. Peering out, he saw a sturdy young man and a
peasant girl with a pretty little face enter the building.

'We won't be disturbed here,' said the lad.

'It's the old brick-works,' she said anxiously.

'Yes. Do you like it?'

'A workman died here in an accident. Ever since then it's
been haunted.'

'Forget all that nonsense, and let me hold you in my arms.'

She pushed him away. 'No, not here. This place scares me.'

'Come on, don't be a child!'

Kel moved the brick-moulds. The sinister creaking froze the
love-birds where they stood.

'Did you hear that?' she asked. 'It's the ghost!'

She fled, and he followed her.

Much relieved, Kel hoped that they would tell everyone
about the incident.

The hours passed slowly. Dark thoughts haunted him: Bebon and Nitis arrested and imprisoned, total failure, victory for the killers . . . Then at last, just before sunset, he heard the voice he had been longing to hear.

'It's me, Bebon. You can come out, Kel.'

What if he was being forced to talk, surrounded by a horde of soldiers? No, he would have found a way of alerting his friend. Kel emerged from his hiding-place.

Beside Bebon stood Nitis, looking more beautiful and more radiant than ever.

'The guards are looking for you everywhere,' said the actor. You've been accused of stealing sacred items and damaging a shrine. That's another death sentence for you.'

'Nobody followed you?'

'North Wind would have signalled to let us know.'

Nitis stepped forward, her expression sombre. 'Here is my copy of the papyrus.'

Kel sat down in the scribe's position and applied the amulets' code. And this attempt was crowned with success. He read the message aloud:

The present situation is disastrous, and we cannot endure it much longer. That is why we have decided to act and set the country back on the right path, taking account of new realities. To wander off into the values of the past would be a grave error. Only technical progress and a profound alteration in the exercise of power will enable the country to extricate itself from the rut. You, to whom this declaration is addressed, will be able to help us and we undertake to provide you with the help necessary to bring our common plans to fruition. However small it may be, one last obstacle worries us: the Divine Worshipper. Even reduced, her powers are not negligible. We must be wary of her and keep her carefully distanced from events. We, that is—

Kel broke off.

'Go on!' demanded Bebon. 'We are going to find out the identities of the conspirators at last.'

'They've used another code,' said Kel. 'The rest of it is incomprehensible.'

'Try harder!'

Kel exhausted all the combinations provided by the amulets, but without success.

'The ancestors illuminated the first part of the papyrus,' said Nitis. 'The Divine Worshipper holds the key to the second, which contains the names of the conspirators and the recipient of their message.'

'It could be King Ahmose himself,' said Bebon. 'He might rely upon a section of his advisers in the hope of eliminating the conservatives and increasing the Greek influence.'

'What if the opposite is true?' argued Kel. 'What if, disapproving of Ahmose's policies, the supporters of tradition have decided to overthrow him and return to true independence by driving the Greeks out of the country?'

'That's nothing but an idealistic dream. We'd no longer have an army.'

'A new pharaoh might know how to raise the necessary troops. In the time of the Queen of Freedom, we succeeded in driving out the Hyksos invaders.'*

'Who can the leader be? Udja? Henat? Or Judge Gem?'

'We mustn't waste our time in vain speculation,' advised Nitis. 'We simply know that this text ought not to have found its way to the Interpreters' Secretariat. Its author was afraid it would be deciphered, and decided to murder all the scribes.'

'Their accomplice and informant must have been my friend Demos,' said Kel.

'And there we have the Greek connection again,' Bebon pointed out.

* See Christian Jacq, *The Queen of Freedom*, 3 vols, Simon & Schuster.

'Demos was paid well to act on behalf of an Egyptian notable. Once he'd killed the scribes, he himself was killed in Naukratis in order to point suspicion at the Greeks and destabilize Ahmose.'

'This document does not mention the king's helmet,' noted Nitis.

'That information must be in the part we can't read,' said Bebon.

'We have the proof of Kel's innocence,' said Nitis.

'Yes, but we cannot make use of it.'

'But we have achieved the first step. We must go to Thebes and meet the Divine Worshipper. Her intervention will be decisive.'

Bebon scratched his head. 'It'll be a dangerous journey, very dangerous. The conspirators will soon know that Kel has deciphered the first part of the papyrus and is trying to reach Karnak. Road and river routes will be watched, and they will make sure that the Divine Worshipper is out of reach.'

'You know every cubit of the Nile Valley, don't you?' said Kel.

'Don't exaggerate.'

'This is our only chance: to see the ruler of Karnak. She will decipher the end of the papyrus and save Egypt.'

'We'll all be killed before then,' prophesied the actor.

'If you feel this adventure is doomed to fail, I—'

'Oh no, don't start that again! Yes, it's bound to be a failure, but so what? I'm free to move around and I won't be seen as less brave than a moralizing scribe who's been sentenced to death several times.'

'I'll try to find a boat to take us,' said Nitis, 'and see what I can find out about the security measures that have been put in place between Memphis and Thebes.'

Kel dared to take her hands in his, very tenderly. 'Be extremely careful, won't you?'

'Stay here. I'll be back as soon as possible.'

80

The deputy senior ritual priest had not stopped cursing the vile individual who had attacked him and stolen several ancient and priceless amulets.

'Judge Gem wishes to see you,' a guard informed him.

'The head judge?'

'Himself.'

'I thought he was in Sais.'

'He has just arrived.'

Proud to be so appreciated, the deputy almost ran to the judge's office. After searching him, an assistant showed him in.

'Do you recognize this man?' Gem asked harshly, showing him a portrait.

'Yes, yes, I think so.'

'You think so or you're certain?'

'I'm almost certain.'

'Is this your attacker?'

'Yes, it is.'

'What is his name?'

'Er . . . I don't know.'

'That's surprising,' grumbled Gem. 'He was working for you and you didn't even know his name?'

Finding himself suddenly in the position of the accused, facing a scornful magistrate, the deputy's face fell. 'The thief was only a simple *ka* priest, but my superior liked him and—'

'I have already questioned your superior,' cut in the judge. 'It is your testimony that interests me. According to your deposition, you caught him in a shrine of Khufu's funerary temple, and he was in the process of stealing amulets and a papyrus.'

'That's correct. Thinking only of my duty, I tried to prevent him and take him to the authorities. The brute struck me violently and then fled.'

'The chests in the shrine still contained the papyrus and four gold amulets. What exactly did your attacker steal?'

'Lots of other amulets.'

'How many?'

'Difficult to say.'

'What did they represent?'

'I don't know.'

'Are you absolutely certain that the boy stole some ritual items?'

'Logic would suggest—'

'So you aren't certain.'

The judge's vehemence frightened the priest for a moment.

'No, not entirely.'

'Thank you for your cooperation. Now leave.'

Gem had gathered some new facts. According to his superior, the deputy was a greedy man, capable of slandering anybody in order to obtain promotion. His testimony was therefore suspect. Nevertheless, Kel had tried to steal a treasure necessary to the conspirators who wished to take power.

The judge had that treasure before him. Four traditional amulets charged with magic, and yet left where they were. And a coded and indecipherable papyrus. Was it linked to the document mentioned by the dying head interpreter-scribe?

If he really wanted to steal these items, why had Kel not killed the deputy? It would only have been one corpse more. Was he trying only to sabotage the restoration of the temple of Khufu, or had he come to retrieve a vital document? The second solution must be the correct one.

So Kel had succeeded in deciphering the text and abandoned the document itself, which was now of no further use. The judge must consult scholars in order to find out the content of this enigmatic message.

Summoned as a matter of urgency by their leader, the conspirators looked most unhappy. This time, the affair had taken a turn for the worse.

'That damned scribe continues to make fools of us,' said one anxious conspirator. 'And now he has the key to the code.'

'You're wrong,' said the leader. 'He may not even have deciphered the papyrus dating from the reign of Khufu.'

'We must not underestimate him. Adversity has hardened that boy. We thought we could make use of a naive young man and deliver an ideal blow to the legal system, and now here we are facing an adversary who is determined to discover the truth, even if it costs him his life.'

'Let us assume the worst,' proposed another conspirator. 'Kel has discovered an alarmist prophecy and has realized that the old Egypt was threatened with upheavals. He is unaware of our names, our true intentions and our plan of action. Several times in the past, seers have spoken of the perils of the future. This ancient text did not necessarily concern our own era. From the point of view of an educated scribe, is it not merely an exercise in style? And even if the little snooper considers it important, he will come up against an insurmountable wall. He will never obtain the key to the code.'

'Unless he knocks at the right door.'

'You know very well that it is out of reach.'

'I am not so sure about that.'

'Only the Divine Worshipper could enable Kel to break the code. First he would have to acquire that information; then he would have to get to Thebes and obtain an audience; finally he would have to persuade that elderly priestess to help him and become his ally. Despite his persistence, and the incredible luck he has enjoyed up to now, that is impossible.'

'We must ensure that he cannot get to Thebes,' decided the leader.

'It already is. All routes, by both land and river, are strictly controlled.'

'A false sense of security!' protested the anxious conspirator. 'The authorities have failed to capture Kel in Sais or in the Delta, and now he is in Memphis, where he's had no difficulty hiding.'

'According to our information, he does not know the South. If he takes the risk of going to Thebes, he will soon be spotted.'

'What if he has help?'

'Kel isn't the leader of a network of rebels, he's merely a scribe who has wandered into the middle of something which is too big for him.'

'At this time, he constitutes a real threat.'

'Then we shall continue to assume the worst and imagine that he goes to Thebes. We'll easily be able to dispose of him before he sets foot in the sacred city. After all, the guards and soldiers have been ordered to kill him on sight.'

'What if escapes from them and succeeds in convincing the Divine Worshipper that he's innocent?'

'That's most unlikely!'

'Since the beginning, we have underestimated this young man. Continuing to do so could well be disastrous.'

'What do you suggest?'

'Only an alliance between the Divine Worshipper and Kel can prevent us from attaining our goals. Either we kill him, or we—'

'Kill the Wife of Amun, the ruler of the god's sacred domain? Surely you aren't thinking of that!'

'If Kel gets too close to her,' replied the chief conspirator dryly, 'there will be no other solution.'

330

81

Memphis was buzzing with activity. There was nothing unusual about the presence of the royal couple, but the arrival of the entire Sais court provoked a kind of fever among senior officials, anxious to give complete satisfaction.

Udja's sternness was particularly alarming for lovers of routine who were used to enjoying their sinecures. Assisted by Pefy, the imposing Udja examined the accounts of the various state secretariats, checked that jobs were being done efficiently, and made acerbic observations, the prelude to painful reforms.

Henat, who spoke little but was just as alarming, watched and made notes. During a meeting with senior officers from the Memphis guards and the principal informers, he confined himself to listening before uttering a cutting judgement: results were inadequate. In other words, there were transfers in the offing.

And the order came: all routes were to be kept under strict and permanent surveillance, all rest days were cancelled until the murderous scribe was arrested, and there would be a large bonus for the man who brought the fugitive back to Sais.

General Phanes inspected the various barracks, and lectured officers and men, reminding the Greek mercenaries of the importance of their work. The announcement of an increase in pay enhanced his popularity.

Although weary, Judge Gem proceeded to hear numerous witnesses, who were convinced that they had seen Kel the scribe. He checked every lead scrupulously. But in vain.

Nitis's task was proving more difficult than she had foreseen. Hiring a boat seemed a simple matter, but it meant declaring the destination, the number and names of the passengers, and obtaining permission from the forces of order, after the travellers had been questioned.

Clearly Judge Gem feared that Kel would leave for the South, or even Nubia, where he would try to rally the tribes to his cause. And the preventative measures taken formed an effective barricade.

Nitis approached a sixth captain, a bearded fellow from Elephantine. He had a large trading-boat, capable of transporting heavy loads.

'Would you be willing to take passengers?' Nitis asked him.

'That depends on the number and the price.'

'Three persons.'

'Men?'

'Two men, one woman and a donkey. You may fix your own price.'

The captain stroked his beard. 'The woman, is she married?'

'No, but she's unavailable.'

'Pity. Nevertheless, the proposition is still quite tempting.'

'Although everything is entirely above board, these travellers wish to avoid the security checks.'

'What? That's impossible.'

'What a shame. Goodbye.'

'Not so fast, young lady! Experience makes it possible to, er, resolve certain impossible situations, and I've no lack of experience. But the price will be high, very high. At the moment, the river guards are very jumpy, and I don't want to cause myself problems.'

Clearly this particular captain was not fanatical about legality.

'How much?' asked Nitis.

Greedy eyes alighted on Nitis's throat. 'At least three necklaces like yours.'

'Very well. You shall have the first when we leave, and the other two on arrival. And no raising the price.'

Jewellery like that was worth a small fortune! 'Are you serious, beautiful lady?'

'When do we leave?'

'The day after tomorrow, when we've finished loading. But before then, you must bring me the first necklace.'

'When?'

'Tomorrow, at the fifth hour of the night. You will come aboard and join me in my cabin. The men on watch will be informed. If you do right by me, I will do right by you.'

'I shall see you at the fifth hour.'

Hiding her joy, the priestess left the port.

Near the Temple of Ptah, where she was to take part in rituals, a voice made her jump.

'Nitis! I've been looking for you everywhere.'

'Menk . . .'

'His Majesty ordered me to come to Memphis to prepare for the great Festival of Hathor. He feels my experience will be useful to the local priests. Given your excellent reputation, would you be willing to help me?'

'Of course.'

Menk, carrying out lowly duties on the king's orders? It was possible . . . but it might be a lie. If that was the case, he was taking the initiative, hiding behind a mask, and trying to lure Nitis into a trap.

'I have dreadful news for you,' he said quietly, 'and I do not know how to tell you in a way that spares you too much pain.'

'Tell me, Menk.'

'High Priest Wahibra is dead.'

The shock was indeed dreadful. Nitis had lost her spiritual father, the sage who had taught her everything; and she felt a terrible void within her. Nothing could ever fill it.

'He passed away in his sleep,' explained Menk. 'Because of his fall from favour, the mummification was carried out quickly and the burial was discreet.'

'Were the rites conducted correctly?'

'Don't distress yourself: Wahibra's soul departed in peace. I understand your sadness and I share it. And, unfortunately, I have another piece of bad news. The palace has just appointed a new High Priest of Neith, an obscure ritual priest whose skills are inferior to your own. The disappointment is unanimous, but we cannot argue with the king's orders.'

So, the sacred domain of Sais had closed to the young Superior of songstresses and weavers. The new High Priest would soon transfer her to an obscure post wholly lacking in influence.

Had Wahibra died a natural death, caused by extreme fatigue, or had he been killed? A pharaoh could not carry out such a crime, at the risk of damning himself. But there were the conspirators. They mocked the vengeance of the gods, and killed all their opponents without mercy.

'I shall plead your cause with the authorities,' promised Menk, 'for the injustice is flagrant. To my mind, it will be only fleeting. One day, Nitis, you will become High Priestess of Neith, to everyone's delight.'

'What does my career matter?'

'Do not yield to sadness, and please help me for as long as necessary. Then you will be able to spread your wings again.'

Menk regarded the young woman's silence as acquiescence. In reality, she was thinking of her dead master, of his teachings and his example. From the paradise of the Righteous, he was sending her an urgent message: continue to fight to make Maat shine forth, do not accept injustice, and re-establish the truth.

82

North Wind's braying awoke Bebon. 'Someone's coming,' he told Kel, shaking him. 'We'd better arm ourselves.'

The donkey did not bray a second time, so there was no danger.

Nitis appeared, looking very sad. 'Wahibra is dead,' she said, with a sob in her voice.

'They killed him,' said Bebon.

'And they have closed the doors of the Sais temple to you, haven't they?' said Kel.

'A new High Priest has already been appointed, on the government's orders.'

'He will let them search everywhere; they will find the original coded papyrus!'

'Perhaps if they do find it, soiled as it is by countless murders, they will be satisfied and stop pursuing you.'

'No, they won't. I have to die, then they will have a free hand.'

'Let us venerate Wahibra's memory together,' said Nitis, 'and ask for his help.'

She recited prayers of transformation, spoke the seven words of Neith, and called for the peace of the setting sun to be upon the High Priest's soul-bird. Communing with all the sun's forms, it travelled with the stars and the planets on a continual voyage of discovery across the paradise lands of the afterlife.

Then she and her two companions shared a modest banquet in honour of the dead man, during which she spoke about the high points of his teaching. Despite his lack of interest in matters theological, Bebon was impressed by the young woman's clarity and depth of thought.

'You should succeed your master,' he said.

She managed a faint smile. 'He demands more than that of me. Wahibra believed in Kel's innocence, and we must fight to establish the truth. I have found a boat and I have enough to pay for our transport.'

'What is the name of the boat?' Bebon asked.

'The *Ibis*.'

'I'll accompany you to the first meeting.'

'No, you mustn't. I have to ensure the captain's full co-operation. His men will be watching the quayside – you'd be intercepted, and our transaction cancelled.'

'What if he attacks you?'

'When he has checked the value of the necklace, all he will think about is the other two.'

'But those are your jewels as a priestess,' said Bebon.

'That is the price of our journey. Only the Divine Worshipper can still prevent the worst from happening.'

'Will she agree to receive us?' Kel wondered anxiously.

'We must be optimistic,' said Bebon.

'This evening,' said Nitis, 'I shall sleep here. Menk is pursuing me, and I suspect that he is linked – consciously or not – with the conspirators. I would prefer to avoid him.'

Kel could not get to sleep. He was searching for the best arguments to dissuade Nitis from joining in this mad adventure, which was doomed to failure. He had nothing to lose. She, on the contrary, had such a commanding personality that she was bound to be destined for high office. To link her fate with his made absolutely no sense. She had already run too many risks and must not compromise herself any further.

True, he loved her with a boundless, unfathomable love. She, on the other hand, regarded him only as a victim, so he could not let her sacrifice her life for him. He would talk sternly to her, to stop her making a fatal mistake.

Suddenly someone appeared. It was she. He closed his eyes and then opened them again. She was still there.

'Nitis . . .'

'Can't you sleep?'

'I – I was thinking about you.'

'You want to persuade me to give up, don't you?'

'You must.'

'Would you take away my freedom? I am a woman of Egypt, not Greece.'

'I shall not escape a tragic end, Nitis. And have no right to condemn you to the abyss.'

Very slowly, she came closer to him. Kel stood up, and Nitis took his face in her hands, with a heavenly gentleness.

'Since the birth of our civilization,' she said, 'a woman has been free to love whomsoever she wishes, when she wishes. The day that prerogative disappears, the world will be reduced to slavery.'

'Nitis . . .'

'Are you really certain that you love me?'

'Nitis!'

She slipped the thin straps of her linen dress down over her shoulders. The fragile garment dropped to the ground.

Naked, she allowed herself to be embraced by a man who was mad with love for her, who feared he would be clumsy, but was unable to contain his desire. And they were filled with the happiness of their union.

83

'I'm sorry to wake you,' said Bebon, 'but the sun's been up for a long time. And here's some breakfast – nice, if not regal: a stale flat-cake and some lukewarm water.'

Kel couldn't believe his eyes: Nitis lay beside him, loving, abandoned. So he hadn't been dreaming after all.

'I don't want to spoil things,' said the actor with mock solemnity, 'but if you carry on living under the same roof, you'll be husband and wife.'

'You are the witness to our union,' replied Nitis, smiling. 'From now on, our destinies are linked.'

Kel could not speak. In that moment of supreme joy, all unhappiness disappeared. If in his heart, in his consciousness, he preserved the truth of that moment, no destruction could ever damage it.

Nitis, Kel and Bebon spent a wonderful day, in which time did not exist. Crime, conspiracies and danger no longer existed. The sun illuminated a sky of perfect blue, swallows and falcons gloried in the space, and the enthusiasm of youth wiped away the anguish of the future.

'Don't go,' begged Kel, hugging Nitis tightly.

'We must obtain the Divine Worshipper's help,' she reminded him. 'One boat journey, and hope will become reality.'

'You take too many risks.'

'The captain of the *Ibis* regards me as an unimportant go-between. All he wants is his profit, and he'll take us to Memphis in exchange for his fee.'

'But—'

'In Egypt a wife does not submit to her husband. Do you remember the maxim of Ani the sage? "Under no circumstances may the male permit himself to reproach her unjustly, for the mistress of the house ensures that everything is in its proper place."'

They kissed passionately, then Nitis left their refuge and headed towards the port.

Kel shook Bebon. 'Wake up!'

The actor emerged from a delicious dream in which thorns were not sharp and snakes did not bite. 'Are we under attack?'

'Nitis hasn't come back.'

Bebon opened his eyes. Day was breaking. 'Hasn't come back?'

'Something must have happened to her.'

'Wait, don't assume the worst.'

'Something must have happened to her,' repeated Kel, devastated.

'Don't jump to conclusions.'

'We must go to the port immediately.'

Bebon sat up. 'The guards and the army are looking for you.'

'I want to question the captain of the *Ibis* and find Nitis.'

'Very well.' It was pointless trying to reason with a man who was madly in love, he thought resignedly.

'Leave this to me,' urged Bebon. 'The less you show yourself, the better.'

Kel held back, while his friend climbed the gangplank of the *Ibis*.

A sailor stepped in front of him. 'Where are you going, my lad?'

'I want to see the captain.'

'You don't disturb the captain just like that. Who are you, anyway?'

'Tell him it's about a priestess's necklace.'

With a suspicious look, the sailor walked slowly to the cabin and knocked several times on the door. It opened. After a long conversation, he returned to Bebon.

'The captain says he will see you.'

Bebon had met countless crooks of this kind. Shady, drink-sodden, ready to sell his own mother and father: the captain of the *Ibis* was a magnificent scoundrel.

'Have you got the necklace?' he asked.

'My employer brought it to you herself.'

'That was the first part of the fee. I want the second before taking the merchandise on board.'

'Normally, one pays on arrival.'

'I've changed the rules of the game. At the moment, the risks are running high.'

'Did my employer agree to the change?'

'Of course, So where's the payment?'

'I haven't received any instructions,' said Bebon.

The captain's face hardened. 'What does that mean?'

'I haven't seen my employer yet.'

'Oh. Well, that's your problem. If I don't get the promised fee, I won't do the job.'

'You haven't bumped her off by any chance, have you?'

The captain turned purple in the face. 'You're talking nonsense, my lad! Me, I do trade. In view of the risk, I intend to be paid a fair price. Killing customers? That would ruin me.'

'I don't think she would have agreed to an alteration in the contract.'

'Well, you're wrong! Faced with the circumstances, she adapted to them. So she decided to go to the Temple of Ptah to fetch what's owing to me and bring it to me this evening. That undertaking reassured me, I must admit. When people are serious, you can always reach an understanding.'

'Correct, Captain.'

The shady fellow smiled. 'Payment this evening, departure tomorrow. Done?'

'Done,' confirmed Bebon.

Kel could no longer stand still. Striding along the quayside, he was about to climb aboard the *Ibis* when his friend disembarked.

Kel seized him. 'Where is she?'

'According to the prince of crooks, she has gone to the Temple of Ptah.'

84

'You really do look like a scribe,' mused Bebon. 'If you speak in a refined way, you'll prove that you're a person of quality, and all the doors will open to you.'

Kel was ready to overturn the biggest pillar in Memphis to find Nitis. If the captain had not lied, he would soon embrace her.

He presented himself at the entrance to the vast domain of Ptah.

'I have come to carry out monthly service,' he told the gatekeeper.

'In what capacity?'

'Pure priest, dealing with offerings of wine.'

'Write your name in the register.'

Kel wrote '*Bak*', which meant 'servant', in fine hieroglyphs, with a skilled hand.

Impressed, the gatekeeper let him pass.

Kel approached a scribe. 'I have a message for Nitis, Superior of the songstresses and weavers at the Temple of Neith in Sais.'

'Ask the head ritual priest. He will know where she is working.' The scribe pointed out the priest's official quarters.

Several priests were waiting to go in. Controlling his impatience, Kel waited his turn.

At last, an assistant invited him to enter.

The chief ritual priest of the Temple of Ptah was an elderly, stern-looking man. He looked suspiciously at the young scribe.

'I do not know you. Who are you and what do you want?'

'I have come from Sais to give a message to Nitis, the—'

'I know her. She did stay here, but she left the temple three days ago.'

'Where may I find her?'

'She has probably returned to Sais. Next!'

So the captain of the *Ibis* had lied. He must go immediately to the port and make him talk. Nitis was probably being held captive on board.

Kel told Bebon the facts. North Wind led the way, selecting the shortest route.

The quays were swarming with people. Goods were being loaded and unloaded, and wealthy customers were haggling over prices. Where the *Ibis* had been berthed, there was now another boat.

'You must have got the wrong place,' said Kel.

'Unfortunately not.'

Bebon questioned a dock-worker. The *Ibis* had left Memphis in the early hours, heading south.

'Did you see a young woman on board?'

'All I saw were the usual crew members,' replied the dock-worker.

Kel was devastated.

Bebon led him away. 'We must go back to our hiding-place.'

North Wind immediately set off in the right direction, avoiding the guards who were patrolling the city in groups of three or four.

'If she is dead,' murmured Kel, 'I shan't outlive her.'

'We have not reached that stage yet,' said Bebon. 'It is clear that Nitis has been kidnapped. The captain of the *Ibis* would appear to be the likely culprit.'

'Then we must go to the South and get her back.'

'But what if it's a decoy? He may have handed over Nitis to the real kidnappers, who have taken her back to Sais. Judge Gem, the guards and Henat's spies could well be implicated. And there are other possibilities.'

'We'll question a thousand people if we have to, but we will find the right trail.'

'You are forgetting that you're wanted for murder. Wouldn't it be best to go to Thebes and ask the Divine Worshipper for help?'

'I don't care about the coded papyrus, or the conspiracy! All that matters is Nitis.'

'Everything is linked, my friend.'

His mind in a fever, mad with anguish, Kel refused to yield to despair. He could feel the presence of his wife, the warmth of her body, the sweetness of her love ... No, she was not dead!

'Nitis has fallen into a trap involving several people,' he said. 'There must be witnesses, or even accomplices, here in Memphis. They think there's nothing I can do. They are wrong.'

Not as wrong as all that, thought Bebon. He was worried that a disastrous failure which would lead them to the abyss, but he would not abandon his friend, however beset by misfortune and injustice. True, their enterprise was becoming frankly insane and their chances of success were virtually non-existent; but the gods might continue to protect them. Perhaps the gods' anger would finally do harm to their adversaries?

Besides, Bebon loved to gamble. There was nothing more terrible than a boring, well-organized life. Thanks to Kel, there was no risk of that.

North Wind rubbed himself against Kel, wanting to be stroked. The donkey looked solemn but not despairing. He transmitted a powerful energy to the young man, and an unfaltering determination.

Yes, Kel would find Nitis and prove his innocence. Yes,

they would savour intense moments of peace and happiness together, in the shade of a canopy, gazing at the setting sun as it bathed them in its light.